ROGERS PARK

MARK POPLE

BLACK ROSE
writing™

First printing

This is a work of fiction. Names, characters, businesses, places, events and incidents are either the products of the author's imagination or used in a fictitious manner. Any resemblance to actual persons, living or dead, or actual events is purely coincidental.

ISBN: 978-1-61296-531-4

PUBLISHED BY BLACK ROSE WRITING

www.blackrosewriting.com

Printed in the United States of America

Suggested retail price $16.95

Rogers Park is printed in Adobe Garamond Pro

PRAISE FOR *ROGERS PARK*

"*Deliciously candid and refreshingly irrepressible. Mark Pople is one of the most interesting new voices on the scene. His story rolls of the page with intriguing vitality.*" - **Roger Paulding**, author of the *Jazzed* series and the *Seney Chronicle* series

"*Pople's sharp prose style—rich with descriptive detail and hints of the hardboiled detective genre—fuels a story that grips its reader tightly and recreates a Chicago neighborhood as it once was. The sturdy brick apartment buildings, dingy alleyways, and brutal winter winds of his Rogers Park build just the right atmosphere for the layers of mystery, malaise, guilt, and redemption that unfold within. Balanced out with wry humor, these elements all come full circle by the end, with some great twists and turns along the way.*"- **Jennifer Malkowski**, Ph.D. in Film & Media from the University of California, Assistant Professor of Film Studies, Miami University

"*Mark Pople's literary thriller, Rogers Park, is a classy crime noir homage to Alfred Hitchcock. Pople's Chicago is dark and gloomy; the late winter desolation chills the reader as Casey trudges the streets to and from the el-trains to his apartment. Casey is a marvelous character. He's a witness to a brutal crime and becomes the target of a deranged killer. The transfer student, Zachary, whose invitation to go out and socialize with some kids from school goes horribly wrong, is the perfect supporting character for the beleaguered teacher. Pople tells the story of Rogers Park through these two characters, and it works so very well. Rogers Park has the ambiance, suspense, and darkness that Hitchcock loved to portray on film. I think he would have loved this book. Rogers Park is most highly recommended.*" - **Jack Magnus**, Readers' Favorite

"*Mark Pople has written an engaging suspense thriller that I enjoyed from the first sentence. Definitely recommended. I shall look forward to reading more from this author.*" - **Jane Finch**, Readers' Favorite

For Jordan and Jessie

MANY THANKS TO:

Reagan Rothe and the team at Black Rose Writing, for publishing my debut novel.

Roger Paulding and the Monday Morning Critique group, for your keen eyes and your willingness to give me an occasional kick in my literary ass.

Jennifer Malkowski, for being the first to read *Rogers Park* from cover to cover before it even had a cover.

The citizens of Rogers Park, for understanding that authors sometimes intentionally butcher geography in the name of artistic license.

ROGERS PARK

Life hasn't much to offer except youth,
and I suppose for older people,
the love of youth in others.
- F. Scott Fitzgerald

ONE

BRIAN

"Consequences be damned. The son-of-a-bitch must die."

Wait, that can't be right. Let me try again.

"I'm going to kill Daddy and I don't care if Mommy gets mad."

Yeah, that's probably how I said it. But I can't be sure. My six-year-old-child voice eludes me twenty-four years later.

I didn't say those terrible words out loud, but that didn't matter. I thought them like a grownup. Damn, I was proud. I understood that Big Bird and Elmo deserved credit for teaching me sharing and warning me about stranger-danger. But the theory that murder could be a viable solution to problems? I came up with that one all by myself.

"He's so advanced for his age." That's what the neighbors always said.

The resolution-by-murder epiphany came to me when I was six. My brother Jonathon knelt beside me in our Rogers Park condo. I'd never seen his eyes so misty, his usual smile so unusual. Something was wrong. The Guns N' Roses backpack our mother gave him for his eighteenth birthday was slung over his shoulder. The zipper strained to contain the bulky contents.

He tousled my hair. "Don't worry, Brian. I'll see you again, little buddy. Be good. And take care of Mommy." Then the part I remember most clearly: "But when you can get out, get out."

He pivoted on a knee and flipped his middle finger at our father who sat with his back to us swirling watered-down scotch and ice slivers in his highball glass. Jonathan stood a moment and looked at the back of the balding head.

Our mother stood by the front door, a feather of a final blockade. Jonathon wiped the back of his hand across his mouth and moved toward her. He whispered something in her ear, brushed a tear from her cheek before kissing it.

He was gone.

. . .

Three years later my father left. He didn't bother with the kiss.

My mother never remarried. "Why would I do that?" she asked me recently. "Men are a bunch of shits. All they do is leave." A pause followed this remark, allowing 900 miles of interstate separating us to pave with guilt.

Once again I'd been reminded. I hadn't yet killed my father.

I still live in Rogers Park, the bowels of North Chicago. Unlike some city neighborhoods boasting "park" in their names, this urban enclave actually has a so-called park, although in February it's a lonely place. The brown grass is crisp and brittle, frosted white. Bare trees silhouette a faint horizon where Lake Michigan, dressed in grey, mingles with grey sky. At the eastern edge of this winter wasteland is evidence that humans once roamed these parts. A cement wall, graffitied by the city's best, drops to a crumbling sidewalk running parallel to the Lake Michigan shoreline. This is the point where the park — and I use the term loosely — becomes a beach — and I use the term loosely.

From this graffiti wall, take a stroll fifty yards east and you'll find yourself in Lake Michigan, not where you want to be in February. Stroll half a mile west and you'll find me, Brian Casey, emerging from the elevated Morse Avenue train station. You can't miss me. I'm the guy squinting into the wind, the idiot without a hat. I have a satchel-style briefcase slung over one shoulder, a gym bag full of sweaty basketball clothes over the other, and an unwritten novel in my head. Yeah, I'm a true renaissance man.

It's Tuesday afternoon. Eighteen degrees. Down from a balmy twenty-four this time yesterday. I zip my jacket to my chin, jam my hands into my pockets, and aim myself toward Lake Michigan for the last leg of my afternoon commute, the three-block powerwalk to my one-bedroom apartment on Pratt.

I hate this time of year.

Five minutes into my walk I stand at the opening of the Farwell-Pratt alley, a bleak yet irresistible shortcut to the backdoor of my building. As always, I pause to convince myself I'm not beholden to dangerous shortcuts. A gust of wind scolds me. *Make up your mind, asshole.*

I turn into the alley.

It hasn't snowed recently, but plenty of crusty black stuff still clings to corners. The old apartment buildings, generously referred to as vintage, rise from the alley like dirty ashtrays frosted white on top of grey on top of charcoal. They lean into the sky and the fire escapes jut out like disease. I'll be home in three minutes, but God, how I hate these alleys.

As though rising from the underworld, an old woman, cotton ball of white hair, emerges through a basement door. She struggles up the steps of the shallow stairwell and perches at street level, thirty feet away. Winded from her six-step climb, she peers up and down the alley. White breath puffs from her mouth.

"Here kitty." She sets down a saucer. "Here kitty kitty."

I don't see any cat.

My attention is hijacked from this riveting scene by footsteps clanging on a fire escape above. I look up. A black spot hurls toward me - a boulder - an asteroid - What the—

The stuffed trash bag booms onto the closed side of a double steel dumpster and explodes. I stumble and trip over a pothole, my ass scraping the jagged pavement. Candy wrappers dance around me. Aluminum cans bounce and spin before rocking to a stop. I gather myself and raise my eyes to the bombardier leaning over the fire escape five or six stories above. His hand is over his mouth in an attempt to restrain laughter. It's not working. "Holy shit." His cackles fall on me. "Sorry, man. You okay?" He disappears without waiting for an answer.

I'm sitting in a frozen alley, dazed, surrounded by garbage. Please let this be the low point of my life.

Cursing my weakness for shortcuts, I pull myself to my feet. The alley is quiet until I hear the cries of what I assume is the mystery cat, but then I remember: mystery cats don't cry in Yiddish. I turn to the empty stairwell. The old woman has disappeared but her voice remains, rising from below. Brushing the Farwell–Pratt alley from my hands, I hurry across and lean over the railing. She's on the stairwell's floor, whimpering, trying to push herself up. She struggles to an elbow but collapses. Her terrified eyes locate me and the cries intensify. I catch my reflection in her glasses and understand why. I'm a silhouette, a shadow looming over her. She probably thinks I'm God or the Devil come for her. If so, she couldn't be more wrong. I'm far from omnipotent and I rarely judge. I'm Switzerland on Prozac.

I hurry down the steps. "It's okay. You hurt? Here, let me help."

I reach to take hold of her arm. She slaps my hand away. I wait a moment before extending it again, this time as though to pet a rabid dog. The old woman either realizes she can't get up without me or the pearly light surrounding me convinces her to accept her mortality. I pull her to her feet.

"You okay?" I ask again. No answer. She doesn't seem hurt.

"Alright then," I say. Having answered my own question and excused myself, I start up the steps.

"Your tush," she calls after me.

At least that's what I think she said. I turn to face her. "Excuse me?"

"Your trousers are torn. I see your tush."

I allow myself a moment of flattery because to notice this she must have been checking out my ass. I'm cool with it. Why should dirty old men have all the fun? I reach behind and locate the flap of khaki, the torn boxers, the flesh. I withdraw my hand and look. At least there's no blood.

"Come inside, young man," says the old woman. "I'll fix them for you."

I wouldn't normally allow myself to be drawn into a strange apartment, even by a little old lady who clearly has the hots for me. But my walk home today has been far from normal. I've almost been crushed by a Hefty Bag from Heaven. A new pair of pants are ripped, and now the cold has found its way to my exposed ass.

What else could possibly happen?

The old woman leads me through the building's basement, past what first appear as dungeon stables for incarcerated horses, then, once my eyes adjust to the darkness, take the form of storage areas fronted by wooden gates. She chugs along, her head easily clearing the jungle of shirts, sheets, and unmentionables hanging from clotheslines stretched across the room. She leads me up a flight of steps and down a dim hall.

I follow her into her apartment and my well-trained libido slaps me across the face. A much younger woman, twenty-something, lounges on a floral couch. She flips through a glossy edition of *Cosmopolitan*. She hasn't noticed me yet. I take advantage by allowing myself to stare. I like what I see: schoolgirl freckles and wispy brunette bangs, a little bit of Rashida Jones.

Thank you, trash bag bombardier.

My next instinct is to thank myself for accepting the old woman's invitation. Had I declined, I wouldn't be ogling the girl I will court, marry, impregnate, grow old with, and die beside. Am I jumping the gun? Maybe. But I deserve this jaunt through the hypothetical future. I'm proud of the rare occasions when I fling caution to the wind, as long as there's a kite string attached.

The young woman's toes snuggle between the couch cushions. I clear my throat to announce my arrival. She looks up, does a double take when she sees me but doesn't stand or put down the magazine.

"Grandma, who's this?" she asks, mildly curious.

The old woman looks at me and gasps. She has no idea where I've come from or why I'm standing beside her. I'm an intruder, one who follows helpless old ladies into their apartments.

"Oh." A snap of recognition in her eyes. "This young man helped me. I fell down."

"Grandma." The young woman stands. "Are you okay?"

"Yes, I'm fine."

I reach to help Grandma out of her coat. She slaps my hands away again.

"Grandma, could I speak to you for a moment?" The granddaughter raises her eyebrows and jerks her head. The old woman slinks across the room. "Grandma, you don't invite strange men into your apartment." She aims the words in my direction. The old woman stares at the floor.

I clear my throat. "Uh. Excuse me, ladies. I'm Brian, Brian Casey. I live around the corner on Pratt. I don't want to make anyone uncomfortable, so if we're good here, I better get going." *Please ask me to stay.*

"Rubbish." The old woman shakes a boney finger at me. "You're not going anywhere until I fix those trousers."

"Trousers?" the young woman asks.

I wait for Grandma to respond but she hasn't heard the question. She glares at me, daring me to attempt an escape. I take a deep breath and begin. "One of the neighbors was too lazy to carry his trash downstairs. Dropped it from a fire escape but missed his target."

Mocking the notion that her grandmother and I almost met our maker, the young woman furrows her brow. She crosses her arms and nods. I don't mind that she's messing with me. Like I said, she's a little bit of Rashida Jones.

"When the trash bag exploded on the dumpster," I continue, "your grandmother and I ended up on our backs."

"And?" she asks.

"Well, and this."

I turn and wave the flap of material, giving her a quick glimpse of the ass cheek underneath. In my head I hear that old-fashioned burlesque music, the kind accompanying an overweight stripper shaking her tits, making the tassels attached to her pasties twirl like pinwheels. The young woman raises her hand to her mouth to stifle a laugh. She must hear the same music. We're already kindred spirits.

"So, Grandma, let me get this straight. You not only invite a strange man into your apartment, but you expect him to take his pants off too? Really, Grandma, I didn't think you had it in you."

"He helped me," the old woman pleads.

I raise my palms. "Thanks anyway, Ma'am. I better get going." With deliberate slowness, I start for the door. *Please ask me to stay, again.*

The young woman waits until I have my hand on the knob. "Okay, hang on there, Mr., uh, Casey is it?"

"Brian," I answer.

"Brian." She places a hand on her hip to compliment her scanty Mae West impersonation. "It's just a little unusual, you understand."

"Sure, I understand."

"Besides." She sits and tucks her toes into the cushion gaps. "You look pretty harmless."

Five minutes later I'm sitting on the faded couch, a lanky stranger engulfed in Ol' Grandad's huge wool pants. The pants, produced from some neglected closet, are too wide and too short. I can't cross my legs without them riding up my ankle to mid-shin, exposing my lily-white legs and mismatched socks. The fabric bunches in all the wrong places and the wool makes my legs itch. I'm trying not to scratch but God, this is unbearable. Shifting positions seems to help. *Let's try this. There, that's better.*

The "ahem" beside me reminds me I'm not alone on the couch. I sneak a peek at the young woman. Our eyes meet, then flick away. Shit. How long has she been looking at me like that?

The grandmother's name, I've learned, is Clara. Uncovering the young woman's name has become a game. She's teased me with, "why don't you guess?" and "what do you want it to be?"

Finally, Clara gives it away. "I'd be happy to fix the holes in your jeans, Rachel, while I have my sewing kit out."

Rachel rolls her eyes. "The jeans are supposed to be this way, Grandma. Besides, what do you expect me to do? Climb into those big old pants with Brian?" She winks at me. I make a conscious effort to tame the budding erection in Ol' Grandad's pants.

Derrick Rose had a great game last night.

Clara settles into a paisley armchair and threads a needle. Rachel lifts her legs onto the couch. She stretches her feet toward me. Her toes tickle the fabric of my temporary trousers before tucking themselves again into the warm cushion gaps.

She knows she has my complete attention. I make an effort to direct it elsewhere. The apartment drips nostalgia. A painting of a rabbi hangs crooked above my head. On the wall to my right, photographs: a black and white father or uncle in a military uniform and slick hair, soft and dreamy female cousins in flowery dresses and lace, a Buddy Holly-like husband or brother in skinny tie and horn-rimmed glasses. And above these, the grandchildren beaming away in stark, intruding color.

"All done." Clara chimes, holding up my khakis.

I change out of Ol' Grandad's pants and the three of us sit and talk for fifteen minutes. Determined not to overstay my welcome, I excuse myself.

Rachel walks me out, not through the front, but down the dim hallway toward the basement. I'm a second-class citizen, the help, relegated to using the servant's entrance. Doesn't matter. She assumes I want to leave the same way I came in, and she's right. It's cold, and the alley still serves as a shortcut. I also don't care because my cell phone now houses Rachel Gold's phone number. Did I mention how much I love the alleys?

The hallway is not only dim, but narrow. Rachel lays claim to the middle. With no room to walk beside her, I find myself two steps behind. No complaints. I don't mind the view.

She spins around. "You know your pants look ridiculous, right?"

Shit. Did she just catch me checking her out?

She smiles. "Hmm. And I'm not even the one with the Frankenstein stitches on my ass."

We reach the end of the hallway and take the steps leading to the basement door. Rachel stands, head cocked, waiting for me to open it. I reach for the handle. She shifts her body, making the knob inaccessible without the crook of my arm brushing her waist. My face inches toward her. *Say something, anything.*

I lower my voice to appropriate the distance. "Where was your grandfather?" The whispered question feels wrong, as though I'm casing the joint.

She leans close, confidential. "He died two years ago. Grandma still keeps his stuff. Why do you ask? Did you channel his spirit while you were wearing his pants?"

"As a matter of fact. . ." I let the words drift into silence because I have no idea where I'm going with them.

Giggling, she backs away. "So tell me, Brian Casey, what is it you do when you're not being a hero?"

"Well, it's a full time job, being a hero, but when I can find the time I teach how to read between lines."

How smooth is that? This is my go-to line, used to establish my position as not only Advanced Placement English teacher, but transcendentalist, one with the ability to train young minds to find value in negative space. I wait for Rachel to ask for more, but she's not taking the bait. My go-to line is left hanging on the hook. We zigzag through the basement laundry. She brushes aside a wet pair of slacks. They swing back in my face. *Did she do that on purpose?* Challenged with the possibility of assault by more wet laundry and awkward silence, I'm compelled to continue.

"I teach high school students how to analyze rhetoric and think critically." My words chase her, desperate to be heard. "I teach Advanced Placement English."

She turns. "Ooh, practically a professor." Mae West is back, with a touch of sarcasm to boot. "I'll bet you're a super teacher."

"Yeah. And if I'm a super teacher and a hero that makes me a superhero."

"Only if you're super and heroic at the same time."

We reach the door leading out to the stairwell. Rachel leans against it, facing me. Her legs are spaced, arms crossed like a regular tough. Nobody's going anywhere until all her questions are answered.

"What do you do for fun superhero?"

I'm speechless, seduced by this brunette pixie, intrigued by the juxtaposition of her leading question and defiant posture. She's keeping me guessing. I'm flattered she's making the effort. Her question is clearly an invitation to flirt. *Say something sexy, seductive.*

"For fun? I write."

Coward.

Rachel raises her eyebrows, waits for more.

"A novel."

She still waits.

"Uh, haven't actually done much writing yet. It's still kind of in the planning stage." Regretting having introduced the topic, I glance to my right, hoping to find a new one in the dark storage areas. A disassembled bicycle stares back at me. *You're on your own pal.*

Rachel blocks the door, waiting. I'm not off the hook yet. I take a deep breath, preparing to use the well-rehearsed tag line that will eventually appear on the hard cover edition on Barnes & Noble's new voices in fiction table. "It's about a tormented man on a quest to find and kill the father who deserted him as a child."

"Wow," she says. "Nothing like a little light-hearted reading to brighten one's day. Where'd you come up with an idea like that?"

"It was easy. I lived it." I pause for effect. "I grew up here in Rogers Park. My dad walked out on my mom and me when I was nine. Went out for a pack of Marlboros and never came back."

I look down at Rachel. I've touched something. She looks away, her first sign of vulnerability. Her eyes, independent of her head, turn back to me.

"Sorry."

"Yeah. Long time ago. Not much I can do about it now except kill him on paper."

She bites her lip, nodding. She starts to move from the door, but raises a finger to make one last point. "I want to read this book."

"Haven't written it yet."

"But when you do . . ."

"Of course."

Cold air and the pungent odor of alley sewage greet us as we step outside and climb the steps of the stairwell. The trash surrounding the dumpster has faded in the darkening alley. Bouncing on the balls of her feet, Rachel hunches her shoulders, rubs her hands. "You seriously grew up here?" She peers down the alley as though I'd been spawned in a gutter and raised by a pack of rats. "Again my condolences. Place is just teeming with shady characters. I mean, c'mon. A guy ends up in an old lady's apartment because people are trying to kill him with trash bags? Give me a break." She dismisses the alley trash with a wave of her hand.

This is her comfort zone, the teasing playful jabs. It's my turn. I'm supposed to say something clever about her toes or *Cosmo* or the torn jeans. My brilliant comeback eludes me. She knows this. Still, I'm not ready to say goodbye. She knows this too.

"Brrr. Freezing." She skips down the steps. "Alright, Superhero. Call me. And watch out, Chicken Little. I hear the sky is falling."

The door's swinging closed behind her. *Say something clever - quick - before she's gone.* "Hey, I'll bet that's the first time anyone's been called superhero and Chicken Little in the same sentence."

She pokes her head through the opening. "Pretty sure that was more than one sentence, Mr. AP English teacher. Besides, maybe there's some hidden meaning. Try reading between the lines."

• • •

19

My bedroom window has no respect for fire codes. It resists opening, rejecting recommended lubricants and requiring a combination of side-to-side jiggling, super human strength, and a complete disregard for the possibility it may never again close. It's held in place by a vice-like frame painted too many times over too many decades. My first and last attempt to open this window was the day I moved into this apartment three years ago, the coldest day of that winter. My intention was to fling the window open, defying the cold air to challenge my independence as I basked in the aroma of my new Rogers Park alley. Instead, after straining for ninety seconds to raise the window three inches, I became a desperado, struggling to close it as subzero temperatures invaded the room.

Determined not to be bullied into using my window as merely a looking glass, I developed the habit of placing my palm on the pane each morning for my weather report. That'll show that window frame who's boss. On this particular Wednesday morning, the window pane forecast calls for cold with a chance of more cold. What a surprise.

I'd like to spend the morning writing. Last night my muse informed me that if Jackson, my yet-to-be-written novel's protagonist, were to have an encounter with a falling trash bag, this could serve as an inciting incident, one contributing to the search for his estranged father, Sebastian. The writing, however, will have to wait because I have a 7:30 appointment with twenty-eight teenagers who would also rather be someplace else. Once again, my job will interfere with my life.

I teach in the suburb of Northbrook. This makes me a reverse commuter, a lonely predawn figure on the northbound platform of the Morse el station. Across the tracks, dozens of Rogers Parkers stand under the cold white lights of the platform waiting for the red-line to carry them south to their offices in downtown Chicago. They no longer find it strange that I'm headed the wrong direction. I've become familiar, the guy in khakis from the wrong side of the tracks.

Just stay away from our daughters.

By 6:45 I'm in Northbrook, powerwalking two quiet blocks to

Booker High School. This is suburbia at its best or worst, depending on your opinion of suburbia. Tree lined streets border frosty lawns. Yellow lights glow in breakfast nooks where Dads sip coffee and Moms pack lunches for kids in Spiderman jammies. Marshmallows in the Lucky Charms always disappear first.

Superheroes, leprechauns, and two-parent families.

This is the strange world I pass through on the last leg of my morning commute.

.   .   .

My classroom at Booker is a dungeon, cinderblock walls and no windows. Two lonely posters grace the back wall: Oprah Winfrey and Johnny Depp for America's Libraries. The celebrities smile from their glossy perches, encouraging reluctant readers to read. The posters were checked out from the school library on day one. They remain my sole decorations on day ninety-eight. I should care more about the appearance of my classroom, but I don't. My female colleagues understand. They know decorating is not my forte. Some even find it endearing.

Poor Brian. The bachelor needs a woman in his life.

If any of these female colleagues were remotely attractive, I might use my clueless bachelor status to get laid. Instead I let the old biddies bring me baked goods. As for my classroom, no worries. What I lack in taste I make for in apathy.

I've spent the last forty minutes of my second period conference grading the remaining AP synthesis essays that spent the past week stacked like unpaid bills on my desk. As always, I placed my best writer's essay on the bottom. This will allow me to spend the rest of the day congratulating myself for planting seeds of insight into yet another young mind. After gracing this final essay with the red comment "Very nice. Well-developed argument," I wrap a rubber band around the stack, toss it into the out box for my fourth period class.

Before my one free period ends, I check my email: the usual meeting reminders, student inquiries, and a message from an English-challenged parent: "Mr. Casey, please execute my son, Vikash, for his absence on yesterday." Tempting, but I doubt a jury of my peers would accept this email as justification for homicide. So much for the idea of narrowing my overcrowded first-period class by one student.

"What would be an acceptable form of execution anyway?" I joke with Clinton Magby, my friend and English department colleague, as we stand in the hallway between classes, "death by rhetorical analysis?"

"Know what you should do?" he says, "Save all of the creative excuse notes. Publish a book someday."

"Been done."

"Okay, how about this? You're an Alfred Hitchcock buff, right? And a writer. Turn it into a story. A teacher takes the message literally, kills a student. The guy's completely deranged."

"Like Norman Bates."

"Who?" he asks.

"Norman Bates. *Psycho.* Remember? Killed Janet Leigh in the shower?"

"Whoa, hold up, Kemosabi." Magby raises his hand in benediction. "Did you say Janet Leigh in the shower? A little respect please, a moment to process the image." He takes a deep breath.

Here we go.

I shrug my shoulders to passing students as they gawk at Magby. His grin is wicked, eyes closed, hands Halleluiah raised. I'm ready to duck into my classroom if he fakes an orgasm.

He opens his eyes. "Alright. I'm done."

If Magby's hoping for a reaction, he won't get one from me. I've known him for two years. Now something at the end of the B-wing catches his attention. "Jesus Christ. Take a look at this." A student meanders toward us. He's taken off his sweatshirt. It dangles from his hand and drags the floor. He strolls the hallway in a tank top, a wife beater. The world is his ghetto and dress codes are for pussies.

"Hey, dude," Magby calls to the approaching student, "you know this is a school, right?"

"Yeah."

"Then put that sweatshirt back on, or start pumping some iron."

The kid glares at Magby, but chickens out. He pulls the sweatshirt over his head and continues on his way.

"Unbelievable," Magby says. "There's a candidate for your Hitchcock-style execution."

The bell sounds to signal the beginning of third period. Within five minutes, I'm standing in front of my Advanced Placement geniuses discussing a quote from F. Scott Fitzgerald's *The Great Gatsby*.

"So," I begin, "when Nick Carraway says, 'life is much more successfully looked at from a single window, after all,' what's he implying? And do you agree with this implication?" A few hands rise. I wait the customary five to seven seconds, allowing others to think and respond. I call on a student from whom I've come to expect an interesting response, a discussion starter.

"Focus your energy on one thing and you'll be more successful," she says.

"Yeah, don't spread yourself too thin," another student adds.

"Okay," I say. "If that's what he means, do you consider it sound advice, and why or why not? Don't forget Nick called himself 'the most limited of all specialists, the well-rounded man.' Is he contradicting himself?"

"Yeah, if you're well-rounded you're not a specialist," a boy calls to my left. They've stopped raising hands. This is fine. The discussion is now flowing.

He continues, "It's a - wait - what do you call that? Like a contradiction?"

Someone in the back helps him out. "A paradox."

"That's right," I say. "It's a paradox. But Nick's a smart guy. He's not conflicted, at least not yet, so if he calls himself a specialist, but also says he's well-rounded and looks at life through a single window, what's the consensus?"

23

"Sounds like he's confused."

"Kind of a hypocrite."

"Like a teacher asking you to bring the whole world into your writing while his world is completely shaded by some dead movie director."

The class is silent. This response has come from the back corner of the room, from my annual anti-establishment student, the one who knows he's smarter than everyone in the room, including me. He's pushing my buttons, trying to draw me into a debate. I won't allow it because I'll lose. Half of the students look at him and half at me, waiting for a response.

"Alright, Matthew," I say. "You got me there. I am most definitely an Alfred Hitchcock junkie. But even if one has a passion, he can occasionally step out of those shadows and into the sunlight." I'm careful not to phrase this as a question so no answer will be required. My response satisfies the class. I've addressed his comment without taking offense. I'm once again Mr. C., the teacher with the cool demeanor, the one who never raises his voice. I turn to the other side of the room and change the subject.

"How might this be connected to Nick's character trait of reserving judgment?"

I feel Matthew's eyes. He sees through my ruse.

Matthew Dials is right. My passion for Hitchcock does shade my world. I approach each stack of student essays with a glimmer of hope that someone, anyone, may have made a Hitchcock reference as part of their argument. I'm not delusional. I'm aware these kids were born decades after the release of any Hitchcock movies. But I've made my passion for Hitchcock clear as well as my stance that ass-kissing is an approved classroom activity. I can't help but think someday I will see such a reference, and with this I will have found my prodigy.

At noon, Magby and I, the male contingent of the English department, sit in the lunch room. I'm consuming standard bachelor lunch fare of peanut butter crackers and a Diet Coke. Magby won't offer me part of his turkey sandwich. This precedent was set early in the school year when he said, "Donna makes me these turkey sandwiches every morning, and they're made with love, Brian. They're small compensation for surrendering my bachelorhood. Giving up my freedom was bad enough. Don't ever ask me to give up my turkey sandwich."

For the record, I never asked for a bite.

We sit discussing our mornings. Magby answers me through a mouthful. "Matthew Dials? Yeah, he's in my advisory, little prick." He wipes a dab of mayo from his chin with the back of his hand.

"But the kid's got it going on up here." I tap my head. "Listen to this. Back in September he wrote something about his great-grandfather, who I guess had just died. Man, can't believe I still remember it. You know it had to be special."

"What'd he say?"

"Something about his great-grandfather sitting atop too many generations, and the hollow nature of the youth on the bottom not allowing his history to penetrate and stabilize their base, resulting in Matthew being crushed by his death."

Magby's mouth hangs open. I wish he'd close it, at least until he's swallowed the mashed potato-like contents.

"Anyway," I continue, "I get the impression Matthew's father rides him hard about his grades. But the kid needs to learn that disrespecting his teachers isn't going to earn him any favors."

The subject of Matthew Dials fades away. We eat for a moment in silence.

Magby is younger than me in years, but older in life. Married, and with a toddler, he tends to deflect questions about his family, preferring to discuss my bachelorhood. I decide to throw him a bone. I tell him about my eventful walk home the previous day, about Clara and Rachel.

"Is she hot?" he asks.

"Seriously? That's the first question you're going to ask? There's more to a woman than looks."

"Is she hot?" he asks again.

"Yes. She's hot." Leaning closer, I whisper, "horn dog."

He smiles and shrugs, crumples his lunch sack and tosses it wide of the trash can. "What does she do?"

"Not sure. She was pretty evasive, like she was determined to make me work for information."

He picks up his keys and stands. "Well sure. If she knows you're interested, and of course she does because you're pretty much an open book, why should she be in a hurry to tell you anything. Sounds like she wants to see you squirm."

Magby's right, except for the "open book" part. But I'm glad he believes this about me. It's easier to hide skeletons in your closet if no one bothers to open the door.

· · ·

At 3:30 I step from Booker High School into long afternoon shadows. I turn my collar up against the wind, duck my chin. I cross the faculty lot and start down Redding, the residential street leading to the Smith Street el station. Near the end of the block, I detour left across a stretch of hard-packed dirt, the Booker Bobcats end zone. Before ducking under the steel bleachers backed by a wooded area at the far end of the football field, I glance to my left and right. No one around. I step under.

The sunshine slices through the bleachers, striping my clothes and striping the ground. I gaze toward the far end of the steel benches. He's not here yet, but I'm not surprised. He knows I'll wait. Why should he hurry? I pace, watching honest teachers file out of the building 150 yards away. I see him approaching. In no hurry, he strolls toward me.

"What took you so long?" I ask. "Cold out here."

"Whatever. Here you go." He hands me the pill bottle. I shake it. It feels light.

"How many are in here?"

"Two dozen. That's all I could get."

I open the bottle. "What the fuck are these?"

"Percocet."

"Percocet? Why? Where's my Vicodin?"

"This is all I could get. Don't want 'em? Here." He extends his hand for the plastic bottle.

I reach into my pocket and place two folded bills in his palm. He walks away.

"Matthew," I call after him. He turns. "Don't ever call me out like that in class again."

"Whatever, Teach." He scoffs. "Just be sure you step out of those shadows and enjoy the sunlight. Say hi to the master of suspense for me." He disappears around the end of the bleachers. I open the bottle, shake out two pills, place them on my tongue, and swallow.

Addiction: a compulsive need and use of a habit-forming substance.

I've committed this definition to memory and repeat it to myself daily to justify my state of denial. The use of "compulsive" and "habit-forming" together is incongruous. Compulsive implies obsession. One could not unconsciously obsess, yet a habit is an unconscious pattern of behavior. I'm not consciously obsessed with forming any unconscious patterns of behavior, so clearly, I'm not an addict. See, who needs rehab? Not Advanced Placement English teachers. We need only words rendering themselves open to interpretation, used insightfully out of context. It's amazing how an analysis of diction and syntax can prove you right, ease your burden, and sooth your pain. Kind of like this bottle of small white pills rattling in my pocket.

My love affair with Vicodin began last summer as I recovered from a knee injury suffered during a game of pick-up basketball. We hit it off instantly, Vicodin and me, and now I only hope Percocet won't throw a wrench into our relationship. We all know how messy these love triangles can become. Of course I never intended for my supplier to be a student. It's not as if I entered class one day and said, "Okay, let me see a show of hands. Who has questions about their synthesis assignment and who has access to pharmaceuticals?" Instead, I learned of a kid who could *hook me up*. This kid turned out to be one Matthew Dials, a young man I had not met, a young man new to Chicago. Imagine my surprise, and his, when one week after our first transaction, he strolled into my Junior Advanced Placement English class on the first day of school.

Wise beyond his years, Matthew immediately recognized the delicacy of the situation, said nothing to me until we met under these same bleachers two days later.

"No worries, Teach," he said. "Your secret's safe with me."

And, as far as I know, it has been. In fact, the arrangement is quite accommodating. We've got each other's backs. I met his no-nonsense father at fall open house, and Matthew has made it clear it cannot be known that his days helping out at his dad's pharmacy involve more than stocking shelves and answering phones. We've also come to an understanding that the generous gratuities he receives are payments for his discretion and grade inflation is not part of the deal. After all, some things are sacred. You don't kiss a hooker on the mouth, and you don't corrupt grades, even the grades of students from whom you purchase drugs on school grounds.

TWO

ZACH

Rogers Park is not at all as Zach Mondini's parents told him, nothing like Atlanta. First of all, it's cold, damn cold. Each time Zach steps outside, the air pricks him with a thousand tiny frozen needles. To make matters worse, the stinging intensifies once he escapes the cold. This is when the numbness subsides and the thousand tiny needles are pulled from his earlobes and the tip of his nose.

West Rogers Park High School is where Zach finds this painful refuge on weekday mornings. The school is a brown brick monster, a block-wide rectangular head with a hundred beady eye-like windows. The front entrance is centered and wide, a mouth with tongue-like steps thrusting downward to gobble him up. Zach's first day was last Thursday. Accustomed to the shopping mall appearance of schools in suburban Atlanta, he was surprised by the governmental feel of this building. If not for the other students dragging themselves through the doors, he might have thought he was ascending the steps of city hall.

His parents told him adjusting to his new high school would be easy. After all, they said, he's such a great kid. So easy to get along with. He'll make new friends in no time. But what would you expect? Parents see their children through rose-colored glasses. Who could blame them for feeling this way about Zach? Ranked number seven in Drury's 486 member senior class. Never been in any kind of trouble. Yeah, he's the greatest kid in the world, a God-damned angel.

By lunchtime on his first day at West Rogers, Zach had confirmed his greatest fear: joining a new school in February of his senior year was like arriving at a party full of strangers after the liquor is gone. Everyone has hooked up or passed out. The only potential friends are party crashers, those not invited in the first place. And now, five days in, he can count those new friends on one woodshop teacher's hand.

Upon returning home that first day, his mother greeted him with a smile. "Hi, Sweetheart. How'd your first day go?"

"Fine, Mom." He hurried past her to the bathroom, not because he had to piss but because his face would betray his unhappiness. After an unnecessary flush, Zach slipped into his room and locked the door. His mother didn't need to shoulder the burden of his unhappiness. She didn't want to move from Atlanta to Chicago, but she was dealing with it the best way she knew how. If she could put on a brave face, he could do the same. It was his father, the selfish bastard, who forced them to move. Accepting a position at Alverez & Marshal including a thirty percent increase in salary was too much to pass up, and he deflected his selfishness by calling the move a necessity now that Zach was college bound. After all, his father pointed out, The University of Pittsburgh, where Zach is to study Sociology next year, is closer to Chicago than Atlanta, so he will, in fact, be closer to home.

Yeah, that's great, thought Zach. Except this place is not my home.

Ten days earlier, as they stood surrounded by packing crates in their ranch-style Atlanta home, Zach's father had tried to justify the move to his wife.

"Think how close you'll be to your favorite niece," he said. "You always called Rachel the daughter you never had."

Zach's mother looked up from the dishes she was bubble wrapping and laying in a box. "Nice try, Tom, but the Rachel angle may work a little better on someone else." She winked and nodded toward Zach.

"Christ, Mom. Let it go. She's my cousin."

"Second cousin." His mother folded the box closed and stood up. "And that doesn't mean you can't have a little crush on her."

Zach watched as his father stood with his mouth agape.

"I'm just teasin', Honey," his mother said. "I know you're over that." She picked up a sharpie to label the closed box. "It will be nice for all of us to be close to Rachel."

Zach didn't need to ask how close. Three blocks north and eighteen blocks west, a neighborhood called Lincolnwood. Couldn't be more than a twenty minute drive, even in city traffic.

THREE

WINSTON

Winston Longstreet gazes at family photos climbing the wall to his left. Why hasn't he come around more? Spent more time here at home? His East Rogers Park apartment is only five blocks away. Who cares if the old man wants nothing to do with him? Mom has given him an open invitation. And then there's Micah. Micah's always glad to see him.

See me now, Micah. Open your eyes. Please.

Winston leans forward on the straight back chair. He stretches his long back, grips the cold rail of the hospice bed that strategically faces the TV. A simple turn of the head permits a window view of the frosty bungalows and barren trees lining Fargo Street. Winston turns from the window. Shitty view. He surveys the living room furniture that's been moved to accommodate the bed. The place barely looks familiar. Nothing's where it's supposed to be. Couches don't belong shoved into corners. Nine-year-old boys don't belong on death beds.

He slides his chair forward, closer to his sleeping brother and further from the urine bag hooked to the rail of the bed. The bag is fed by a catheter tube snaking from under the blanket. Micah's cheeks are sunken, his bald head the color of ash. It blends into the dingy pillow as though the surrounding Mylar balloons and stuffed animals have sucked away the color.

Winston glances at the clock on the mantle. He's going to be late for work.

Whatever.

A throat is cleared behind him. He turns. His mother stands in the doorway clutching her robe closed with one hand, a cup of coffee in the other. Her eyes are heavy with lack of sleep.

"Winston, Honey, how long have you been sitting here?"

"Don't know. Since about six I guess." He stretches his arms to the ceiling.

She sets the cup down and steps into the room. "You seen the time?"

"Yeah, I know."

"Don't you need to get going?"

Winston stands up. "I guess so. God forbid I keep old man Jones waiting. His morning coffee ain't gonna pour itself."

He looks down at Micah. "When he wakes up will you—"

His mother raises a palm. "I'll tell him you were here." She moves closer, puts her hand on Winston's shoulder. "But you know what? I'll bet he already knows. As much as you mean to your little brother, I'll bet he already knows."

Winston reaches down and adjusts the blanket under Micah's chin. "I don't get it. He seemed so full of life a couple days ago."

His mother runs her finger over the Jones Automotive logo on Winston's grey jacket. "I think we need to remember what the hospice nurse told us, Winston." She bites her lip. "Children with cancer live until they die." She takes a deep breath, gathering herself. "They don't dwindle away like older people."

Winston kisses her on the cheek. "You okay, Mom?"

She nods. "Go to work, Honey."

"Okay. Call me if . . . well, you know. Just call me. Got a long shift, then I'll head home and clean up. I'll be back later."

He starts from the room. His mother calls, an exaggerated whisper from behind. "Oh, Winston, hang on." She tiptoes past the sleeping boy, opens a cabinet and removes a blue gift bag stuffed with orange tissue. "Micah remembered your birthday. He knew he might not be awake for you this morning."

Winston pulls the tissue from the bag and pauses, smiling at the contents. He slides out a green and yellow baseball-style cap. He turns the cap's logo to face his mother. "Green Bay Packers."

"There's a card too. Micah wrote it himself."

Winston opens the card and reads aloud. "Happy birthday to Winston a great big brother and cheesehead."

Something rises within him, catches in his throat. He blinks away the tears and turns from his mother. He gazes though the window. It will all outlive Micah. In two months the bare trees will spring to life. His '08 Mustang, parked at the curb, is good for another twenty thousand miles. That old bitch Mrs. Lofton across the street will probably see one hundred.

FOUR

BRIAN

Yes, The Great Gatsby's Nick Carraway called himself "the well-rounded man," but he's got nothing on me. If being a pill-popping, novel-procrastinating, basketball-playing, English-teaching, Hitchcock junkie doesn't say well-rounded, what does?

Like Nick, I'll soon turn thirty. As a literary character, Nick will remain forever thirty. I, however, will age. I guess I should look on the bright side. Had I achieved my childhood dream of playing professional basketball, radio sports talk hosts would say I'm about to be on the wrong side of this number. Then again, if you're going downhill in your thirties, you might as well do it in one of the classic sports cars you've purchased in your twenties.

It's Thursday afternoon. As is the case each Tuesday and Thursday, I carry my gym bag from my classroom in the front of the building to the boys' locker room in the back. While thirty may start the downhill slide for pros, for the six of us who meet to play basketball after school, the age is perfect. Most skilled players in their early-to-mid-twenties are diehards, still competing against younger players. Many of those in my own age range, twenty-seven to thirty-three, lose sight of priorities. They shun basketball for wives, children, and thirty year mortgages. The older basketball players are, well, older and have wives and knees yelling at them to slow down, take it easy. So here we gather, three teachers and three coaches in the prime of our fantasy careers, meeting in a high school gym to recapture our former glory in a biweekly game of three-on-three.

At 2:45 Magby strides into the locker room with a flurry of confidence. "Gentlemen of the physical education department, prepare to be taken to school."

"If memory serves me correctly, Magby," says Coach Barry Dolan, "we took you to school on Tuesday and you flunked out big time."

"That's because Brian here couldn't find his game." Magby puts his hand on my shoulder as I sit on the bench pulling off my loafers and socks. "But today, my friends, the tide will turn because our friend Mr. Casey has found inspiration."

"Yeah? What kind of inspiration?" asks Dolan.

Magby puts his hand to his mouth as though he's about to tell a secret. Then, in his loudest voice yet: "Brian met a girl."

There's eye rolling and laughter from the others. Dolan shivers with mock fear.

"C'mon, Brian," says Coach Nick Atway from his locker. "I thought I told you to stay away from your students."

"Alright, enough," I say, slipping on my hightops. "Let's play some basketball."

The camaraderie among our group is such that is rarely found in high school gymnasiums. If any of Coach Dolan's trash-talking varsity basketball players were to stroll into the gym, the backslapping and sportsmanship would make them cringe. It's only Magby who brings an edge to the proceedings. There's no roid-rage here, and while Vicodin and Percocet are not performance-enhancing drugs, they work wonders for tolerating the Clinton Magbys of the world.

As usual, the six of us attempt to recapture the former glory each claims to have lost. The common ground upon which our sneakers squeak is remarkable. We all played basketball in high school, but for reasons beyond our understanding were spurned by recruiters for The Kentucky Wildcats and North Carolina Tarheels. This, I suppose, could be forgiven, but to have been overlooked in every single NBA draft? To be cheated out of our million-dollar destinies? Each of us has suffered like no other. We understand, however, that one must adapt, so now we teach and coach, playing the cruel hand life has dealt us.

At 3:50 I limp from the school, through the gymnasium doors, and across the faculty parking lot. Tuesday's loss has been avenged. For the other five of us, this came at the cost of Magby's gloating as we dressed in the locker room. For me, although I found my game, the victory comes at the cost of a sore knee, a jammed finger, and an inflated ego. Two of these will be relieved by the pills I'll pop as soon as I'm out of sight. The inflated ego will be fed and encouraged to balloon as I relive the breathtaking moves I made this afternoon, the incredible athleticism on which the Chicago Bulls are missing out.

I board the el at the Smith Street station with my briefcase and gym bag. Two women nestled among Neiman Marcus and Macy's shopping bags chat away on a torn vinyl bench. I can't hear their words but I don't need to, for they couldn't be more obvious:

Look, Francesca, he's carrying a briefcase AND a gym bag. He's everything I ever wanted in a man.

I see that, Desiree, He's so much more of a man than any professional athlete because he's a professional AND an athlete. Doesn't need to combine the two.

I can't resist, Francesca. I have to go talk to him.

Oh no you don't, Desiree. He's mine.

I sit on a bench two rows in front of them and stretch my long arms across the back of the seat to let them know there's plenty of me to go around. I catch a snippet of their conversation, something about "fifty percent of the clearance price." Francesca and Desiree have changed the subject for fear of me overhearing how awesome I am. Yes, my finger and my knee do feel much better. And that ego? Well, let's just say finding my game now encompasses much more than basketball.

For the rest of this afternoon, this ego will serve me well as I step out of a comfort zone normally limited to a direct route from the Morse el station to my sorry excuse for a bachelor pad. Today, as Robert Frost would say, I'll take "the road less traveled." When I arrive in Rogers Park and descend the steps of the station, I'll make two stops. Sure, I'll arrive at my apartment later than normal, but no worries. It's not as if my "Honey, I'm home" is going to be met by a glass of wine thrown in my face because I didn't call and now the dinner's ruined.

Don't give me that "Honey, I'm home" crap, Mr. Brian Casey. All you care about is playing basketball with your friends and visiting that old lady. How old is she really, Brian? Are you cheating? Tell me the truth.

The speaker in this horrifying scenario is the bitch I have not yet married and hopefully never will. She is, of course, drop-dead gorgeous, but this doesn't outweigh her shortcomings, the most glaring of which is her failure to appreciate that I'm primed to give the most interesting man in the world a run for his money. The old lady mentioned, the lucky recipient of my company, is one Clara Gold, fellow trash bag dodger.

The train grinds to a halt at Morse. I sling my bags over my shoulder and skip down the steps to street level. There it is: Morse Flowers, such a creative name for a florist on Morse Avenue. The flowers are yellow, red, and pink. They beg for the light that fights its way through the film and grime on the storefront window. Still, compared to their surroundings, they're brilliant. Color exists in the other windows, but mostly in the form of signs printed in large block letters: CHECKS CASHED, LAUNDRY, GYRO.

The flowers will be for Clara, a gesture of gratitude for a Frankenstein scar on a pair of slacks that will from this point forward serve as an artifact in the Brian Casey museum at 406 Pratt Avenue. If, as I mentioned earlier, Rachel Gold becomes the woman I grow old beside, these slacks will be produced for show-and-tell with the grandchildren. "These are the pants I wore when I met your grandmother, kids, after almost being killed by a plastic twisty-tied UFO."

The idea to bring flowers to Rachel's grandmother is brilliant. I'd like to say it was mine, but it actually came from Magby, causing me to once again wonder how a married man could be so good at being single.

This is how it will go down:

Tears will well in Clara's eyes when I hand her the flowers. She'll see the gesture as a sign that chivalry still lives among the younger generations. Next, she'll call Rachel and say, "the nice young man from the alley brought me flowers today." Rachel will be flattered, viewing the gesture as drenched with ulterior motive, an attempt to impress her by sucking up to her grandmother. She'll be right.

The potential to flatter two women with one gesture. Like I said, brilliant. Thank you, Clinton Magby.

At the florist's recommendation, I purchase a dozen peach gladiolas and carry them proudly. To the other pedestrians I'm a doting husband, thoughtful boyfriend, or at the other end of the spectrum, a refugee, begging forgiveness after being banished to the dog house. I select choice A.

When I reach the alley, instead of taking yesterday's shortcut, I continue to Lakewood, the street connecting Pratt and Farwell. I approach the front of Clara's building with the intention of locating her name on the listing next to the buzzers. I glance at the dozens of names. No Gold among them, no first initials serving as clues. Rachel's grandmother must have a different last name. This possibility hadn't dawned on me yesterday as I followed Rachel from the apartment. I didn't think to look at the number on Clara's door.

Cut me some slack here. I had other things on my mind.

I stand on the doorstep facing the iron and glass door. The pathetic reflection of a guy with an armful of flowers and nobody to give them to stares back at me. I'm sure I could press random buzzers, find my way into the building that way, but still I'd be lost, not knowing which door is Clara's. I walk back to the street and look at the building. A couple pushing a stroller passes by. Now I am in the doghouse, and even an armful of pink gladiolas hasn't allowed me to gain access.

Plan B: I walk to the end of the street, turn left, and start into the alley. Perhaps if I knock on the door in the stairwell someone will be hanging clothes from the lines or rummaging in the storage areas. If so, maybe they'll be brave enough to open the door to a stranger. Then, perhaps muscle memory alone will guide me through the basement, up one flight of stairs, and to the correct door.

If I can't get in, I guess I'll continue home and end up with a bouquet of peachy-pink gladiolas trespassing in my apartment. I have nothing resembling a vase. I'll likely end up with twelve gladiolas protruding two-at-a-time from six Bud Light bottles. If nothing else, it's an excuse to drink a six-pack. Sure, the Percocet may object, but I'm a firm believer that it's important to let new family members know who's the boss.

I start into the alley. As though synchronized, a silhouette turns into the slice of daylight at the other end. From a distance it's ET walking his bicycle. We approach each other. A rendezvous awaits, the schoolteacher with enough heart to bring flowers to an old woman and a friendly alien with the extra-terrestrial power to make it happen.

We're fifty yards apart. ET morphs into an old man pushing a shopping cart. A single arm guides the cart. Where the other arm should be, a tattered sleeve hangs loose. A dozen or so aluminum cans bounce and click like restless children each time he wrestles the cart over a pothole disguised by dirty water. He reaches the sight of Tuesday's trash bag explosion. The dumpster is surrounded by two-day-old garbage that appears disturbingly at home.

He stares at the trash. I stare at him.

The flaps of his unsnapped galoshes hang around his ankles. His pants are bunched and half tucked into the rubber boots. He wears his ratty wool coat like an old bathrobe.

Twenty feet from him, I'm invisible. He's done nothing to acknowledge my presence. I wait, hoping he'll move on because I'm cradling a dozen peachy-pink flowers and I'm about to knock on a door in an alley stairwell and I planned on doing it with no one else around.

The old man kicks pieces of trash toward the dumpster. Others items he drags with his feet, using the galoshes as a push brooms. Determined not to abort my mission, I descend the steps and knock on the door, softly at first. No response. My head is at street level. I stretch my neck and glance at the old man scraping with his heel, trying to dislodge a wet page of *The Chicago Sun Times* plastered to the ground. I knock again, harder. No response. *One more time. Then I'm giving up.* I rap on the door, this time using the side of my fist instead of my knuckles.

"Maybe she ain't home."

I spin around, startled by the closeness of the voice. The old man is leaning over the railing of the stairwell. I'm reminded of the image I saw in Clara's glasses as she laid in this stairwell two days ago. He's a faceless shadow lording over me.

"Is she pretty?" The words fall on me like dust from the top shelf of a neglected bookcase. He has no idea the flowers are for an old woman rather than a romantic interest. Let him think this. Maybe he'll move on.

"Yeah." I lift the flowers from the crook of my arm and let them hang by my side, a more masculine way to hold peachy-pink gladiolas. "She's pretty."

"That's nice kid," he says. "Better make the most of it 'cause someday nobody will give a damn." He pauses. "You know, this town was pretty too 'til we gave it to the kids and they started droppin' bombs on it." With his single arm, he gestures to the fire escape above, then to the broken glass and wet trash in the alley.

"Now nobody knows," he says. "And nobody cares." He waits a moment for me to respond.

"Sorry," is the only word I can muster. It's not enough. He sighs and his head drops.

I'm trapped, sandwiched in a stairwell between a locked door and the silhouette of a stranger. Because I have nowhere else to go, I climb the steps and for the first time we're face to face. His nose is large and crooked like that of a fighter KO'ed too many times. His eyes hide deep in the shadow of his untamed brow and a jagged scar travels from the edge of his nose to the curve of his jaw. I'm frozen by his features. He shrugs his shoulders, waiting for me to say something. He waves a thick hand at me in a gesture of disgust and picks up a single handful of the wet paper towels and candy wrappers he'd maneuvered into a small pile. He tosses these into the dumpster before turning to look at the remaining trash. His work has just begun.

It would be easy for me to leave, to become a member of that apathetic generation. I could turn my back on him, mosey down the alley as though the daylight glowing at the other end would burn away my shame. But I don't. Instead, I lay the gladiolas against the wall. The old man watches as I scoop up a Doritos bag and a banana peel and toss them into the dumpster. Next, I pick up a crushed Sprite can. I drop it into the cart. He nods to me and puts his galoshas back to work, guiding the wet trash toward the dumpster. We don't speak a word.

I hadn't intended to help him pick up every piece of trash surrounding the dumpster, but I do. What I intended was more of a symbolic gesture: help him out a little and be on my way. But my new role of friend to the elderly has empowered me. I'm a trailblazer, crossing an uncharted bridge that connects generations, and it's kind of cool that I'm crossing it in silence. It's creating more of a moment.

The old man and I work together until the alley is as clean as could be expected of a Rogers Park alley. Now, having restored his faith in humanity, I take advantage of the opportunity to give him a simultaneous nod and wave, a double gesture. If that doesn't say *my work here is done*, nothing does. A smile fights through his bitter facade. He's either thrilled to have found a young person who shares his vision of a proud Rogers Park or he's amused by my corny, dramatic exit. Once again I select choice A. I pick up the gladiolas and walk away.

• • •

Having failed in my first attempt to deliver flowers to Clara, I text Rachel the following day: "What's grandma's last name?" Not quite the scenario I planned, the one in which Clara would call Rachel to let her know I brought her a bouquet of beautiful peachy-pink gladiolas and Rachel should get to know me because I'm a combination of Prince Charming and Sir Lancelot.

Within five minutes, Rachel texts her response: "Wiseman," and my mission, at least the first part, is accomplished.

Before heading home to retrieve the gladiolas that have rested in my kitchen sink for twenty-four hours, I stop at Clara's building and once again scan the names next to the buzzers. Wiseman. There it is.

. . .

For a moment, as I stand in Clara's doorway holding the flowers, she appears confused. Am I a delivery boy? Have I knocked on the wrong door?

"Hi, Clara. I wanted to come by and thank you for being so kind the other day, for sewing my pants."

A spark of recognition flickers in her eyes. "Oh, yes. It's Brian isn't it?"

I hadn't expected her to remember my name. "That's right. Hope I haven't come at a bad time."

"No no. Come in, young man."

I hand Clara the gladiolas. Her reaction exceeds my expectations. Her eyes light up like Miss America presented with her bouquet.

When was the last time anyone gave this woman flowers?

She insists on making me coffee. When I offer to help she lays down the law: my assistance is neither required nor welcome. The coffee has a cinnamon flavor. It tastes like Christmas, which strikes me as ironic as I sit under the still-crooked Rabbi painting. I ask Clara about the photographs spanning decades on the wall to my right. My questions climb her family tree until they reach the top branches, their predetermined destiny.

"And that's Rachel, right?" I ask, pointing to a photograph of a young woman in cap and gown, clutching a diploma against a backdrop of downtown Chicago.

"Oh, do you know Rachel?"

Now *I'm* confused. "Yeah, she was here on Tuesday, Clara, when you sewed my pants."

She sits forward in her chair. "Yes, of course she was. Please forgive me. I just need to be reminded of things sometimes."

"That's okay," I say. "Sometimes I forget I'm not Lebron James." The reference is lost on her and once again she's confused. Our conversation strikes me as absurd. I consider telling Clara we're stuck in a "who's on first" comedy routine, but that wouldn't be fair because it's not her turn to be confused. I return to the subject of Rachel.

"What does she do? What's her job?"

"Some kind of artist." Clara does a double take, glancing at the gladiolas she'd placed in a vase twenty minutes ago. For a moment, she's seeing them for the first time. "Oh my, those flowers are so beautiful."

I clear my throat, redirecting her attention. "What kind of art?"

"Oh, I don't know, young man, modern art I guess. Everything with you young people is modern."

"Where does she live?" I ask.

"In Lincolnwood, with a roommate, I think."

"Does she visit you often?"

"Yes, she visits about once a week." Clara stands, placing her cup and saucer on the tray. "Rachel's so sweet. I know she'd rather not spend her time with an old lady like me. But she really is the sweetest girl in the world."

• • •

I've only been back in my apartment ninety minutes when I take a call from the sweetest girl in the world. The gladiolas have worked their magic and Clinton Magby is a genius.

"That's so awesome you brought her flowers," Rachel says. "Not a lot of guys would do that for an old woman."

"Maybe I'm not 'a lot of guys.'"

"Well, whoever you are, if you're trying to impress me, it's working."

I imagine Rachel's face on the other end of the line, biting her lower lip, twirling her hair, nervous yet excited about this thoughtful new man in her life. She continues. "And to say that you'll stop in and see her every Tuesday. That's so sweet."

What? Wait. Did I say that?

"You know, you just keep this up and you might get lucky," she says, lowering her voice to a seductive whisper. Then a giggle. "Seriously, you're so sweet, Brian, but every Tuesday? You don't have to do that."

I had at no point told Clara I'd see her every Tuesday. Perhaps she's more of a shrewd old bird than I've given her credit for. This fragile little old lady is becoming larger than life, a romantic comedy movie character played by Betty White, feigning senility to serve the double purpose of playing matchmaker for her granddaughter and assuring herself of a visitor on Tuesday afternoons. Or perhaps it's Rachel who's playing me and I'm falling victim to the feminine wiles of the seductive granddaughter who hopes for someone to relieve her of her weekly visits to Rogers Park. Hell, maybe it's a conspiracy and I'm about to be pinned to the mat by a grandmother-granddaughter tag team. Doesn't matter. If I go along with this, everyone will come out a winner. Clara will get her visitor. Rachel will get her break. And me? Do the words "get lucky" ring a bell?

"Gotta go," Rachel says. "Talk to you soon, superhero."

She clicks off before I can say goodbye.

Having completed step one of Operation Make Brian Irresistible - OMBI to those in the know - and armed with an assortment of amusing anecdotes and irresistible banter, I call Rachel the next day. One ring — two rings — three rings — shit. My script is rendered useless as her voicemail greets me. I find myself composing an impromptu response.

"Hey Rachel. Brian Casey." *Idiot. She knows your last name.* "Uh, just thought I'd give you a call to - uh - to let you know that if you need a superhero, just use the bat signal. Alright, call me back if you want."

Mental note: compose voice mail response ahead of time. Batman is not a superhero.

Having left Rachel with, "call me back if you want," I now have no choice but to wait for her to call me back, but only if she wants.

I do wait, for three days.

By Tuesday afternoon, I've all but given up. I'm hauling my usual Tuesday bags from the el station. Because I had allegedly promised, and because it's part of my OMBI contingency plan, I've decided I will stop in to see Clara. Perhaps she'll call Rachel again to remind her of my awesomeness.

I'm about to press the old woman's buzzer when my phone rings. I dig it from my pocket and look at the screen.

Finally.

"Do you like blues?" Rachel asks in lieu of a traditional greeting.

"Sure," I answer, "but I also like reds and greens." *Did I really just say that?*

"I was talking about music, Brian. Blues music."

"Yeah, I know, I was just trying to . . . never mind."

That night, at Rachel's invitation, I hop on the el and meet her at Charlie's, an Uptown blues club. I considered telling her I don't frequent clubs or bars on school nights, but to avoid adding *prude* to my newly-established status of *idiot*, I responded without hesitation: "Sounds great."

At eight I meet her in the parking lot and together we step into Charlie's. The club is a converted diner. The band, Smokin' Al and the Dogs, is performing Eric Clapton's "Nobody Knows you when you're Down and Out" on a make-do stage at one end of the rectangular building. The vinyl barstools that once accommodated spinning kids consuming milkshakes, burgers, and fries, are now populated by eclectic characters drinking beer, downing shots, or both. A businessman in a dark suit has had a rough day. He's shed his jacket, unbuttoned his top shirt button and loosened his tie, oblivious to the fact he's rubbing shoulders with a biker sporting a black leather jacket accessorized with looped chains. A Willie Nelson look-alike knows everyone in the place, as do the Smokin' Al groupies who yell song requests and call out to the band members by name. The diner's booths have been replaced with high tables and bar stools facing the stage.

Rachel and I may be the youngest in the club. The band consists of four middle-aged men in blue jeans, sunglasses, and flannel shirts. The guitar players and bass player stand stationary on the stage. Their only movements, save the fingers that dance on the necks of their instruments, are occasional knee bends or shoulder scrunches as the music and the emotions carried with it surges through their bodies. The base pounding the air rattles my bones.

The band leaves the stage after completing their first set. Rachel taps me on the shoulder. Ears ringing, I bend close to hear her tiny voice.

"Hot in here," she says. "Let's get some air."

"Seriously? It's thirty degrees outside."

She puts her mouth close to my ear. "I promise you won't feel cold for long." The liquor on her breath moves across my face and fills my nostrils. She stands up and starts for the door. I take the hint.

We step outside. "Did you drive here?" she asks.

"Uh, no." I withhold the small detail of not owning a car.

"Good, me neither. That'll make it even more fun. C'mon."

She takes my hand and tugs me through the parking lot from car to car lifting door handles. "Locked—Locked—Shit, it's cold—Alarm light flashing—Locked—Locked—Damn, why are people so paranoid? What do they think? People are going to jump in their car for a quick fuck?"

We reach a pickup truck in the back corner of the lot. Rachel has become so accustomed to moving from car to car, she almost fails to realize the handle has lifted and the door has opened.

"Oh. Jackpot."

We climb into the pickup. Her mouth meets my mouth, and her hand meets my crotch. She climbs on top of me, and she was right. Within two minutes, I'm no longer cold.

FIVE

ZACH

"Your name's Zachary, right?"

Zach's heart jumps. He didn't expect to close his locker and find a dark face forcing a smile on the other side.

"Yeah, that's right, Zach Mondini."

The boy nods absently. "I'm in your English class. Saw you join last week. Where you from, dude?"

"Atlanta."

"Atlanta? Moved all the way from Atlanta in the middle of your senior year?"

"Yeah. Sucks."

The boy turns his attention to the closed locker next to Zach's, hopeful his next words will slide through the metallic slats like dead presidents from an ATM. When the withdrawal doesn't come, the boy clears his throat and glances over his shoulder. A girl, Indian or Pakistani, standing with two other girls, gives him a sideways look and waves him ahead with the back of her hand, egging him on.

Zach nods toward the girl. "Who's that?"

"Huh? Who's who?"

"That girl who just signaled you."

The boy looks back over his shoulder. Now, with both of them looking at her, the girl rolls her eyes and gives the boy an exasperated look for blowing her cover. She turns back to her friends as though she'd never abandoned their conversation.

"Oh, that's my girlfriend, Priya."

"What's she doing?" asks Zach. "Why's she waving you on like that?"

Avoiding the question, the boy turns back to the closed locker and fiddles with the combination dial. Then he lets his confession spill. "Listen, I'll be honest with you, dude, she's been bugging me to talk to you. She feels sorry for you. Says you look like a lost puppy."

Zach shakes his head. A lost puppy. So much for the idea of West Rogers not being large enough to accommodate his machismo.

The boy spins the locker's dial. "Anyway, I wouldn't let her come talk to you herself because I don't know you. I didn't want you to get the wrong idea about her, so she's making me do it, and here I am."

"Terrific," says Zach. "I'm a charity case. Can't exactly say I'm thrilled, but at least you're honest."

"Honest? Dude, funny you should say that 'cause my name's Abe, well, Abraham." He extends his hand. Zach shakes it.

"I'm supposed to invite you to join us after school in the park, to hang out," says Abe.

"*Supposed* to invite me?"

"Uh, yeah. Sorry." Abe nods toward Priya, who rolls her eyes at him for blowing her cover, again.

Zach sighs. He's being adopted by a high school girl with PINK printed across the ass of her Victoria's Secret sweatpants and a copy of *Beowulf* tucked under her arm, and she's sent her pussy-whipped man servant to do the dirty work. A lost puppy; how insulting. Now if he can only resist the urge to flounce up to her, tail wagging, and lick her face.

Making a conscious effort to suppress his excitement at the prospect of a new group of friends, Zach shrugs. "What park? And who would I be joining?"

Abe smiles. He's a tour guide about to share his vast geographical knowledge of the grid that is Rogers Park. "Head north from school," he says. "Take Farwell or Pratt east toward the lake. You'll end up in the park." Proud of himself, he turns to Priya and gives her a thumbs up. Mission accomplished. He turns back to Zach. "We'll be there around four. Me and Priya and some friends. Park's pretty deserted in the winter. Bunch of pussies in this town can't handle the cold. Anyway, just look for the non-pussies gathered around a bottle of vodka. Hope you can make it, Zach."

Abe starts to turn but spins around. "Oh, I forgot to ask. You do drink, right?"

"Sure."

Until recently, this would have been a lie, but during the first half of his senior year at Atlanta's Drury Hills High School, Zach formed new friendships, coming to the long-overdue realization that even AP students are entitled to a little fun. Besides, what was the harm in a once-a-week drinking binge to go along with his other college prep courses?

• • •

At 3:15 Zach arrives home. The door to his new Rogers Park home clicks shut behind him.

"Zach? That you, Honey?" his mother calls from the kitchen.

"Yeah."

He enters the kitchen. His mother stands over the stove, stirring a pot of spaghetti.

"How was your day?" she asks.

He drops his backpack onto a chair. "Not bad. Heading out in a while. Gonna hang out with some new friends."

"That's great, Zach."

Her tone is too enthusiastic. Something's up.

She lifts the wooden spoon from the pot, extending it toward him. "What do you think?"

He tastes. "Delicious, as always."

His mother turns back to the stove. "So, Rachel called me today, to shoot the breeze." A pause. "She's got a new boyfriend," She peeks over her shoulder to see Zach's reaction. "A high school English teacher named Brian, works in suburb called Northbrook."

Zach suppresses the pang of jealousy. Ridiculous, expecting a girl – no, woman – like Rachel to be interested in him. It's time to suck it up and let go. If his cousin's happy, he should be happy for her. His mother faces him now, the wooden spoon dangling in her hand, her eyes offering a consoling hug.

"It's okay, Mom. Really." He picks up his backpack and turns toward his room. "I'm happy for her."

. . .

Zach waits until 3:55 to leave his house for the park. It would look pathetic, not to mention desperate, if he arrived before Abe and his friends. The last thing he wants is to be seen wandering around like a lost puppy.

He zigzags northeast until he reaches the intersection of Sheridan Road, Rogers Park's main thoroughfare, and Farwell Avenue. He crosses Sheridan, passes a row of brownstones, and enters the park he hadn't known existed. The wind howls from Lake Michigan. The frozen needles have become daggers and Zach is tempted to join the pussies Abe claimed can't handle the cold. He pulls his beanie over his ears and ducks his chin. After following the sidewalk and moving fifty yards closer to the lake, he notices the group of six or seven huddled bodies gathered under a barren tree. Abe was right. It is easy to spot them, too easy if they're doing what he said they would be doing.

Abe emerges from the pack to greet him. "Awesome, you made it."

He introduces Zach to Priya and the others, three more boys and two girls, all seniors at West Rogers except for Winston, an alumnus three years removed. Each greets Zach with a smile and a puff of white breath.

The girl named Ashley passes him the bottle. The liquor burns his throat. He makes what he knows is an acceptable reaction, merely a wince, that of a drinker experienced enough to handle the liquor but honest enough to acknowledge that vodka bites.

Abe beckons Zach aside. The two boys stroll to the sidewalk and stand facing the lake. Abe gestures toward the beach and the narrow pier extending into Lake Michigan.

"Summertime we'd at the end of the pier. Too much wind out there now."

"Who brought the vodka?" asks Zach.

Abe nods to the group. "Winston, the tall guy in the Packers cap." He leans close, lowers his voice. "Dude just lost his little brother to cancer a few days ago. He seems like a different person. Nobody's sure what to say to him."

Zach glances at the group over his left shoulder. Winston's green and yellow cap rises above the rest. He's laughing with the others but his eyes prowl the surroundings, angry, almost wild. They fall on Zach, who looks quickly away.

"Get your sorry asses over here." Winston raises the vodka bottle to the two boys. "This shit ain't gonna finish itself."

Abe nods to Zach. "C'mon."

The rest of the afternoon is a blur of booze and wind. At 5:15 Zach says goodbye to his new friends, for the most part a good group. But the jury's still out on the older guy, Winston. There was something fragile there, like a twig that'll snap if you step on it. Zach shivers. Got to be tough to lose a little brother.

His equilibrium hijacked by vodka, Zach somehow finds his way home. And while he barely remembers dodging the rush hour traffic on Sheridan Road, he does remember the names of his new friends, the ones he can now count on two woodshop teachers' hands.

Maybe Rogers Park won't be so bad after all.

SIX

WINSTON

It's one a.m. Sheridan Road has gone to bed. Winston Longstreet leans against the door of the closed Rogers Park Cleaners. His face is engulfed in shadow beneath the bill of the Packers cap which juts forward from the hood of a black sweatshirt. The hood protrudes from a grease-stained jacket with a logo, Jones Automotive, stitched on the chest.

Winston shuffles his feet. He takes a deep drag on his cigarette and exhales. The smoke crawls over the bill of the cap. It drifts into the yellow light above the door and like everything beautiful, disappears.

I miss you Micah. God, how I miss you already.

In the buzz of the streetlights he hears a whisper. Micah's voice saying his name.

He shivers. *Get a grip. Remember why you're here.*

He lowers his head and spits on the old man sleeping under the cardboard blanket at his feet. Nothing but another wasted life. Years, decades, stolen from his little brother. Using his boot, Winston nudges the cardboard aside to reveal a wedge of face beneath a tattered Chicago Bears beanie. The sleeping man's nose is large and crooked. Snot, crusty and frozen, clings to the nostrils and grey stubble of the upper lip. The exposed skin is weathered and blotchy, a convoluted network of tiny cracks. But no amount of cracks can hide the deep scar etched across the side of the old man's face.

Christ, what a pathetic sight.

Winston kicks the man's black rubber boot. "Wake up." The man stirs but doesn't open his eyes. Winston kicks again. "I said wake up."

The old man groans. He opens his eyes and gasps. Confused, he shakes his head, blinks hard. Is he dreaming?

Winston leans forward so he's blocking the light from above. His shadow engulfs the old man's face. Winston feels a surge from within. How awesome, to have the power to play God. Too bad he can't turn his voice into a booming echo from the heavens. He leans closer. The shadow on the man's face grows. Winston doesn't speak. He has plenty to say but it can wait. God works in mysterious ways.

The old man struggles to a sitting position and the cardboard falls to the side. He raises his hand, his only hand, to defend himself against the monster towering over him. The other sleeve of the man's ratty coat, empty as his life, drapes over the fallen cardboard. Winston scoffs. Is the fact that this geezer's missing an arm supposed to make him feel better? It doesn't. So what if part of this loser has been taken? God should have finished the job.

The old man's terrified eyes dart left and right. Winston lifts his foot to the man's shoulder. He boot shoves him back onto his lone elbow and crouches, glaring down at the waste of a human being. He takes another drag of his cigarette before flicking the ash. It floats onto the face of the old man who waves it away with a fingerless glove.

"What's your name?" Winston asks, leaning into the terrified face.

"Why?" The cracked lips tremble. "What do you want?"

"Your name." Winston slows the words. They fall like a dark fog. "I want your name."

"Elliot."

Winston lowers himself to the concrete step because even God needs to sit his tired ass down sometimes. He pulls the hood forward, concealing his face. He's still God, but now disguised as the Grim Reaper. The old man leans away, his mouth moving in confusion or silent prayer.

A lonely car, stained with salt, creeps through the Sheridan Road slush. The driver does a double take when he sees the strange pair sitting in the doorway. Winston flips his middle finger at the driver who speeds away leaving a cowardly cloud of white exhaust.

Winston sighs. "This where you live, Elliot? In the doorway of the . . . what is this place?" He cranes his neck to read the lettering on the door above. "The Rogers Park Cleaners?"

No response.

He takes another slow silent drag.

"Fucking shame, don't you think, Elliot, how some people waste their lives when others don't even get a chance to—"

A gust of wind whips past. A howl. Micah's voice, crying. Winston springs to his feet and onto the empty sidewalk. "I'm here Micah." He turns frantically to the north, to the south. He raises his voice. "I'm here for you. I'll always be here."

The wind dies. Winston drops to his knees. A fast food wrapper dances across the sidewalk in front of him and comes to rest. Sheridan Road is quiet and empty. Micha is gone, again. The muscles in Winston's shoulders tighten. His chest heaves. He raises his voice to the heavens. "You fucking took the wrong person." The words echo down the empty street.

Wiping the back of his hand across his mouth, Winston raises his head. What is he doing? Why is he kneeling on a frozen pavement, letting his rage seep into the sidewalk cracks? Letting it go to waste. He takes a deep breath and lets the anger take over. Nothing can stop him: not grief, not conscience, not God. He rises from the sidewalk, a mercenary from the underworld.

When God's doing a shitty job, do it yourself.

He closes his eyes, allows his blood to boil in preparation for the well-deserved terror he's about to inflict on the wasted life behind him. He turns to face the old man.

The doorway of The Rogers Park Cleaners is empty. The cardboard blanket, dragged and discarded, rests on the sidewalk, rocking in the night breeze.

SEVEN

BRIAN

Innocence is born with us. It wanders away from our adolescence, returning to knock on our middle-aged doors while we're too busy or pretending not to hear. Finally, it is allowed re-entry into our lives in old age, provided it wipes its dirty feet on the doormat. - Brian Casey

Yes, one day I will be one of those writers whose profound quotes appear in italics at the start of chapters in great novels. For now, I'll just put it here.

•   •   •

Eleven days have passed since I got laid in a pickup truck. It's a lazy Saturday afternoon. Rachel lies on my bed beside me. We've seen each other four times since our rendezvous at Charlie's. She intrigues me, and part of this intrigue is inspired by this five-foot-two-inch pixie's ability to make a six-foot-two man feel small.

Rachel is, as Clara said, an artist, and it has nothing to do with her ability to create warmth in a frozen pickup truck. Rather than an artist in the traditional sense, Rachel is a decorative artist, one with the ability to take a tray of watered-down paint and a rag and turn a plain vanilla wall into suede. Her occasional canvas paintings are accent pieces created with a certain client's living room in mind. Don't tell her I said so, but to me this reeks of selling out. I imagine most purists would object to the idea of art being created for the specific purpose of matching the furniture.

But who am I to judge? A pill-popping high school teacher with an unwritten novel.

While I have yet to introduce Rachel to my fun-loving personal demons, she knows of my passion for Hitchcock and doesn't mind sharing my bed with the two of us on this lazy afternoon. She stares at my framed Hitchcock poster, a contoured silhouette of a portly genius. She rolls onto her side, facing me.

"Didn't he make most of his movies back in the '50s?" she asks.

"As a director, starting in the '20s, all the way through the early '70s"

"Kind of cool that you're into something from before your time."

She pauses, letting her fingers brush my shoulder. "Makes you interesting, and a little strange. Most people who are into the past feel like they were born at the wrong time. Is that how you feel?"

"Don't know. Maybe."

Lying back, hands locked behind her head, she addresses the ceiling. "I'm guessing this book you're writing has kind of a Hitchcocky feel about it. Am I right?"

"Hitchcocky is not a word."

She flips over onto her elbows, leaning into my face. "You said you're looking for people to use as models, right? For your book? I'm going to help you find these characters"

"Why would you want to do that?"

"Sounds like an adventure."

"I don't want adventures. I save those for my dreams. In real life, adventures can be a pain in the ass, and my ass has a low tolerance for pain."

"Oh yeah, I forgot." She lies back, hands behind her head. "Your whole mantra is avoid this, and once you're done avoiding this, avoid that. At least that's what you say, Mr. Brian Casey, but I think there's an adventurous little gnome inside of you struggling to get out."

"Why would you think that?"

"Because you let my grandmother lead you into her apartment. Because you asked me for my phone number. And, oh yeah, there's that small detail of you fucking me in a stranger's pickup truck. If you really want to live this simple life free of commitment and risk, you wouldn't have done any of those things."

All of this is true. My uncomplicated life has taken some unusual turns.

"Alright," I say. "I admit when I take some chances, it's liberating, but I'm still going to attempt to keep things simple, avoid complications. It's an art not many mortals have mastered. I like to call it. . ." *quick, think of something.* "I like to call it creative avoidance."

She rolls her eyes. "Uh huh, and how does that work?"

I think for a minute.

"Well?"

"Hang on. I'm thinking. Okay, hypothetical example. Let's say I get to work in the morning. Still dark outside. I'm walking toward the school, maybe thirty yards from the door. Another teacher, a woman, is behind me about twenty yards. I figure I'll reach the door in about nineteen seconds. The woman's pulling a large rolling bag, so there's some lag. Her pace is slower. I'm guessing she'll reach the door in, let's say, thirty-seven seconds. I have to make a quick decision, have to creatively avoid a situation."

"What situation?"

"Well, if we both move at our current pace. I'll reach the door eighteen seconds before her. What do I do then? Do I look like an asshole by letting the door close, forcing her to put down her stuff to open it herself? Or do I hold it for her?"

"Of course you hold it for her."

"Aha, but then she sees me holding the door and feels obligated to pick up her pace because she doesn't want to keep me waiting. This is an uncomfortable pace for her. She might even have a heart attack."

Rachel laughs, pulling the sheet over her head. "Oh please. A heart attack?"

I pull the sheet back. "But you see my point, right? Sometimes common courtesy is not so courteous. If I hold the door, I've sent her an invitation to a party she really doesn't want to attend."

"So how do you creatively avoid this situation?"

"As soon as I notice her behind me, I speed up, so there's a greater distance between us, a more acceptable amount of time between each of us reaching our destinations."

"You're still an asshole. She still has to put down her stuff to open the door."

"Yeah, but if she noticed how fast I was moving, she probably assumes I'm in a hurry. Can't afford to hold the door for twenty-five seconds when I'm already late for a parent conference."

Rachel looks at me, shaking her head. "This is your superpower? The one few mortals have mastered?" A pause. "One more question, Einstein. Is this really how you spend your time? Thinking about this kind of stuff?"

I don't answer because the answer is yes.

"I'm cold," she says, snuggling closer.

I unsnap my jeans, take her hand and slide it inside my jeans, onto my crotch.

"What do you think you're doing?" she asks.

"You said you were cold. Just doing my part, keeping your hand warm. You know me, always thinking about others."

"You mean thinking about ways to creatively avoid others. Yeah, I'm beginning to know you, weirdo." She leaves her hand where I've put it.

• • •

The night at Charlie's was a rarity for me. Not only because I had sex in a stranger's pickup truck, but also because I rarely drink hard liquor. It impairs my judgment, causes me to act irrationally. Besides, my other girlfriend, the one going by the name of Vicodin, objects. If there's one thing pills and women have in common, it's a tendency to inflict painful punishment if you cheat.

So when I venture into Rogers Park's local watering hole, Sheridan Sam's, on this frigid Saturday night it's not because I'm seeking warmth at the bottom of a glass of scotch. Nor is it because I care to join the local drunks for whom Sam's represents a home away from home. It's because I've seen these drunks coming and going, and in a Hitchcockian way they inspire me. Perhaps here I can find a model for Sebastian, the long-lost father of Jackson, my novel's protagonist.

When I venture into Sheridan Sam's, I do so in the name of research.

It's one a.m. when I enter the bar. I close the door against the wind, shutting out the buzz of the streetlights. I'm struck by the silence in the room. A few dark heads turn toward me, sizing me up. I'm a trespasser, but one quickly forgiven. Too lazy or drunk to object to my intrusion, the handful of slumping regulars become disinterested and turn quietly back to their whiskey, gin, and solitude.

Sheridan Sam's is unpretentious and dark. Three dim yellow lights hang above the bar. A naked bulb illuminates a puckered dart board on the back wall. Neon beer signs, Old Style and Michelob, glow smoky blue in one corner and red in another. The atmosphere is heavy with the stench of cigarettes and spilled beer. The bartender emerges from a back room wiping his hands on a rag. He doesn't see me. I climb aboard a stool and wait, drumming my fingers on the bar. He picks up a folded newspaper and leans against the back counter, holding the paper under the light. I'm invisible. I might as well be home in bed. At least there I have the full attention of supermodels gracing my dreams.

The silence is interrupted by a small grunt from behind. I turn and see a shadow in the blue corner coming slowly to life. The bulky body rises from a chair with great effort. Something about the movements, the posture, strikes me as familiar. Then he passes under the light of the bar and I get a quick impression of his face: the large crooked nose, the scar stretching across his cheek like an extended smile line ending at the curve of his jaw. An empty sleeve hangs where his left arm should be.

He brushes past me, moving toward the door.

How long ago was it? Almost three weeks? After leaving this grizzled Rogers Park veteran in the Farwell-Pratt alley that day, I'd scolded myself for not considering him a potential novel character. I should have spoken to him, tried to learn something, anything, about him. After all, we're kindred spirits, charged with the tasks of cleaning alleys and bridging generations. I won't let him slip away this time.

Ignored by the others, the old man reaches the door and pulls it open, allowing the dim glow of the Sheridan Road streetlights to penetrate the room. The cold air rushes in. It brings to life a hibernating bear resting his head on his arms at the far corner of the bar. Grunting, this amorphous figure lifts his head and shouts, "God damn it, Louise. Shut that door." Then the bear drops his head and the hibernation continues.

The old man steps outside into the dull yellow glow. The door swings closed behind him. I'll wait a moment to avoid suspicion and then follow. Looks like my three minutes in Sheridan Sam's has come to an end. I guess they won't be naming any cocktails after me.

"I didn't want a drink anyway," I mumble to the out-of-earshot bartender as I slide from my stool. He looks up from the sports page of The Tribune. He's noticing me for the first time, thinking maybe he should have offered me a drink, *but nah, the stranger's leaving now anyway.*

I step outside. For spite, I hold the door open a split second too long. It swings closed, and sure enough I hear it: "God damn it, Louise. Shut that door."

As I turn to the south I'm greeted by a cold gust of Chicago. I zip my jacket to my chin and squint into the wind. The old man has moved thirty yards down Sheridan. He's pulled a beanie over his head, flipped up the collar of the same tattered coat he wore three weeks ago. He wears the same galoshes on his feet, the unlaced flaps at the attention of the wind.

His pants are again bunched around the top of the rubber boots. Bracing himself, he trudges ahead. The loose sleeve flaps in the wind. I consider calling to him: "Hey Mister. Remember me? I helped you clean the Farwell-Pratt alley," but I don't. If he were to reject my overtures I might lose the opportunity to learn anything about him. No, the circumstances call for a more clandestine operation. I'll follow, just long enough to see where he goes, where his home is, if he has one.

The air bites with cold. I pocket one hand while using my teeth to pull a glove over the other. This is not a night for strolling. While I've always taken pride in my ability to defeat the cold by ducking my head and plowing into it, tonight I don't have that option. Tonight I'm determined to stay a good distance behind an old man who, according to my internal speedometer, is walking in place.

It's late, only a few cars on the road. A cab driver slows, gives me a curious look as I hop and jog in place, attempting to stay warm while keeping a safe distance behind the old man. Waiting until he has my full attention, the cabbie shakes his head - *only nutcases out walking at this time of night* - and speeds away.

The old man reaches the end of the block and to my surprise turns left on Farwell. Surely he doesn't live in a lake-side-of-Sheridan condo. The wrought iron-fronted brownstones east of Sheridan Road represent the closest thing Rogers Park has to prime real estate. I increase my pace so not to lose sight of him.

I turn onto Farwell. I'm in a different world. The hum of the Sheridan Road streetlights is gone. The cold has become dark and quiet and still, the wind buffered by the brownstones lining the street. I gaze to the east, beyond the old man. Although I know this street gives way to a park ending at a beach that borders Lake Michigan, tonight, beyond the dim streetlights glowing in the distant cul-de-sac, there's only black. By the time the old man reaches this abyss, my skepticism about his life as a brownstone dweller is confirmed. He steps over the curb and disappears into the shadows of the park.

I hurry to the cul-de-sac and jump over the curb. The wind has returned. It howls through trees, swaying branches above me. Restless clouds drift like black smoke across the sky, revealing only an occasional wisp of the moon. I squint toward the east. There he is, a shadow fifty yards ahead. Beyond the old man, geometric shapes emerge from the darkness: the grey beach, the black lake, the narrow pier dissecting the lake.

I wait for him to stop and bed down on the only remaining bench, the last refuge for anyone who, for whatever insane reason, is drawn to this winter wasteland in the middle of a frigid night. Instead of stopping, he plods on through the darkness, past the bench and graffiti wall, onto the open beach.

I pause when I reach the bench.

We're not alone. A flash of a camera, distant voices and laughter interrupt the night. Ahead to my left, five or six teenagers huddle, partiers, secure in their assumption it's safe to get wasted on a cold beach late at night. They don't see me, but they've spotted the old man. They're pointing and laughing. Oblivious or unconcerned, the old man trudges ahead, across the beach and onto the narrow concrete pier stretching into the blackness of Lake Michigan.

The sight of the old man starting onto the pier is too much for the teenagers to resist. They move toward him, stumbling, laughing and shoving each other. Then they're on the pier. They've narrowed the distance. I'm a spectator to what strikes me as a scene from a twenty-first century remake of *A Clockwork Orange*: a gang of misguided youth pursuing an old man onto a frozen pier in the middle of the night.

I step from the sidewalk onto the beach, straining to see the old man. His image blends in and out of the distant darkness. Upon reaching the end of the pier, he stops and turns to the south. He rests his forearms on the railing and stares into the black water. My attention snaps back to the teenagers as a scream – a battle cry – comes from the cluster of dark bodies. Then, as though shot from a cannon, one of the figures breaks from the pack and charges toward the end of the pier. He slides into the old man. For a second the two shadows become one. Then the taller of the two lifts the other by the legs. He flips him over the rope and into the water with a silent splash.

Common sense screams at me to turn and run the other way but conscience propels me forward. I rush onto the pier shouting something asinine like "Hey." The other teenagers turn and see me coming. I'm body-slammed into the railing. Pain. Blackness. Nothing.

. . .

Seconds, minutes, maybe hours later, I regain consciousness. My face rests against cold gravel. I spit out dust, blink hard. Lifting my head, I attempt to shake away the cobwebs. The pain in my skull screams at me to stop.

How long was I out?

The scenario returns to me piece by piece: the bartender ignoring me at Sheridan Sam's, the cab driver turning to look at me as I did my strange dance behind the old man, the flash of a camera, the laughter of the teenagers. The Teenagers? Where are they?

Hoisting myself onto an elbow, I squint to the west. There they are, running away in the distance. The dark images disappear into the shadows of the park. I struggle to a knee. My head throbs. I tug a glove from my trembling hand and touch the lump above my left ear. Tender and painful, but no blood.

I clutch the twisted steel rope that serves as a railing. There's no way the rope caused the lump on my head. I must have hit the iron post. I try pulling myself to my feet. An irresistible force knocks me back down. I kneel on the pier, clutch the rope, and vomit. I'm in a vortex, spinning. Did I really see what I think I saw? The old man, what's happened to him? It was only a few minutes ago, wasn't it? Is he still in the water? Splashing? Freezing?

Determined, I drag myself to my feet. I use the steel rope to hoist myself toward the end of the pier. I gaze into the black water. Nothing. I stagger toward the shore, straining my eyes to where dark waves lap onto a darker beach. Nothing.

My next instinct is to call 911 – the correct instinct – until I begin to anticipate scenarios. What if someone at Sheridan Sam's saw me come in, sit three minutes, and follow the old man out into the night? What about the cab driver who saw me follow him down Sheridan? What if someone saw me turn on Farwell and follow him into what should have been a deserted park? These questions chase me as I rush up and down the pier searching for the proverbial needle - or in this case old man - in a haystack that goes by the name of Lake Michigan.

I yell at the water, "Hey. Can you hear me? Hey." I stumble down the pier calling into the water. I stand and yell from the beach.

How will I explain myself? Why am I here?

The teenagers. Perhaps they left some evidence. I scavenge the dark beach, unsure if I'm looking for something to show the cops or to justify their existence to myself. I find nothing, not a beer can, not a cigarette butt, nothing. Will anyone believe my story? The only evidence I have of anything is a bump on the head that could have just as easily been caused by a slip on the icy pier.

I look at the sky. No answers up there.

I stopped believing in God years ago. But as I stand on the frozen beach I wish I hadn't. I wish it wasn't my place to worry because it all happens for a reason. But it doesn't. I can think of no reason why an old man distraught over the apathy of a younger generation should die by their hands. What had he said in the alley that day? "Nobody knows, and nobody cares."

I sit on the arctic sand, raise my knees, and lay my head on my forearms. Helplessness can be humbling. I'm not big enough for a world where nature, human or otherwise, has the power to remind us we're pawns, our lives don't matter. The old man's dead. He must be. Only one arm, dumped into a frozen lake, his clothes heavy and wet. Besides, what will I do if the body washes up at my feet? Will I feel obligated to dispose of it, to get rid of the evidence of someone else's crime?

Hours pass: two, three, maybe more. I sit and stare at the dark expanse of water and darker space above. I'm still here on this frozen beach because I have to believe a miracle will happen and if I leave I'll miss it. At any moment the old man will rise like a messiah from the lake. He'll be alive. I'll be saved.

I snap myself to reality, turn and look behind. Rogers Park is still asleep, but for how long? They'll want to know why I didn't report this when it first happened. It's too late now. That ship sailed hours ago.

Eventually, I give up on my miracle. I've waited too long to do anything but leave. I want to be home. Instead of the wind and waves, I want to hear the rattle of a pill bottle. I want to climb into my bed and wake up from this nightmare. The eastern sky is beginning to show the first signs of light on the Lake Michigan horizon. I take one last cursory look at the expanse of water. I turn and walk back through the park. Once I reach Sheridan Road I'm a hit-and-run driver. I've left the scene of the crime, and like a Rogers Park window painted shut, I know this window of opportunity, the opportunity to do the right thing, is closed forever.

EIGHT

ZACH

It's been a long time since Zach cried. Even saying goodbye to his friends in Atlanta, to life as he knew it, he hadn't shed a tear. He understands and accepts this. He's an adult now, desensitized, and a wall eighteen years in the making blocks him from childish emotions.

But last night was different. Last night the wall crumbled and the tears flowed freely.

It's almost six a.m. Zach lies on his bed and repeats the words to the ceiling. "I shouldn't have been there. I knew that asshole was trouble." He'd hesitated when Abe told him Winston Longstreet would be at the beach with them, but caved when promised they would stay just long enough to catch a buzz.

He rolls onto his side. A camera rests beside him on the bed. It wasn't a dream.

Again, he goes back to the beginning.

They met on the beach at one a.m. as planned: Abe, Winston, Zach, and two other boys. Huddling against the cold, they danced in place and shared a bottle of vodka. Winston snapped pictures with a digital camera smaller than a deck of cards. This, he claimed, was his way of "chronicling a bunch of frozen pussies who can't handle their liquor."

Anderson was the first to see the old man. "Dudes, check it out. Who's that?"

They all turned and watched the unexpected figure emerge from the nighttime shadows of the oak trees and plod onto the open beach. A loose sleeve flapped in the wind. He struggled forward as though pulling an invisible plow.

Winston stepped from the pack to get a better look. "Wait a minute. I know this loser. What's his name?" He pondered a moment. "Elliot. That's it. He's garbage, sleeps in doorways on Sheridan." Winston held the bottle to his lips and took a long swig. After watching the old man reach the pier, he added, "Where the fuck is he going? C'mon."

Full of bravado and vodka, they followed Winston toward the pier with the understanding they were just going to mess with the old man. Zach had no desire to participate, but he was the new guy, so he followed, trying to convince himself he wouldn't let things get out of hand. They started onto the narrow pier. The wind blew harder. Zach swore the pier was swaying, but dismissed the idea as vodka-induced. Still, clutching the twisted steel rope and pulling himself forward, he couldn't help feel he was crossing a rope bridge over a deep canyon. He threw up in his mouth and spat. Hoping to regain some sense of sobriety, he gulped the cold air.

They reached the halfway point of the pier. The old man had struggled to the end. He leaned forward on the steel rope, gazed into the water below. Winston turned to Zach and the others with a wry grin. "Let's see if he can swim."

Abe laughed at Winston's joke, but the laughter faded abruptly as Winston pivoted, pumped a fist, and sprinted away from them. His battle cry defied the wind to slow him down and by the time he reached the end of the pier the roar had faded into the night.

Zach watched, frozen with vodka and horror, as one of the two distant shadows disappeared over the edge and the other threw his arms skyward in triumph. He was struggling to process what he'd seen when out of nowhere the other guy came from behind, emerging from the dark, shouting and running toward them. Zach barely had time to turn around before he saw Anderson pile drive his shoulder into this man. The man's head made a horrifying ring as it cracked against an iron post.

Winston was running toward them from the end of the pier. The other boys ran toward the beach. As though caught by a wave, Zach ran with them. At the base of the pier, he looked over his shoulder and slowed. Winston had stopped. He was bending over the unconscious man, going through his pockets. Then Winston was up and running again, sprinting toward Zach. Zach increased his pace, the others ahead of him, Winston behind. Swept up in a nightmare, Zach chased the other boys through the park and past the brownstones. It was so easy to run, the wind at his back, each step carrying him closer to safety. And while he swore he could hear the cries of the man struggling in the frozen lake, the voice was drowned out by Winston's threats approaching from behind.

"Keep moving, motherfucker. Run."

Zach reached the others who had stopped, ducked into the doorway of The White Hen pantry and were bent over, hands on knees. Zach struggled to find his breath although he knew it was there because it showed itself in short white bursts from his mouth.

Anderson raised his head to face Winston as he approached. "What the fuck, Winston? What the fuck?"

Winston bent over, caught his breath. Then he straightened his tall frame. "Shut up and listen." He waited until all eyes were on him. He looked at each boy in turn, his measured words falling on them with threatening precision. "This never happened. I swear to God I'll fuck you up if. . ." Winston's words continued, but Zach couldn't hear them. They were drowned out by the voice screaming in his head.

Go back. Call the cops. You've got to do something.

It was close to two a.m. Winston continued his rant. It occurred to Zach that a group of young men gasping for breath in the middle of the night could draw unwanted attention, but from who? There were no pedestrians, and the driver of the only passing car looked away, choosing not to confront a nocturnal band of teenagers. The others were talking and arguing, but to Zach their words were nothing but background noise. He stared at the ground.

"I'm going home," he said to a crack in the sidewalk. The lack of acknowledgement from the others made him unsure if he'd spoken these words aloud. He raised his head and looked at Abe. Their eyes met for an instant. Abe turned quickly away.

Ignoring Winston's continuing threats, Zach crossed Sheridan and started north, knowing he'd double back once the others were gone.

From behind the edge of a building on the corner of Sheridan and Farwell, he watched and waited. Abe was gone, but Winston remained, talking to the other two. Several times, Winston stepped from the doorway of The White Hen Pantry, strolled to the corner, and glared toward the park in the distance.

Zach clenched his teeth. "Go home assholes," he whispered to the three boys a block away. After a ten-minute eternity they went their separate ways. None came his.

The rush back down Farwell and through the park was a new nightmare. The street was longer. The cold, colder. And while murder can do wonders for sobering you up, it doesn't mix well with vodka. Twice Zach had to stop running and bend over, splattering vomit onto the sidewalk. When he reached the bench resting atop the graffiti wall, he strained his eyes toward the pier. Nothing. The man they left in an unconscious heap was gone. He looked to the right on the chance the old man might have struggled ashore, and his vision caught slow movement in the darkness. Fifty yards to his right, not twenty feet from the water, a shadow sat hunched over. It could have been a rock, but rocks don't sway back and forth in agony. Zach crouched behind the bench and watched, not knowing what he hoped to achieve, but knowing he had to watch.

The man sat and rocked. He gazed at the sky. Several times he got up and walked the length of pier, staring into the black water before returning to his seat on the beach to continue his rocking. Zach wanted to console this man, tell him he was sorry, he was a victim too. He struggled to keep his emotions in check.

He's okay. At least physically, he's okay.

Zach leaned against the bench. He drifted in and out of a troubled sleep. Each time he awoke, the man was still sitting on the frozen beach. At first Zach thought he was dreaming when the figure stood and walked his direction. He shook himself, rubbed his eyes. It wasn't a dream. Zach scampered behind the bench and ducked low. He couldn't control the shivering, the pounding of his heart. The dark figure shuffled toward him. Then, with only twenty feet of darkness between them, the man made a left turn onto the sidewalk and into the park.

Zach kept a good distance behind as he followed the man through the park and onto Farwell. It wasn't until he was fifty yards from Sheridan Road that Zach noticed it. It almost called to him, a glint of light reflecting from a streetlight onto the silver edge of a small metallic rectangle. He moved closer to the object and bent to look at it. A camera, nestled beside the iron fence fronting one of the brownstones. Zach picked it up, looked from side to side, nobody. Behind him, nobody. He slid the camera into the pocket of his coat and like a guardian angel followed his subject home.

NINE

WINSTON

It's Sunday morning, 6:15 a.m. Winston stands at the base of the Rogers Park pier. A cold grey mist rises from Lake Michigan. The sky on the horizon is the color of ash and fades to charcoal above. If only Micah hadn't died. He would have thought this was beautiful: the mist, the sky. The kid had a knack for finding beauty in natural things. Nine years old, yet saw the world through the eyes of an artist.

Winston shivers. *Refocus. Remember why you're here.*

He's walked the length of the pier three times and through the park twice without any luck. Now the flashlight's battery is running low. The white light he'd used to sweep the ground to his left and right has faded to a dull yellow and his search, for the time being, has become impossible.

Still, the camera has got to be here somewhere.

If he waits a little longer, until the dull grey on the horizon lifts into the sky, he may have enough natural light. Maybe then he'll spot it. But he can't stay too long. After what happened four hours ago, he better not be seen here this morning. Before long, the old Russian couples in fur hats will be strolling through the park. People with no lives will be walking dogs.

Keep looking. A little longer.

He starts down the pier for the fourth time. The unused light tower at the end is coming into focus, silhouetted against the dawn. He squints into the wind. Too much vodka. Too little sleep. For a moment he thinks he sees a shadow clinging to the railing, dangling above the water.

Did last night really happen? Did he really kill a man? .

He shuffles the loose gravel under his feet. A few pebbles he kicks into the water. So what if he did kill that bum? If God doesn't take the right people, he'll have to do it himself. There are those who deserve to die and those who don't.

Micah's voice whispers through the wind. "Thank you, big brother."

Winston turns to the west. Rogers Park is coming to life, more yellow lights appearing in windows. It's time to go. If he doesn't spot the camera on the way back, he'll accept that it's gone. He starts down the pier, sweeping the gravelly surface with his eyes, his hope swept into the cosmos like the whiteness of his breath.

It was one hour ago that Winston sat up from a drunken sleep and sensed something wrong, something left behind. He checked the pocket of his jacket. His camera wasn't there. He checked the floor, under the bed, the hallway outside his room. No camera. He sat on the bed and rubbed his temples. His head pounded with vodka regret. His mouth felt stuffed with cotton. Still, he couldn't let the discomfort stop him. He had to go back to the pier.

Within two minutes Winston was out of the house running, dragging his hangover like a ball and chain through the dark streets of Rogers Park. He was unsure what he'd find upon his return to the beach. The unconscious man whose wallet he lifted, would this man, Brian Casey, still be there? Would he be standing with cops on the beach next to the lifeless body of an old bum washed ashore? Would those cops be holding a transparent bag with a single piece of evidence, the camera?

Winston's mother had given him the digital camera as a gift a year ago for his twentieth birthday. It housed a year's worth of his life, but more importantly, the last year of Micah's. Sure, there were images from last night that could prove to be problematic, but Winston had been the one snapping pictures and so would be absent from them. Instead they were pictures of Abe, Anderson, Spenser, and that new kid. What was his name? Zach?

Now the sky on the horizon is starting to glow orange. Winston takes a final stroll down the pier and through the park. Nothing.

Why hadn't he saved the contents of the camera to his computer? How could he be so stupid? He replays the images in his head: He and Micah together at Navy Pier before the cancer, waving foam fingers in the Wrigley Field bleachers, Micah, bald and smiling, propped in a living room hospice bed as though all was right with his world.

When Winston reaches Sheridan Road, he pauses. Only one explanation, only one place the camera could be. He reaches into his jacket, removing the wallet he'd lifted from the unconscious man four hours ago. He flips it open to the driver's license: Brian Casey, 406 Pratt Avenue, apartment 3B

TEN

BRIAN

Six times a day I'm a traffic cop. As teachers, during the passing periods at Booker High School, the expectation is that we stand outside our doors hurrying students along and ushering them like sheep into classrooms, a monotonous task to say the least.

Today every pair of eyes avoids mine for fear I may recognize them from an incident on a dark pier. All laughter is the laughter of despicable teenagers preying on the elderly. Every shoulder braces, preparing to slam me into an iron post.

I'm haunted by Saturday night.

I can see Magby standing by his doorway three doors down from my own. He's reprimanding a male student, waving his finger. His raised voice draws attention from passing students. I wonder what happened to set him off. Doesn't matter. I'm not surprised by anything anymore. Since Saturday night, I'm convinced I'll never be surprised again.

Later, I ask Magby about his altercation with the student.

"The little shit," he says. "Kid's been chewing and spitting tobacco juice in my classroom. After he left class yesterday I noticed a brown spot on the carpet back by his desk. Dabbed it with a tissue, and it was wet, so I know it was him. Told him I'm going to come to his house and spit nasty stuff all over his carpet. Fucking kids. This is not what I signed up for."

I don't tell him about the "fucking kids" who drown old men for fun. I haven't told anyone about what happened two nights ago. I'm still trying to convince myself it never happened.

•   •   •

It's the following Saturday. I'm on my way to Rachel's apartment in Lincolnwood. I've asked her to lunch. "Got to talk to you,'" I said. "Tell you about something that happened last weekend."

I'd spoken to Rachel but not seen her during the week. It wasn't easy, resisting the urge to tell her about the incident. I'm hoping her reaction will make it worth the wait. Sympathy sex could be a nice little bonus. She suggested eating at a place close to her and asked me to come to her apartment. She had a few errands to run but would be home by noon.

I arrive at 12:10 and ring the bell. An unfamiliar voice answers through the intercom.

"Who is it?"

"Brian Casey. Is Rachel home?"

"Brian? Okay, she told me you were coming. She's not back yet. Hang on. I'll buzz you up."

Wearing blue sweatpants and a baggy t-shirt, a disheveled but gorgeous blonde opens the door. I'm reminded of Hitchcock's quote about blondes making the best murder victims because "they're like virgin snow that shows up the bloody footprints." I'm tempted, but decide telling this young woman she'd make a wonderful murder victim is probably not the best opening line.

This, I know, is Chelsea. Rachel had told me about her roommate, a store manager at Northbrook Court, a suburban mall no more than a mile from Booker High School. What Rachel didn't tell me was that

Chelsea's eyes are the color of water lapping onto a Bahama beach. A strange wave of relief washes over me as I realize a traumatic incident on a dark pier has not superseded my ability to appreciate what's really important in life.

"Hi there. I'm Chelsea." She extends her hand. "Come on in. I guess Rachel should be home soon. Maybe got caught in traffic. Want something to drink?"

"Nah, thanks. I'm fine."

"Well, I don't mean to be rude, but I've got to get ready. I'm on my way out. Make yourself at home."

I watch Chelsea walk away. While I've seen my share of women walk away from me, this time I don't mind. In fact, I hope she comes back soon so I can watch her walk away again.

I sink into a couch to wait.

In the corner of the room an easel holds a canvas with abstract splashings of blues and greens. The subject matter of this painting is obviously open to interpretation. That is, unless you're an art connoisseur like me; I instantly recognize the image as an old man drowning in a lake. Next to this easel, on a table covered with a plastic cloth, lie scattered tubes of paint and an assortment of brushes. Other brushes rest in a cup of cloudy water. A shirt, a man's size, hangs on the edge of the easel. It's rolled at the sleeves and covered with paint smudges.

Rachel comes in. "Hey superhero." Crossing to me, she bends and kisses me on the cheek. "Sorry I'm late. Give me five minutes to freshen up." Another attractive woman excuses herself from me. If I didn't take so much pleasure in watching them walk away, I might acknowledge this as a disturbing trend.

Chelsea comes back into the room first, hair brushed, wearing blue jeans and a red sweater. She smiles at me as she opens a closet door.

"Nice meeting you, Brian. Have fun." She puts on her coat and walks out.

• • •

"She's pretty, huh?" Rachel asks as we step out into the crisp afternoon.

"Is she?" I give her a tiny grin. "Didn't notice."

"You are so full of shit."

I slip my arm through hers. "Okay, I guess she's pretty. But I prefer cute little brunettes with smiles curling at the corners, green eyes, and a smattering of freckles across their nose."

She looks up at me. It's a look I haven't seen before. I'm experiencing a breakthrough. Rachel Gold is having a bashful moment. The only other times my words had been followed by silence were when they had fallen flat and the silence had been calculated, a ploy allowing her time to step on those words and crush them, along with my spirit, into the sidewalk.

She gathers herself and pretending to be unmoved, slides her arm from mine. "Yeah, you better pile on the flattery, buddy. You've got some competition now."

"Yeah? Who's that?"

"My adorable cousin Zach. He's had a crush on me since puberty. His puberty, not mine. His family just moved here from Atlanta." She raises her eyebrows, a stern warning. "Eighteen and legal. I'm tellin' ya, Brian, competition."

Playing along, I shake my head, overcome by despair. "Damn. That's what I get for falling for a cougar."

We step into The Olympus Grill, one of Lincolnwood's fifteen-million Greek cafes, and find a table by the window. Rachel is quick to comment on the playful mural filling the walls, animated Greeks dancing and throwing plates. Opa! White buildings and blue water fill the background. "Love the passion in here," she says. "Can't leave a place like this with a care in the world."

I slide her chair out. "Hold that thought." I take my seat, lean forward, and wiggle my fingers for her to do the same.

She props her chin in her palm. "Ooh, must be something juicy."

I glance at the other customers. If any of them happen to be film historians, they must see our image as undeniably Hitchcokian. We're silhouettes of conspiring young lovers in an urban café, about to whisper across a table in front of a bright window where only the outsiders looking in can make out our faces. The camera would zoom in on our silhouettes as a portly man passes by outside, Alfred Hitchcock himself, choosing this opportunity to make his traditional cameo.

"Hey, space cadet." Rachel shakes my arm. "What's going on?"

I lean closer. "Something happened last Saturday night. Something bad."

Her eyes widen.

I start at the beginning. I tell her about meeting an old man in the Farwell-Pratt alley two days after I met her, an old man with only one arm, a crooked nose, and a long jagged scar on his face. She looks at me, head cocked, eyes squinting. She thinks I'm using her as a guinea pig, seeing how she'll react to an outrageous character description. Then, after our order is taken, something in my tone must convince her of my sincerity. Her expression changes to one of concern as I tell her about my visit to Sheridan Sam's and the rest of my misadventure.

"Why didn't you call the cops?" she asks.

"I waited too long. Started thinking about how I'd explain why I was there. Besides, what could I tell them? I couldn't identify those kids. It was too dark. They were all bundled up."

I gaze from the window. The street is busy with Saturday pedestrians. A father and son pass by. The little boy is holding onto Daddy's sleeve, tugging, trying to get his father's attention. It occurs to me how quickly people disappear, and I understand I've experienced my second life-defining moment, only this time a man is not just gone, but dead.

Hold on tight kid. Tug a little harder.

"Why didn't you go to the hospital?" Rachel asks, breaking my trance.

"I'm fine. It was just a bump on the head."

"Yeah, a bump that caused you to black out. You should have gone to the ER."

I dismiss her concern with a wave of my hand. Concussions happen. For real men, life goes on. "Okay" but listen. There's one more thing." I lean in again, this time closer. "When I got back to my apartment there was a note in my mail slot."

"A note? What did it say?"

"It said, 'say anything, and you're next'."

"Oh my God, Brian. How'd they know where you live? Did they take your wallet?"

I nod. "Didn't realize it until I got back to my building."

The waiter delivers our food. With complete disregard for the fact that I have a beautiful woman hanging on my every word, he fusses around the table, wiping a wet spot, straightening the condiments. I'm tempted to throw my plate at him. Opa! After he leaves, Rachel stabs at her Greek salad, attempting to unite the lettuce, tomato, onion, and feta on her fork. We eat for a moment in silence. My incredible story has rendered her speechless, or so I think. She raises her head, her expression mockingly serious.

"Why is it you keep finding yourself around old people who have fallen and can't get up?"

Unbelievable.

I let my mouth drop so she'll recognize my disapproval of her flippant attitude and throw herself at my knees, begging forgiveness.

"He didn't fall," I say. "He was thrown from a pier."

"Oh, c'mon, Brian. Lighten up. It's kind of exciting." She returns to her salad but stops, dropping her fork and grabbing my arm. "Ooh, got a great idea. Use something like this as the last scene in your novel. What's your main character's name? Jackson, right?"

I nod.

"Listen to this," she continues. "Jackson follows an old man down a dark pier because - I don't know - think of that part later. Anyway, the old man falls from the pier. Jackson rushes to help, but as he's reaching for the old guy's hand, he recognizes him as his father and lets him sink into his watery grave."

She leans back, open palms. *This novel writing business is a piece of cake.*

I'm at a loss. How can I be angry with a woman who thinks like Hitchcock? Her idea has turned a traumatic event into an opportunity. I visualize the film, the one based on my novel, the one Hitchcock has returned from the grave to direct because it's just too good for him to stay dead. In the closing scene he directs the camera to focus on each face: Sabastian's crooked smile from the water as he recognizes his long-lost son reaching for him, then Jackson's reaction as he recognizes the man who deserted him as a child. Next, Hitch directs the camera to zoom in on the hands as the one above releases the one below. Finally, one last image of Sabastian's terrified face as he sinks into the black water.

I look at Rachel a moment in silence, pretending to be unimpressed, pretending to be upset that she's not bursting into tears at the idea of my life being threatened, pretending I'm not falling in love with her.

•   •   •

Back in my apartment, I pop open a beer and turn on a basketball game. My mind stays with Rachel. Every time I leave this woman I walk headfirst into a wind of questions blowing me back in her direction.

I remember being told by my high school art teacher that mistakes do not exist in art. Well, if as Oscar Wilde pointed out, it is life that imitates art rather than the other way around, I suppose for an artist, mistakes do not exist in life. Rachel has a way of embracing mistakes, seizing moments in their various degrees of discomfort or trouble and splashing them onto the canvas of her life. Me? I'm a blending color, burnt umber or something like that. She'll squeeze every oily ounce of me onto her palette and use me as she pleases.

I wash down the remainder of my philosophy with the final sips of beer. I can't help but imagine Rachel would be thrilled to know my time away from her is spent trying to attach meaning to our time together.

She's won again.

Determined to reclaim a sense of autonomy, I cross the room and check my voicemail. Two messages, the first from my mother in Houston.

"Hi, Sweetie. Haven't heard from you in a while. Give me a call when you get a chance so we can catch up."

The second voice is unfamiliar. "Hello, Mr. Casey. My name is Josiah Coffee. I'm a student at Howard High School. A friend of mine that goes to Booker gave me your name. I'm calling 'cause I want to take the AP English test in May to try to get college credit, but I'm not in an AP class. My friend said you're a real good teacher, so I was wondering, do you do any tutoring? I just need—"

Beep. Message deleted.

Tutoring? I'll pass. Who's got the time? I've got a woman to figure out, a murder to process, and a father to kill. Hell, even my regular March job of armchair college basketball analyst has been put on hold because this year March madness has taken on a whole new meaning.

• • •

The next afternoon, Rachel and I sit over a greasy pizza box at my kitchen table.

"It's like this," I say. "The human body is made up of mostly water, right? So it has about the same gravity as water."

She washes down her final bite of pizza with a sip of diet coke. "Okay."

"And how quickly a submerged body rises depends on the amount of air trapped in the clothing, but heavy clothing or heavy boots adds to the gravity, might keep it submerged for a while."

"Uh huh." Her eyes drift to the ceiling.

"It depends on how quickly some kind of gas forms. Putre-fac-tive gas I think it's called. Anyway, this gas decreases the gravity. Makes the body rise. The colder the water, the longer it takes." I try my best to sound as though this is common knowledge, as though Wikipedia doesn't exist.

Rachel leans forward on her elbows, chin in palms. "So, Professor Casey, will this information be on our final exam? And is it true that you accept sexual favors for extra credit?"

She's in no mood to discuss forensics. It takes me an entire nanosecond to decide to play along. "As a matter of fact, Ms. Gold, I do accept sexual favors. Come by my office later today and I'm pretty sure we can figure out a way to bump your grade from an F to an A."

"An F? Why do I have an F?"

"Sorry, but you haven't yet mastered my anatomy."

She pouts. "But, professor, I thought I aced my midterm, the one I took in that cold pickup truck."

"Yes, you did do quite well, but now that I know what you're capable of, I know you can do even better." I wave my finger, a stern reprimand. "I'm not going to give up on you, Miss Gold. I'm going to push you to reach your full potential."

My phone rings, bringing an end to our little game. I hear Pat Sajak's voice in my head: "That's it folks. That sound indicates our time is up. And the winner of this episode of "Sexual Role Play" is Brian for his portrayal of Professor Casey."

The ringtone continues. Rachel looks at me. "Gonna get that?"

"Nah." I slump in my chair. "Probably this kid calling again about tutoring. He called yesterday and earlier today. Doesn't even go to Booker. Got my name from a friend."

"What does he want your help with?"

"Getting ready for the AP test."

"And you don't want to help him?"

"It's not that. I'm too busy."

She leans back. "You should help the kid out, Brian. Make some extra cash so you can take your girlfriend out to fancy restaurants? I'm sure she'd love to be wined and dined."

"Yeah, I'll bet." I toss my remaining crust into the pizza box. "Oh, speaking of wining and dining, I forgot to ask. A friend of mine from work wants us to go to dinner with him and his wife this week. How's that sound?"

"Hunky-dory."

"What night's good for you?"

She considers. "I don't know. Tuesday?"

"Ok, I'll tell him."

She sips her diet coke. "Who's your friend?"

"Clinton Magby." I can't help but smile. "Magby's going to say Tuesday's perfect. We play basketball against some coaches after school on Tuesdays. If we win, he'll get to brag to you women about how the teachers licked the jocks."

"He'd say that?"

"Wouldn't be the first time."

"I like him already."

Rachel leans forward on her elbows. "So, Professor Casey. Do I really have to wait until later to come to your office?"

Commercial break over. Game on.

"Now, Miss Gold, you know I'm about to give a lecture. If you want to earn extra credit, you're going to have to work around my penis - I mean my schedule."

She chuckles, reaching under the table and placing her hand on my inner thigh. "Bet I can change your mind."

I let out a great sigh of oppression. "You young people today. The concept of patience is lost on you. Everything has to be now - now - now."

She stands up and peels her sweater over her head, dangles it in the tips of her fingers and lets it fall to the floor. She sashays toward the bedroom, winking over her shoulder.

I take the hint.

"Sit there," she says, taking my shoulders and lowering me to the bed. She backs up five feet and unbuttons her blouse. It could be the sexiest thing I've ever seen. She slips the blouse from her shoulders, twirls it, and tosses it at me. It brushes against the side of my face and I catch her scent. It slides onto my shoulder and floats to my feet. She reaches behind and unhooks her bra. It falls to the floor.

"Should I keep going, professor?"

I fake a yawn. "Meh. I guess so."

"Then call him back."

"What? Call who back?"

"The kid that wants tutoring. You want me to keep going? Call him back. Tell him you'll help him."

"Seriously?"

"Yes. Seriously."

"Okay, I'll call him tonight." I stand and move toward her.

"No." She pushes me onto the bed and unsnaps her jeans. Her fingers locate the zipper and lower it two inches. It's the new sexiest thing I've ever seen. "Call him back now," she purrs.

If it's true that weakness for a beautiful woman makes a man more of a man, then I'm Rambo, John Wayne, and every real man in between. I'm putty in the hands of the woman standing topless before me. Rachel's breasts are small but shapely. Her erect nipples – thank you Chicago for staying chilly in March – are aimed at me like a couple of Cupid's horny little arrows. But it's her face, her parted lips and green eyes that have me mesmerized.

I pat my empty pocket. "Alright, I'll call him, but I have to get his number. Phone's in the other room. I'm allowed to go get it, right? I mean, you will still be standing here in my office half naked when I get back, right, Miss Gold?"

"Who knows, professor? I may be all-the-way naked."

I stroll out of the room. Once I'm out of her sight I move like a man on fire. I retrieve the phone and don't slow down until I reappear in the bedroom doorway. Rachel is now "all-the-way naked." I'm surprised by my own reaction. Of course I'm turned on. But it's also an affirmation of her feelings for me. It's one thing for a woman to be naked under the covers or in a dark room, but to be standing before me completely exposed on a Sunday afternoon represents a different kind of commitment: total honesty, full disclosure. I'm not sure if it's my heart or penis that's moved the most by this.

Rachel nods at the forgotten cellphone in my hand, clears her throat. "Oh, right."

I make the call. "Hi, is this Josiah Coffee?" Rachel struts toward me. "Hi Josiah. Brian Casey, returning your calls." She drops to her knees. "Got your messages about tutoring, and yeah, I'd be happy to help you out." She unsnaps and unzips my jeans, pulling them and my boxers down below my knees. "Uh yeah, how about if we start on Friday?"

Rachel looks up at me and scowls, shaking her head. "Sooner," she whispers.

I cover the phone. "What? Sooner?"

"Sooner," she repeats.

"Um, wait a minute, Josiah. How about Wednesday?"

Rachel scoots back on her knees. "Sooner."

I press the phone against my chest. "This kid's going to think I'm nuts."

She reaches for her discarded bra and panties.

"Tell you what, Josiah, how about tomorrow? Can you start tomorrow?" Rachel crawls toward me, puts her hands on my thighs. She grins up at me and takes me into her mouth.

"I'll have to, uh, call you back later with the details," I steady my voice. "Can't really talk right now."

Rachel releases me, shaking her head. "Do it now," she whispers.

"Now?"

Again, she reaches for the panties.

My jeans and boxers are at my ankles, my cock is at full attention, and my phone has found its way back to my ear. "Alright, Josiah. Let's do it this way."

Rachel opens her mouth and takes me in.

The rest of my conversation with Josiah Coffee is a blur. Did we arrange to meet at 3:30 or 4:30? Did I remember to ask him to purchase an *English Language and Composition* practice book? Did I really say, "Shit, that feels good" into the phone?

. . .

The following day I wait for Josiah at The Loyola University library. He said he preferred not meeting at my apartment because he would feel he was intruding. I'm guessing it's because the library is closer to his home. No problem. Loyola, on the southern edge of Rogers Park, is only one extra stop on the red line as I head south from Booker.

Having arrived an hour early, I sit in a chair in the lobby drafting character descriptions on my laptop and mentally undressing attractive coeds. I'm amazed how many of them have Rachel's body.

A voice comes from my left. "Mr. Casey?" I'm snapped from my trance.

"Yes." I stand up, extending my hand. "Nice to meet you, Josiah. Ready to get to work?"

He pats the binder tucked under his arm and shows me the English Language and Composition practice book I did apparently ask him to bring.

Josiah strikes me as a quiet kid. He's polite to a fault, and when I ask him to call me Brian because "Mr. Casey just makes me feel old" he's uncomfortable with the idea. I point in the direction of the reference shelves where an empty table awaits. "Let's have a seat over there. Looks quiet."

He nods.

"Who's your friend at Booker?" I ask.

"Malory Carstens."

This is a name I don't know, but I'm not surprised. Teachers gain reputations, good and bad, not just among their own students, but also among friends of those students.

We sit down next to several archaic rows of Contemporary Literary Criticism. It doesn't take long for me to realize Josiah's focus is remarkable. Unlike me, he remains on task as two cute Loyola coeds stroll by our table and smile. We spend a good part of the hour going over the list of rhetorical terms in his practice book. I explain the format of the Advanced Placement exam: three essays and a grueling multiple choice section that makes the SAT seem like child's play. As the hour draws to a close, we discuss some sample essay prompts, how to approach them.

I nod toward his binder. "Better write this down, Josiah."

He picks up his pencil. I turn the practice book to face him. "For next time, I need you to do a rhetorical analysis timed write. Forty minutes." I tap my finger on the page. "Here's the passage. Read it and annotate. Determine the author's purpose. Write an essay analyzing how she uses rhetoric and language to achieve that purpose. Think outside the box. Look for how she manipulates the reader."

"You want me to do this at home?"

"That's right, Josiah. Even tutoring comes with homework. Got to do timed writes to prepare for the exam, and I don't think your parents want me to sit here watching you write for forty minutes when they're paying me forty bucks an hour."

The kid looks crestfallen that I've questioned his commitment. "Sorry, Mr. Casey. I didn't mean to sound like I'm complaining. I'll do whatever it takes." He pauses. "But if you assign timed writes for homework, how do you know the student's only going to spend forty minutes?"

I give him a tight grin. "I don't. Spend two hours if you want, but you're only fooling yourself. If you want to pass the exam, you've got to complete an assignment like this in forty minutes."

He nods. "I understand. Thanks for your help." He reaches into his pocket and pulls out two crumpled twenties. "Really appreciate this."

I take the forty dollars. "No problem, Josiah. Together we'll slay this beast. I'll see you on Wednesday."

ELEVEN

ZACH

Zach arrives home at six. He opens the door and his senses come alive. Roasted chicken with rosemary. He'd know that smell anywhere.

He lets himself go, closes his eyes and the door gently so not to disturb the moment. He lets the aroma take him back to Atlanta, to Mom standing over the stove in the kitchen. The window faces the magnolia tree in the front yard, the flowers brilliant white in the Georgia sunshine. He loved coming home to that house, to his mother. Dad would never arrive home until later. It was always just the two of them, him and Mom. He'd drop his backpack on a kitchen chair and they'd talk about their day, all the time watching from the window, not minding that the magnolia tree served as second base for the nine-year-old Atlanta Brave wannabes playing outside.

Keep those eyes closed. Soak it in, just a minute longer.

He inhales deeply through his nostrils. Yes, chicken with rosemary, maybe with green beans and long grain wild rice.

His backpack slides from his shoulder and, along with his daydream, thuds on the floor. His mother calls from the kitchen. "Zachary? That you? You're late today, Honey. Hope that's a good sign, making some new friends."

He steps over the backpack and moves to the kitchen. He comes behind her, wraps his arms around her and kisses her on the cheek. She turns, overjoyed. Her smile is radiant in front of the tiny window facing other tiny windows across the narrow alley.

"Love you, Mom."

She throws her arms around his neck. Her sobs are soft and secret. He lets her head stay buried in his neck until they're gone. She pulls away, quickly turning her tear stained cheeks from him.

Again he inhales through his nostrils. "Mmm." He whispers to the back of her head. "How am I ever going to find a wife that cooks like you?"

A hiccup in her stirring rhythm. He knows she's smiling.

In the hallway, the door clicks open and slams shut. His father's footsteps creak on the hardwood floor.

"Zachary, you home?"

"In the kitchen, Dad."

His father appears in the kitchen doorway, coat draped over one arm. He lifts an envelope in his other hand. "Letter from Pitt, Sociology department."

"Thanks, Dad."

Zach carries the letter to the living room and sinks into the couch. Jesus Christ watches him from the crucifix hanging on the wall to his left. Zach tears open the envelope: a list of books and required readings for incoming Sociology majors. He leans back, gazes at the ceiling. What does his future hold? What will he do with a BA in Sociology? So many unanswered questions.

Still, his decision to study Sociology at The University of Pittsburgh was not made haphazardly. His high school introductory course made an impression, helped him understand that a society is a functioning organism and, like a human being, is subject to the manipulation of

91

outside forces. He glances again at the crucifix. One of those outside forces is religion. Catholicism, his own religion - or at least the religion his parents bestowed upon him - he now understands is a negative force, a creed thrust upon children too young to make up their own minds, a tool used to manipulate trusting victims of pedophilia and AIDS.

The crucifix berates him: *Pretend to believe anyway, for your mother, a little longer.*

He's pretended to believe for years.

As a dutiful child, Zach became well-versed in the seven sacraments of Catholicism. Didn't have much choice. Now, at eighteen, only one of the seven strikes him as worthwhile, the sacrament of penance. One must atone for one's sins. Sure, there's a certain hypocritical irony in the idea of paying restitution for the purpose of relieving your own guilt, but still, restitution must be paid. After all, if you're going to suffer the symptoms of Catholicism, you might as well take advantage of the religion's prescribed cure.

The man to whom he will pay restitution is named Brian Casey. Zach knows this because they had both witnessed a murder on a pier. Zach had followed the man home from the beach in the predawn darkness of that horrible Sunday morning. He followed him to the small apartment building on Pratt. Massaging the bump on his head, the man went inside, and from the sidewalk Zach watched him in the yellow glow of the lobby. The man removed a piece of paper from his mail slot. He read it, snapped his head to the left and right and then patted the back pocket of his jeans, checking for a wallet no longer there. After the man vacated the lobby and went upstairs, Zach looked at the names next to the six buzzers. He snapped a picture of the names with his phone and headed home.

With the help of Google and Facebook, he determined the subject of his watch was not Adelle Gentry, accountant for the Law firm of Green and Shuester. Nor was it William Langston, a sixty-three-year-old Viet Nam vet with a shard of shrapnel embedded in his right leg. While a couple of the other names were possibilities, Zach convinced himself that

Brian Casey, AP English teacher at suburban Booker High School, was his man. This was confirmed when Zach woke up early on Monday and set up a pre-dawn reconnaissance. He watched the man emerge from the building and step into the yellow light that bathed the entryway.

Six a.m. Teacher's hours. Yes, Brian Casey was his man.

TWELVE

BRIAN

"Tell you what the problem is," says Magby, emptying the bottle of Cabernet into Rachel's glass. "Erik needs to learn how to execute a simple pick-and-roll. He fucking killed us today. Didn't do shit on offense." Much to Magby's dismay, the teachers failed to *lick the jocks* four hours ago in our game of three-on-three basketball, and as an old SAT analogy problem might point out: victory is to gloat as loss is to cast blame. At least that would be Magby's answer choice.

"Clinton, please stop cussing," says Donna, his wife. She's bored with the conversation and fed up with her husband.

The four of us have met at Amichi's, an Italian restaurant in Evanston. Butcher block paper covers the table, serving the double purpose of protecting the white linen cloth and taunting wannabe Picassos. Crayons have been provided for doodling, or in Rachel's case, for art.

"Donna, how's Justin doing?" I ask, referring to her three-year-old.

"He's fine, Brian. Thank you for asking." She smiles, appreciative of my efforts to change the subject from teachers licking jocks.

"How old is your little boy, Donna?" Rachel asks.

As the two women converse, Magby kicks my leg under the table. He nods toward Rachel, makes his eyebrows dance like Groucho Marx and gives me a nod of approval. I kick him back.

The evening goes well. Rachel and Donna hit it off and engage each other in conversation. This allows Magby an opportunity to cut his final asparagus spear into three pieces, maneuvering these on his plate to demonstrate the correct method for running a pick-and-roll as the defenders, or in this case ravioli noodles, scramble in desperation.

Magby waves his utensils like an orchestra conductor. "Ah no, Giovanni – I dona-wana switch on defense."

His Italian accent is the worst I've heard and he has a ravioli noodle named Giovanni. Got to give him credit though. The dexterity is remarkable, moving six tasty little Italian basketball players with a knife and fork. I'm not even sure what to call this skill. After the asparagus guard has penetrated the defense and made it all the way to the Chicken Rollatini for an easy score, I point out to Magby it may have been easier to complete his demonstration by using the crayons and butcher-block paper.

"You know, old-fashioned X's and O's."

"Yeah, I thought about that," he says, "but I couldn't help but notice how much this ravioli noodle resembles Coach Nick."

We've finished our entrees, polished off a second bottle of wine, and ordered a third when Magby leans forward and whispers to me. "Shit, see who just came in?" He nods toward the door, signaling me to look over my left shoulder. I turn and see a father and son being escorted to a table. It takes a moment for me to recognize the young man with the shock of blonde hair and familiar face. Then it comes to me. Matthew Dials.

"Seriously?" I whisper across the table. "Please tell me he didn't see us over here. I really don't want to talk to any students tonight." No sooner do the words leave my mouth than I notice Matthew and his father making their way toward our table.

"How's it going, Teach?" Matthew says to me, ignoring Magby, even though we've both stood to greet him and his father.

"Teach?" says Matthew's father. "How about Mr. Casey, Matthew? Show some respect."

"That's okay, Mr. Dials." I extend my hand. "Nice to see you again."

"You too, Mr. Casey. And how are you, Mr. Magby?"

"Surviving," Magby says, and he goes on to introduce Matthew's father to Donna and Rachel. I'm terrified one of the women may ask them to join us. Hopefully Rachel has mastered my art of creative avoidance and Donna is simply too embarrassed by her husband to let this happen. I'm tempted to ask Matthew why he's missed class the last two days, but in addition to the danger of this question extending the conversation, I also consider the possibility he may have been skipping. The last thing I want to do is incriminate my drug dealer in front of his father, my unknowing drug supplier.

"I apologize for interrupting your dinner," says Matthew's father. "But I wanted to let you know we've withdrawn Matthew from Booker. He's going to be attending Northshore Prep in Highland Park."

"Really? I'm sorry to hear that," I lie. "Matthew's one of my brightest students." This is the truth, but my first reaction is still one of relief. My third period AP class just became a little more comfortable. It will be a pleasure to know I can take the moral high road, discussing the transgressions of great literary characters without my hypocrisy reflecting back at me from Matthew's eyes.

Of course, with Matthew no longer attending Booker, we may have to conduct our business elsewhere, but no matter, as long as we do still conduct business.

A disturbing thought occurs to me. What if Matthew is being withdrawn from Booker because he's in some kind of trouble? What if that trouble involves his father finding out he's stealing pills from the pharmacy? If so, his father's friendly attitude would indicate Matthew hasn't yet implicated me as one of his customers. But if this is what's happened, Dad would want to know details, and there'd be no reason for Matthew not to turn state's evidence. Worst-case scenario would be for him to do it right here, in front of Rachel, Magby, and Donna.

I'm watching Mr. Dials' mouth move, something about "renewed commitment to his studies. . ." I can't speak because my heart is in my throat. I avoid Matthew's eyes, but I can feel them burning into me, taking pleasure in my torture.

The small talk continues. It lasts an eternity. When Matthew and his father turn toward their table I exhale a sigh of relief. Sitting down, I bump my wine glass.

Rachel steadies the glass. "Brian, what's the matter with you? You look like you've seen a ghost."

Magby leans toward her. "Not a ghost, an asshole." He glances over his shoulder, makes sure Matthew and his father are out of earshot. "The kid's an asshole, but now he can be someone else's asshole." A pause. "Wait. That didn't come out right."

Rachel laughs, I pretend to laugh, and Donna looks ready to murder her husband.

•   •   •

It's Wednesday, third period. *The Great Gatsby's* Nick Carraway wishes he stayed out of other people's business. I wish I stayed in bed. All of the desks in my classroom are filled but one, the desk previously occupied by Matthew Dials.

I stroll the aisles. Each student becomes scholarly as I pass. Fingers move across pages. Pencils rapidly scribble notes.

I break the silence and repeat the question. "C'mon guys, think about it. How is Nick Carraway, as a first person narrator, able to tell us about the conversation between Michaelis and Wilson even though he's not there to hear it?" I reach the front of the room and turn to the class. "Isn't F. Scott Fitzgerald violating the rules of first person narration by doing this?"

A meek voice answers from my left. "Yeah, but maybe Nick heard about it later, 'cause he's telling us the whole story after it happened anyway, right?"

Finally.

"Thank you, Ashley." I turn from her and gesture to the class for more. "But how does Nick know the details of this conversation? Doesn't Fitzgerald need to cover his bases? Is he exercising his artistic license, or does he include any key words, clues, that justify his bending of the rules?"

A hand is raised to my left. It's the only hand raised in the room. Still, I'm reluctant to call on David Hanratty because it's March and by March I know what to expect. Calling on David is akin to letting the air out of an inflated tire, followed by lost time as the air of critical thinking is pumped back into the classroom.

I wait a moment.

Several students avoid my eyes for fear I may call on them. David stretches his arm toward the ceiling. I have no choice. My focus, the focus of the entire class, is about to be abducted from *The Great Gatsby* to whatever's on David's mind.

"What do you think, David?"

"Sorry, Mr. C. I know this is off topic, but is it true that Matthew transferred?"

The class engages in a collective groan. It's March for them too.

"You're right, David," I say. "Way off topic."

"But he did transfer, right?"

My shoulders drop. "Yes, David, Matthew did transfer, and how is that relevant to *The Great Gatsby*?"

His smug smile informs me I've fed him the line he wants. "That empty desk is kind of calling to me," he says, "like a green light across a body of water."

The class groans again.

David beams. "Mind if I take Matthew's desk? I need a new perspective. Might help me regain my focus."

"Don't believe him, Mr. Casey," says the boy sitting next to him. "He just wants a better view of Allison. From over here he's got to turn all the way around to check her out."

David opens his palms to the ceiling. His point's been made for him. "That's what I said, a new perspective. At least I'm honest. I'm not going to wait around like Gatsby. If I want something, I'm going for it." He turns and fist bumps the boy behind him.

The tire is flat. The class's collective attention, along with any insight into F. Scott Fitzgerald's manipulation of first-person point of view, is gone. I slump forward on my podium. My job is exhausting.

David Hanratty grins at me, waiting for an answer. Matthew's desk does need to be filled, and even though David has slashed our academic tires, I'm tempted to reward him for taking the literature and applying it to his life. However, looking at Allison Palmer, the alleged object of David's affection, I see she has buried her face in her hands. She lifts her eyes to me and shakes her head, a pleading look.

I walk to David's desk, place my hand on it and lean close. "As much as I do want you to 'regain your focus,' David, it would hurt my feelings if you're paying more attention to Allison than to me. And I know you don't want to hurt my feelings, so the answer is no."

Returning to my podium, I glance at Allison. She mouths a subtle "thank you."

•   •   •

It's 3:25. The dirt at the ten-yard-line is packed hard, the sparse brown grass sprinkled with frost. For the past seven months of Wednesdays, crossing the fifteen, the ten, the five, has meant scoring. Today, as I step under the bleachers, something feels different. I've crossed the goal line but without the football. Instead, I carry the empty weight of Matthew's desk and empty anticipation. The air is heavy, the sky thick with dull clouds. The bleachers fail to cast their striped shadows on the ground.

Northshore Academy, the prep school Matthew's father mentioned, is in Highland Park, a good thirty minute drive from Booker. Depending on what time this school releases its students, Matthew may be hard pressed to make it here by 3:30, if he comes at all.

This morning I gave my alarm clock the day off as doubt jarred me awake at four a.m. Acting upon the premise that I may end up leaving these bleachers empty handed at the end of the day, I shook only half my usual dose of Vicodin into my anxious palm, opting to save the last handful of precious pills. The decreased dose left me agitated and as David Hanratty would attest, disagreeable.

It's 3:32: I've paced these bleachers too many times this year. The eye-level graffiti scribbled on the rear of the steel bench at the far end is too familiar. 131 steps from end-to-end is too many. I can do better. I'll wait a while for Matthew, but not too long. In order to catch the el and make it to Loyola for my 4:30 tutoring appointment with Josiah Coffee, I need to leave these bleachers by 3:50.

3:36: In the distance the last of the faculty over-achievers pull out of the parking lot; Magby is long gone. The woods behind me are deep and dense enough to accommodate a big bad wolf. I know Matthew likes to keep me waiting.

3:41: I blame Rachel. If she hadn't preyed upon my weakness and forced me to tutor Josiah, I could wait here all afternoon like Miss lonely heart from Hitchcock's *Rear Window*, a jilted woman sitting at a table with dwindling candles and two empty wine glasses. How dare Rachel cause me to sacrifice my own selfish ideals to help another? The nerve.

3:45: I've paced the length of the bleachers. 117 steps is my new personal best. I imagine a pill bottle calling from my medicine cabinet: "Feed me, Brian. Fill me up."

3:48: I consider the number in my phone, the one I entered last summer when I first met Matthew, the number I swore I'd never use.

3:52: I clutch my phone. What if I leave now and Matthew shows up in five minutes? Would he assume our arrangement has come to an end?

3:57: Empty handed, I step from under the bleachers. I've lost my best friend.

• • •

"No problem, Mr. Casey. I'll let it slide this time," says a smiling Josiah Coffee after I've apologized for arriving ten minutes late. "But next time I'll have to write you up for being tardy."

He hands me his rhetorical analysis timed write, a college-ruled sheet torn from a spiral. His essay is written in black ink. The cursive is legible, a good sign.

He sits forward, anxious. "Forty minutes. Went by real fast. Be kind, Mr. C."

I lean back in my chair to read.

Not bad for a first attempt, but still far from what The College Board would consider a passing score on the AP exam. The potential is clear. While it's common for my better writers to slip into moments of ineptitude, gravity seldom affords writers the opportunity to fall up, to capture moments of beautiful prose that have no business hanging out with clumsy phrasing and generic word choices. But somehow these moments, like hoity-toity party crashers, dot Josiah's essay.

We spend the first thirty minutes of our session looking over the passage and reviewing Josiah's analysis. For the remainder of the hour we discuss argumentation, the second type of writing required on the exam. I assign another timed write for homework, this time, argument.

"Bring in outside concrete details for support," I say. "History, literature, current events, even pop culture. But don't let them dominate. Let reason and logic drive your argument."

I glance at the clock on the wall. "Tell you what, Josiah, we've got a little time left. Let's find a random prompt, and take a few minutes to prewrite." I flip through the pages, scanning the various prompts. "Here, try this one." I turn the book to face him. "Spend seven or eight minutes: interpret the prompt, create a claim and warrants, and brainstorm some concrete details."

Josiah picks up the book and leans back in his chair. He mouths the prompt and wiggles his pencil, tapping the eraser end against his chin as he considers his argument. His brow furrows with concentration.

I like this kid, and even though I've made it clear our work together in no way guarantees a passing score on the exam, I can't help but acknowledge my own stake in his progress, the need for a success in my own life. But this is a crapshoot. My classes at Booker, consisting of the brightest kids in a recognized suburban high school, have been preparing for the grueling exam for months, and I'll consider the year a success if sixty-five percent of them receive the minimum passing score.

Still, if I can get this kid over the hump. . .

I suppose if I were a religious person, I'd give God credit for recognizing my need for therapy and sending Josiah my way. But, as is my cynical nature, I dismiss this idea as unlikely unless God is masquerading as Rachel Gold.

Josiah drops his pencil onto the table. "Ok, Mr. Casey. Guess I'm done."

I look over his prewriting.

At Booker, I encourage my students to view their planning from a distance. I advise them to take the advice of Ralph Waldo Emerson, imagining that as they stand on a distant hill, they see not only individual farms, but the landscape in its entirety, using "an eye that can integrate all the parts." I explain this to Josiah, delicately pointing out that when looked at from a distance his prewriting does not create this cohesive landscape.

"Yeah," he says. "I see what you mean. Kind of a mess, huh?"

"No worries, Josiah. We'll work on it."

Our hour comes to an end. With nothing left to say, I stand up. "Alright, I'm sure you got stuff to do and—"

"Not really," he interrupts, his relaxed posture inviting me to stay.

Why not? Nothing and nobody waiting at home. I sit back down. "Nah. Me neither."

I cross my legs and turn to face him as he searches the bookshelves - Business and Finance - for a conversation starter. I break the silence. "What are you into Josiah? Sports? Music? How do you spend your free time?"

"Video games mostly. How about you, Mr. Casey? You married?"

"Not yet. But I'm about to turn thirty. I guess it's getting to be about that time."

"Got a girlfriend?"

"As a matter of fact, yes I do."

"What's her name?"

"Her name is Rachel." I lean forward. "Questions are getting a little personal, Josiah."

For a moment he seems distracted. His blank stare focused on the bookshelves behind me.

"Josiah? You okay?"

"Sorry." With noticeable effort he dismisses whatever was on his mind. "What do you do with your time then, Mr. Casey? Mind me asking that?"

"I play some basketball and do some writing. Watch old movies."

He sits forward. I've peeked his interest. "Old movies? What kind?"

"Ever heard of Alfred Hitchcock?"

"Yeah, I know the name but don't really know nothing about him."

"Don't know *anything*," I correct him. "He was a director, made mysteries, thrillers way back. Also had a TV show for a while. I actually got turned on to him when I took a course in college called The Art of Hitchcock. Can you believe that? I've been a huge fan ever since."

We sit for another ten minutes. I ask Josiah about his family. He dismisses this topic with a mumbled name and a wave of the back of his hand. We turn to the topic of sports and, even though he admits his baseball loyalties lay elsewhere, the distant possibility that the Chicago Cubs may have a winning season. He laughs easily, an infectious laugh that originates somewhere deep in his belly. I could sit here all day with this kid.

THIRTEEN

ZACH

It's 11:30 Thursday, lunchtime at West Rogers Park High School. As was the case at Zach's school in Atlanta, the faculty members assigned to cafeteria duty stroll the aisles like prison guards. The Goth students at the far end of Zach's table have a running bet about how many times U.S. History teacher Mr. Aleman will look at his watch, frustrated by having to perform this mindless cafeteria duty while there are so many other pressing demands on his time. Apparently the bet involves tater tots. Aleman looks at his watch and, on cue, several of the soggy little concoctions are launched like missiles at a kid with jet black hair sweeping across his face. Laughing, he closes his eyes and opens his mouth, inviting the onslaught.

Zach rises from the table. *Can't wait to get out of this place.*

He dumps the contents of his tray into a trash can and steps into the boy's restroom, away from the eyes of duty teachers. The restroom is empty, the perfect opportunity to confirm his suspicions. His mother had planted an interesting seed in his head. The man he'd followed home from the pier, Brian Casey, could this be the same Brian his mother mentioned in the kitchen? The same Brian that Rachel's seeing?

He pulls his phone from his pocket and makes the call.

"Mom, you told me Rachel has a boyfriend named Brian, right? You said he worked in Northbrook. Do you know the name of the school?"

"Zach, honey, let it go. Let your cousin live her life."

Exactly the reaction he expected from his mother. No problem. His lie is prepared.

"It's not that. I met somebody who goes to Booker High School in Northbrook. Said he has an English teacher named Brian Casey. I was just wondering if it's the same guy."

"Well, Rachel didn't tell me his last name, but yes, Booker High School, that sounds right."

Zach returns the phone to his pocket and stares at his reflection in the cracked mirror. Rachel and Brian Casey? What are the chances? But how serious is his cousin's relationship with Brian? Does she know what happened at the pier?

Zach steps from the restroom, back to the cafeteria. He doesn't sit down. Somehow that would slow down time and time is already crawling. Has it really only been thirteen days since the incident? He gazes at the institutionalized students and patrolling teachers. West Rogers Park High School has become his prison, one in which he moves from cell to cell serving a never-ending series of eight-hour-a-day sentences for crimes against humanity.

One hour later, at 12:35, Zach steps from cell number six, Mr. McDougal's AP English classroom, the cell he shares with Abe and twenty-seven teenaged ignoramuses who think they have problems.

He hasn't spoken to Abe since that horrible Saturday night. The eye contact has been fleeting. He's sure Abe feels as he does, that acknowledging each other's presence would tumble the delicate card houses of denial they've spent thirteen days building.

Zach stares into his open locker. A yellow form lodged between two books catches his eye. He slides it out and reads. Two weeks ago this would have mattered. He crumples the form into a ball.

Don't give a shit how my name appears on my diploma.

He tosses the wadded paper into the locker. His Economics text sits atop a stack of books, taunting him. One more cell to visit, then tutoring, then home. He removes the book, swings the locker door closed. His heart jumps. Abe's face, this time without the forced smile, waits on the other side. The mouth is open, but no words escape.

Raising an open palm, Zach shakes his head. "No way. Leave me alone. Leave me the fuck alone. Don't want to talk to you. Don't want anything to do with you."

Abe closes his mouth, lowers his gaze.

Zach turns. He starts to walk but stops, grounded by conscience. The hallway ahead is slick with shame. He turns to Abe, who still searches the floor for a speck of compassion. Zach bends his head. It's there, an undeniable bond forged by shared trauma, a bond that can't be broken by avoidance. Like marionettes having their heads lifted, forced to acknowledge the truth of their wooden existence, they look up and their eyes meet. Abe's eyes are wet, and Zach sees in his pupils the silhouettes of old men engulfed in water.

"He's dead, isn't he?"

Zach clenches his teeth, keeps his voice low. "Of course he's dead, Abe. He was an old man with one arm dumped into a frozen lake. Of course he's fucking dead."

The words "fucking dead" are punctuated by the thump of the Economics book sliding into his backpack. "I gotta go. I'm going to be late for class."

Abe grabs his arm. "What about the other guy? You think he's okay?"

Zach jerks his arm free. His shoulder follows meekly as if to apologize. He looks beyond Abe. The hallway is emptying, students filing into classrooms, teachers hurrying the rest along. In a moment one of these teachers will approach them: *Move along guys. Let's get to class.*

Defeated, Abe turns away. The emotional lifeline, the shared hope he counted on, has been dashed. Zach watches him start down the sterile hallway.

"Abe, hang on."

The B-wing is almost empty now. Beyond Abe, who has turned to face Zach, Mr. Parnell eyes the two boys from his classroom doorway. *Don't make me come over there.*

Zach slings his backpack over his shoulder. "C'mon."

"Where?"

"Just follow me."

Zach hurries toward the main hallway, Abe behind. The tardy bell rings. Zach jailbreaks left at the end of the B-wing. He and Abe duck behind the up stairway, into the empty space normally reserved for class cutters and hormonally-charged make out sessions. Zach takes a deep breath. "Just between us, the other guy from that night, his name's Brian Casey. He's okay."

"What?" Abe's voice echoes in the hollow stairwell. "How do you know he's okay?"

"Shh."

Zach hesitates. How much should I tell him?

"I went back to the beach that night and—"

On the stairs above, a scamper of late footsteps. Zach's raised finger requests patience. Abe waits, eyes alive with hope, hands clutched as though in prayer. After the footsteps fade, Zach moves closer, lowers his voice. "The guy sat on the beach a while. He walked up and down the pier and went home. He's okay."

Abe's dark eyes are wide. Seventh period has been forgotten. To hell with tardies.

FOURTEEN

BRIAN

It's been 48 hours since David Hanratty requested a new perspective in the AP classroom. His seat has not changed, and neither has his penchant for annoyance.

"What're you doing over spring break, Mr. Casey?" he asks, this time breaking my concentration as I take roll at the start of third period.

"Recovering from the last two and a half months," I say, resisting the temptation to add, *of having to deal with you, David Hanratty.*

Such has been my existence at Booker for the last two days. With detox officially on, my tapered doses of Vicodin have left me wired, and with the start of spring break a few hours away, my students are wired too, but differently. It's taken every ounce of my creative avoidance superpowers to stop these wires from crossing, to prevent my precious little geniuses from witnessing the Mr. Hyde living inside my Dr. Jeckyll.

•　•　•

At 4:30 I again meet Josiah Coffee at Loyola for our last tutorial session before the break. At least I assume it's our last session. After all, what teenager wants to have his spring break schedule dotted with AP tutorials? Hell, what teenager wants to even have a schedule on spring break?

We sit at our usual table in the library.

"Okay, this is it, Josiah. Not going to see you for a while after today. Let's see what you've got for me."

He's taken aback. "We're not meeting next week?"

"No, it's spring break." I pause. "Sorry. I assumed that was a given. I'm going to be out of town."

"Oh, okay." He's disappointed and I'm confused.

"You can still practice over the break." I try to sound encouraging. "Why don't you pick a couple prompts from the practice book? Show me your work a week from Monday?"

A week from Monday. The words hit him like a right cross. He slumps in his chair.

"Did you write your argument?" I ask. I glance at the paper in his hand, anxious for the opportunity to look anywhere but into his eyes.

He hands me the sheet, filled front and back. The prompt was to interpret and base an argument on a quote by the Nobel Prize winning Indian poet, Rabindranath Tagore: "You can't cross the sea merely by standing and staring at the water." Josiah has written an argument focusing on motivation, taking the position that motivation should come from within. Nothing about his argument strikes me as insightful. Nothing peeks my interest until I reach his third body paragraph:

Of course, sometimes internal motivation should not even be necessary. For example, when an actress once asked Alfred Hitchcock what could motivate her to connect with her character, he said, "your salary."

· · ·

In late March, darkness descends upon Chicago around seven p.m. I leave the Loyola University library at 5:35 on this Friday evening with Josiah's essay in my briefcase. Next time I'm at Booker, a week from Monday, I'll make a personal copy of the Hitchcock reference that has been so long in coming, yet another artifact for the Brian Casey Museum on Pratt Avenue.

I step from the Loyola quad and turn south on Sheridan Road, the wrong direction. This is not a mistake. It's part of an evolving detoxification strategy. The further I remove myself from my apartment, the further I'm removed from my final dose of Vicodin. Like a baby bird leaving the nest, I'll venture far from the security of my warm apartment and plastic pill bottle, or at least as far as the Exxon station around the corner. The walk back will be difficult, but not as difficult as sitting in my apartment attempting to honor the impossible pledge to "wait just one more hour." I'm treating myself to tough love.

The southwestern shoreline of Lake Michigan runs in a southeasterly direction. Sheridan Road, as though desperate to escape the cold, runs almost straight south. This sprint continues until the street is reminded to obey the old real estate axiom, "location – location – location."

The sprint slows to a crawl and the busy thoroughfare makes a sharp left turn, staying fashionably close to the lake before turning another ninety degrees and scampering south again.

I follow this route as Sheridan wraps around the Loyola University campus and passes by tiny Mundelein College, a private Catholic girl's school where, according to rumor, the girls are not so private. I guess when Billy Joel sang, "you Catholic girls start much too late," he wasn't singing about the student body of Mundelein.

I'm in Edgewater now. High rise apartment and condo buildings line the east side of Sheridan. They back up to the lake like gigantic bouncers waiting to scoop up Edgewater beach party crashers and punt them back to Rogers Park. The sun no longer shines on this side of the street. Only the tops of the buildings glow.

Take your time. Don't turn back yet.

With the dual intention of killing time and accomplishing what has become the bothersome task of eating, I stop and order a gyro at an eatery aptly named Gyro. I try, but can't finish the wrap or greasy fries. I step out onto the street and look up. Sunlight no longer illuminates the tops of the buildings. The sky is dark blue. Dusk. Time to go home.

Within twenty minutes I'm back at Loyola. It's 7:05. Rogers Park rush hour is still in effect. My nose is running, my opioid-deprived head pounding. I'm irritable. I have no sympathy for the impatient drivers who, having left downtown and cruised Lake Shore Drive, now become frustrated by the endless string of traffic lights delaying the start of their weekend.

My steady on-foot progress results in me reaching two consecutive red lights at the same time as the frustrated driver of a BMW, probably on his way home to upscale Wilmette. At the second light he looks at me, shakes his head. I'm supposed to sympathize with him. I don't.

Deal with it, buddy. I'm the tortoise and you're the hare.

I turn left on Pratt. My street is a one-way approaching Sheridan so it's devoid of traffic, quiet and dark. I near my apartment building at the end of the block.

A figure sits under the yellow light on the step of the building's doorway. One of my neighbors? Could be, or perhaps a homeless man hoping to take advantage of anyone feeling generous on this bi-monthly payday. I'm not sure why he'd be soliciting at the end of a quiet street instead of on Sheridan Road, but who knows why people make the choices they make? It's not as if much of anything in my life has made sense lately anyway.

I'm fifty yards away. He hasn't noticed me yet. Creative avoidance, I remind myself. I plan a course of action that'll get me into my building efficiently and with little expense. I slow my pace, turn my back, and open my wallet: a twenty, a ten, a few singles. I remove a dollar bill and clutch it. I'll hand him the single and slip through the door.

Still unnoticed, I reach the sidewalk in front of my building. The man's head is down, covered by a hood. He wears skinny jeans, some designer brand, and unlaced basketball sneakers. They look expensive. He's barely a man, definitely not homeless.

Fancying himself an artist, or perhaps just bored, the stranger doodles on the cement step with a twig. I shuffle my feet on the sidewalk to announce my arrival and to let him know he's going to have to move his ass to let me by. He looks up, slides the hood from his head, and I recognize his face, this time immediately.

"Where you been, Teach?" he asks. "Been waiting forever."

"What are you doing here, Matthew? How'd you find out where I live?"

He scoffs. "You really think it's hard to find out anything about anybody these days? Join the twenty-first century."

Condescending little prick. "What are you doing here?" I ask again.

"Why? Did you miss me? You're probably hoping I have something for you, right? I'll bet you even waited under the bleachers on Wednesday." He leans back on his elbows, casual and confident. "Sorry, Teach. Those days are done. It's your turn to do for me."

Matthew waits for me to respond. I say nothing. It isn't part of his script for me to remain silent. For a moment he appears confused. He's put himself in a defensive position, the yellow light from above illuminating his face, the cement step hard on his elbows. He looks away, finds a pebble on the step, flicks it, then another. When he runs out of pebbles, he has nowhere to look but up. He pulls the hood over his head, engulfing his face in shadow. I'm face-to-face with the Grim Reaper. His voice comes from the depths. "It's like this, Teach. We both had secrets we were keeping for each other, but my secret's not a secret anymore, so I don't really have any reason to keep yours."

He slides the hood back a few inches, waiting for me to respond. When I don't, he addresses the night sky. "Shit. This new school, the teachers all got sticks up their asses. Think we got nothing to do with our free time but homework." He angrily brushes the dust, along with the Northshore Prep faculty, from his elbows.

"So," he continues, "I asked myself how I could ease my workload. Then I thought of you, how you could help me out." A pause. "And you will help because if you don't, I'm telling my father you were my number one customer."

He exhales. There, he got it out, though the last few words ran like cowards. He takes a deep breath before continuing. "I thought about asking you for money, but you're a teacher so I know you don't have any."

His eyes flick at me. He's expecting a reaction to the insult. I give him none.

"My dad is on my case about my grades," he says. "So I tried to think what else you could do for me. Then it came to me. You can be my homework bitch. The rest of this semester's going to be a breeze 'cause you're going to write some essays for me."

I step dangerously close to him. He twitches, but he's not done yet, not until he delivers his grand finale. "Who was that woman at the restaurant with you the other night?" he asks the sky. "Your girlfriend? She's alright I guess. Not much of a body though. Always thought you'd be more of a tit man. Does she know about your little habit, Teach? What's her name? Rachel something? Green? Gold?"

I reach down and grab him by the front of his hoodie. I lift him off the ground and slam his back against the door. His eyes widen in fear and his jaw clenches. He's surprised by my violent reaction. So am I.

I grit my teeth. "I'm not doing shit for you. Go home."

He shakes himself free, staggers toward the sidewalk. When he reaches it he stops, hesitates before turning. Then, as though offering an apology: "You're the best teacher I ever had." His voice has become that of a child. "I already miss your class."

He stands a moment too long, allowing the compliment to linger. He looks at the ground. This is not how he'd seen this going. The snide remarks, the biting script, were all too rehearsed. Now he wants me to tell him I'll help him, tell him he doesn't have to resort to blackmail. A week ago I may have done this, but now he's asking for compassion from a pill-deprived monster of his own creation.

I clamp my lips together.

Matthew turns his gaze across the dark street, perhaps searching for the combative frame of mind he seems to have lost. He can't find it and again stares at the sidewalk.

"Whatever. Don't think I can prove anything? Maybe you better reconsider that." The threat rings hollow as a reluctant moment passes before he turns to walk away. He calls over his shoulder. "I'll be in touch, Teach. Enjoy your spring break."

Fat chance of that.

· · ·

"I'm not going to lie," Rachel says on Saturday morning, making me feel all the worse for having called her to lie about my spring break plans. "I'm disappointed, Brian. I thought we'd be spending extra time together next week."

As has become habit, I wait for Rachel's next sentence, the zinger that will leave me hanging out to dry. It doesn't come. Her sincerity takes me by surprise, leaving me hanging out to dry.

My forehead rests in my palm. The lies tumble to the table. "Sorry. I know it's last minute, but I need to see my mom. She's having a tough time, going through some stuff. It's going to be a cool surprise for her when I show up."

"I understand," she says. "But Houston?"

I'm not sure how I'm supposed to respond to this.

A heavy sigh on the other end. "When are you coming back?"

"Next Saturday."

Silence interrupts the conversation, silence that needs to be filled with truth. You'll make this up to her, I tell myself, but it feels like another lie.

Before making that phone call, I'd considered telling Rachel everything: that the young man she met in the restaurant on Tuesday was more than just a student, that I've been abusing pain killers for seven months, and that I'm planning on spending my spring break in self-imposed isolation attempting to wean myself of the habit. But how would she react? Would she support and help me, or would she reject me outright for not having told her earlier? The answers to these questions eluded me, so I took the easy way out. I lied.

. . .

It's a grey Saturday afternoon. I've checked myself into a converted Motel Six now going by the name of The Skokie Inn. Upon entering the non-smoking room, I'm greeted by the stale stench of a thousand cigarettes. Heavy flame retardant drapes hang to my right. Stained carpet puckers beneath my feet. On the nightstand, a Bible has been provided for the redemption of those who rent the room by the hour. The walls are bare, save a painting of a barn hanging above the bed looking out of place as the cacophony of Skokie traffic invades the room. The barn door is open, and within, a horse pokes his head from a stall to see what all the fuss is about.

I place my bottle of multivitamins on the dresser. These will replenish the nutrients disappearing from my body along with my already-vanishing appetite. I'll force myself to eat, but it won't be enough. In a few minutes I'll head to the Jewel grocery store across the street and purchase two cases of water bottles. I'll consume seven or eight bottles a day, pouring the water down my parched throat in an effort to flush out my system. I'm scared. If I can make it through this week, through day four which I've heard is the worst, I'll be okay.

Sunday: I write without purpose. The words pour from my confused brain, down my arms, and through my fingers as they tap the keyboard of my laptop. Somewhere on this stream-of-consciousness journey these words, at least in their original form, become lost. I glance at the screen as the characters dance from left to right. I pause to read: *Jackson has windy places that live on the edge of his fragile bathroom.* What does that mean? Perhaps some of this may make sense later, or perhaps I should make sure that Jackson's windy places never see "later" and that his fragile bathroom is shattered to pieces. After all, I doubt the memories generated this week will find their way into any Casey family chronicles, at least not by choice.

Monday: I chug the rest of a water bottle, toss it at the overflowing trashcan. My mind generates random thoughts: whoever said a good piss feels better than sex has never had to do it 20 times a day. Did I just hear horse in the painting whisper something? I really should recycle those water bottles. Need to walk, get some air, suffocating in here. I step outside. The traffic rushes by me with incredible volume. I begin to walk, faster, increasing my pace to the point where I'm almost running. I am running. I don't' know where. I don't care. Keep going, one more block, keep that blood flowing.

Tuesday, day four: The horse in the painting - I swear his head is poking further from the stall than yesterday - laughs at me. I've raised the temperature on the thermostat. My life has become a how-to manual: pushups - sweat - hydrate - piss - repeat - pushups - sweat - hydrate - piss - repeat. I've run the streets of Skokie a dozen times, avoiding the temptation to knock down everyone in my path. *Get out of the way. Detox guy comin' through.*

Wednesday: I feel like shit. My stomach is knotted, my head pounding, and my nose won't stop running. I knew I'd experience flu-like symptoms but Christ, please give me the flu instead of this. I try to run, but I'm too congested. I tell myself if I could run all the way to Rogers Park I'd join an old man on the floor of Lake Michigan. I can't imagine feeling well enough in three days to face Rachel or to stand in front of a roomful of disgruntled students on Monday.

Thursday: I take my third hot bath of the day. I soak and think. I've turned the corner and I'm never going back. Matthew Dials is no longer my student, no longer my supplier. He's nothing but— Wait. What's that? He's my blackmailer? Perhaps I haven't turned the corner. Hearing the human voice of the horse in the painting reminding me I'm someone's "homework bitch" is probably not a good indication of sobriety. I close my eyes and dip my head under the bathwater to drown out the horse's laughter.

Friday: I feel better. I see a light at the end of a dark tunnel. I tell myself to look forward. Each day now will be better than the last. The horse is quiet. This could be because the painting is now under the bed instead of hanging above it.

On Saturday morning I return to Rogers Park empty, yet fulfilled. I've lost five pounds and my brain begs for pain medication, but I've gained a sense of control. I once again own my life. I work up the nerve to call Rachel. I dread it, not because I don't want to talk to her - I do - but because I know she'll ask about my trip to "Houston," and the lies I tell will stir in my already queasy stomach. Our communication was limited to texting. I initiated this for fear she may call me first, hear the anxiety and paranoia in my voice. Once I sent that first text, the mode of communication was established. Thank God I could LOL when I felt DOA.

Of course, texting Rachel on Wednesday that I "feel like shit, think I've got a touch of the flu" bordered on the truth in addition to serving the purpose of explaining my weight loss and any lingering flu-like symptoms upon my return to Rogers Park. Thinking I've got all my bases covered, I call her on Saturday afternoon.

"Is your mom doing okay?" she asks.

"Yeah, she's feeling better. She's such a mom. If she goes a few months without seeing me she gets lonely. Feels like all the men in her life have deserted her."

Rachel continues to pepper the conversation with questions about my trip. Each lie I tell is a dagger in my gut, yet the questions keep coming: How was the weather? Do I have a suntan? Do superheroes have to use planes when flying from Houston to Chicago? I do my best to deflect the rest of her questions by focusing on the time ahead.

"Let's get together tonight," I say. "I miss you."

This is not a lie.

•   •   •

During my hallucinatory hiatus in beautiful Skokie, Illinois, I began having a recurring dream. In this dream I'm in bed alone until a one-armed old man, dripping wet, appears in my doorway and crawls into bed with me. I'm not surprised. I've been expecting him.

"Will you help me write this essay?" I ask, but he doesn't answer. "Do you have anything for pain?" Again, he's silent. He never answers these questions. I know this, but I always ask anyway. Then my bedroom window shatters. The curtains blow and flap as a violent storm, rain and wind, pours in. Neither of us reacts in the least.

"Can you swim?" I ask the old man even though again I know he won't answer.

I turn back to the window, squinting my eyes against the wind and rain, and wait for what will happen next. The storm is sucked back out into the night and the shattered glass flies back into place. The window is intact, and the room is quiet. I know the old man is gone, but I turn anyway and find my father, John Casey, lying in his place, appearing as I remember him when I was nine. He opens his eyes, a hint of a crooked smile on his face. Then I'm awake, alone in my bed, and drenched in sweat. I lie in silence, aware that once again my opioid-deprived subconscious has put all of my rotten eggs in one basket and fed them to me in my sleep.

I check the news every day. No dead bodies washing up on Chicago beaches. I've logged on to the Illinois State Police missing persons report, searching the photos for the old man with one arm, the weathered face with the jagged scar and crooked nose. No luck. Perhaps I dreamed the whole thing. It's fading now and feels that way. I should be glad about this, but I'm not. Apparently witnessing a murder comes with the annoying responsibility of acknowledging it happened.

I think about the old man daily, hourly. Who was he? Who was his family? Everyone deserves an identity. Everybody deserves to be somebody. I decide to dignify him. If I couldn't save his life, the least I can do is create one for him. Thanks to me, the old man with one arm now has a history and a family. And hell, even my dead-beat father has a name. Certainly this guy deserves one too.

•   •   •

"Why Walter?" Rachel asks me on Saturday night.

We're sitting on the bench atop the graffiti wall, under the stars. The night is clear and calm. The moon, almost full, shimmers on Lake Michigan. It bathes the beach in front of us with soft light.

I shrug. "Don't know. I guess because it feels like a name with dignity, like Walter Cronkite."

"Walter Cronkite? Alfred Hitchcock?" She turns to me, her eyes narrow with playful suspicion. "Who are you, Brian Casey? Tell me the truth. You came here in a time machine. You're going to kidnap me and take me back to Woodstock. Am I right?"

"Nah." I put my arm around her and draw her close. "I took an anti-aging pill in 1970. I'm really a seventy-two-year-old man. So you, young lady, should be extremely impressed by my ability to maintain an erection."

She laughs. I'd laugh too, but the mention of taking a pill has caused unpleasant movement in my stomach.

"Okay," she continues. "So his name's Walter. Now tell me about this family you've created?"

"His wife – well, widow – is Mary. She's got a great support system, a large extended family that won't allow her to wallow in grief."

"Listen to you, creating characters. Always thinking like a writer."

"Yeah." I turn my gaze to the pier in the distance. "I guess that's what I'm doing."

"Hey, look at me." She waits for me to turn, waits until I've met her eyes. "You know, none of this was your fault, Brian. Things happen that are out of our control. Sometimes we have to let them go."

"I know that," I say. "But it won't let go of me."

We sit on the bench in silence. I'm sure Rachel is freezing and anxious to leave. She's accommodating me, just as she did one hour ago when she accepted the premise of a "romantic stroll" even though she suspected ulterior motives. Her suspicions were accurate. My intention was to take her on a journey I'd taken ten thousand times in my mind. Perhaps this time, I reasoned, if Rachel accompanies me, the next ten thousand mental journeys will be a little less lonely.

We left my apartment at eleven p.m. Instead of taking a direct route to the park, I took her half a block north to where the single window of Sheridan Sam's glows nightly with an Old Style Beer neon sign. We didn't go into the bar. Instead we stood for a minute in the doorway before beginning a slow walk down Sheridan, turning left on Farwell, and entering the park.

Now the world is still. The city behind us has gone to bed. Lake Michigan's sleepy waves brush the beach in front of us and the smell of night lingers in the air. I'm supposed to feel tormented, but I don't. The stars, the water's steady breath, the woman with her head on my shoulder; all these things have calmed me. I'm numb with contentment. I bend my head, whispering into Rachel's soft hair.

"Ever notice how, if you sit on a bench long enough, it becomes impossible to tell if you're feeling the slats of the bench or the spaces in between? The positive or the negative space?"

"Emptiness or fulfillment?"

Her voice is tiny, but I'm sure this is what she's said. I'm speechless. She gets me. What did I do to deserve her?

She lifts her head from my shoulder. "Why'd you bring me here tonight?"

"Because I'm selfish."

"Selfish? How?"

The night has lulled me into honesty. I'm on the verge of revealing the truth about my week of detox. I check myself. One confession at a time.

"I can't do this alone anymore," I say. "Sorry. I shouldn't have dragged you down here. This isn't your issue."

Rachel sits forward on the bench, turning to face me. "Not my issue?" She pauses. "Yeah, it kind of is." She looks at me to see if I understand.

I do, but I want to hear more.

She slows her words for emphasis. "What I'm trying to tell you, dummy, is that I care about you. If you've got a problem, I want to help."

I can tell by the look in her eyes that I don't need to say thank you. I say it anyway.

"Where did it happen exactly?" she asks.

I point to the pier. "The old man walked all the way to the end. I made it about half way before. . . Well, c'mon. I'll show you."

We take a diagonal shortcut across the moonlit beach to where the sidewalk runs east-west and meets the concrete pier. I lead her by her hand. The distant end of the pier is obscured by darkness. The rusty light tower at the end has not been used in years. I imagine Walter having company at the bottom of Lake Michigan in the form of drowned pirates, fisherman, and boaters who have met their demise by crashing into the end of the unlit Rogers Park pier. They're having a jolly old time. Oh, the stories they tell.

"This is where I woke up." I lean against the steel rope and look at the stars. Unlike the wind that howled three weeks ago, only a faint breeze blows. We stand in silence a moment. Rachel gazes to the south, watching the lights of Navy Pier twinkle in the distance. It occurs to me that intimacy comes in many forms. A billion stars above and a million city lights behind, yet we're alone in the universe.

"Hey," I take her face in my hands, turn her to me. "Thank you."

"Thank me for what?"

I answer her with a kiss.

As I lift my mouth from hers, the breeze blows her hair across her cheek. I brush it away, tuck it gently behind her ear. The moonlight caresses her face.

• • •

I lay in my bed, Rachel asleep beside me. My mind is consumed by the familiar image of an old man plodding down a concrete pier. A group of teenagers follow, their adrenaline infused by alcohol and cold air. I ask myself the usual questions. Why did Walter stroll down that pier in the first place? Why was he staring into the water? Was he planning on killing himself? Did the teenagers do him a favor?

I tell myself if Walter climbs dripping wet into my bed tonight, I'll ask him these questions, but I doubt he answers anyway.

FIFTEEN

ZACH

The impending spring break evoked mixed feelings for Zach. He could use a week off from avoiding his partners in crime, but school had served the purpose of occupying his time and distracting his conscience. He'd thrown himself into his studies, attended tutorials, immersed himself in his classes, and now those classes would be gone, for a week.

On Spring Break Friday the bell dismissed his seventh period AP Economics class and Zach stepped into the crowded hallway. There was a noticeable pep in the step of the student body, a buzz in the air.

I wish my teachers had assigned more homework for the break, Zach thought. He looked quickly around to make sure he hadn't thought it aloud.

At home, Zach's late arrival on certain weekday afternoons because of "study sessions" prompted contrasting reactions from his parents. His mother expressed concern about his sullen mood and suggested he get out more, have some fun. His father, on the other hand, let Zach know he was proud of his focused son, and when Zach informed his father that his dedication was motivated by the prospect of gaining enough AP credits to graduate from college in three years, his father was thrilled by the idea of saving a year's tuition. All of this led Zach's father to surprise him that Friday evening.

"Better start packing." His father handed him an envelope. "You leave in the morning."

Zach tore open the envelope, sliding out the single sheet, a printed confirmation for one round trip plane ticket to Atlanta.

He raised his eyes to meet his father's. "Seriously? I'm going home?"

"Home? Well, I wish you thought of Chicago as your home now, but what the hell, enjoy your spring break, and say hello to your friends for me. You've earned this."

It immediately occurred to Zach that this trip must have been his mother's idea and her subsequent wink confirmed this. For her, this was therapy for her homesick son. She allowed her husband to take credit for the idea because that's the way it's done in the Mondini household.

When his father turned away, Zach smiled at his mother and mouthed a subtle "thank you."

He was going home.

Zach saw no reason to stay in Rogers Park over the break anyway. With one two a.m. walk across a deserted Sheridan Road two weeks ago, he'd broken ties with the only group he called his friends. After this, he crawled into a shell. A girl named Chloe tried to pry this shell open by becoming friendly, more than friendly, but Zach would have no part of it. He'd made up his mind he would leave Rogers Park free of commitments and leave no injured parties behind, with the notable exception of those already entombed in the watery grave of Lake Michigan.

But Brian Casey was an injured party, and this gave Zach pause. He and Brian were kindred spirits, both haunted by the image of two dark figures becoming one at the end of a frozen pier. And now, like a coward, Zach would flee Rogers Park for a week, leaving behind a man who had become his watch, his responsibility. He'd been tempted to reveal himself to the teacher from Booker High School many times, but how would he react?

. . .

Eight days later Zach touches down at O'Hare. Spring break is over, and for Zach, not a moment too soon. His week in Atlanta was a disaster. His friends had become shallow ignoramuses, unschooled in the ways of sub-zero temperatures and murder. It took Zach all of one hour in their company to realize that over the course of one month they became children and he became a man. As he spent his fourth restless night on the couch of his longtime friend Chase, it occurred to Zach that Thomas Wolfe was right when he said, "You can't go home again." Atlanta was no longer his home, but a place he would reserve for childhood memories, innocent memories.

Zach spent most of the week anticipating his return to Rogers Park and recognized this as a result of his unfinished penance. The fact that he was not emotionally vested in the reunion registered with his friends. In fact, Chase commented that Zach "had changed," even going so far as to ask, "What happened to you up there, dude?"

SIXTEEN

BRIAN

When Dr. James Naismith invented the game of basketball, nailing that first peach basket to the bottom railing of a gymnasium balcony, I doubt he envisioned the tattooed giants who would become the face of his game. I'm sure he never imagined a league in which spoiled superstars would balk about having to practice as part of their multi-million dollar contractual agreements. And what would Naismith think about trash talk? What does "yo' momma" have to do with boxing out for rebounds? What Naismith probably had in mind was something more like Tuesday afternoon faculty basketball at Booker High School: slow-moving white men with bad knees running simple plays. Then again, I'm sure he never envisioned Clinton Magby.

"Umph," grunts Magby. He regains his balance and bends over, hands on knees. He's had the wind knocked from him by a blindside pick. Catching his breath, he raises his head to his teammate. "Christ, Eric. Call out the screen. You trying to get me killed out here?"

Coach Barry Dolan, deliverer of the pick, gives Magby a playful shove. "Lighten up, Magby. We're just here to get exercise and have fun, remember?"

Magby returns the shove. "Fuck you, Dolan. That was a moving screen. You'd think as head basketball coach you'd know how to set a legal pick."

Dolan drops his head and sighs. He'd like to let this go, but man code dictates a reaction. He approaches Magby, who stands his ground. The two men are face to face, each daring the other to make contact. Atway intervenes, sandwiching himself between them.

"I'm done," says Magby. "This is bullshit." He drops the ball and storms off.

Game over.

As I mentioned earlier, it is Magby alone who brings an edge to our otherwise chummy game. Today's outburst, however, was uncharacteristic even for him. If he was ten years old, I'm sure he would have said, "I'm taking my ball and going home." If today's basketball belonged to him instead of being the property of Booker High School, he may have done this anyway.

In the locker room, Magby forgoes a shower. He retrieves his work clothes from his locker and without acknowledging the rest of us, starts for the exit. The others keep their distance. They're talking low enough not to be heard, shaking their heads and gesturing toward Magby. They've formed an alliance, and it doesn't include me. I'm a victim of guilt by association. They know Magby's my friend, and they hold me responsible for recruiting him when we found ourselves without a sixth player four months ago.

I raise a palm to them. *Don't worry. I got this.* I hurry toward the door, intercepting Magby before he reaches the exit. "What's the matter with you? What was that all about?"

He looks at me without answering.

"What's going on, Magby?"

"Nothing." He pauses. "Personal stuff."

"Everything okay with Donna?"

He avoids the question by laying his slacks on the bench and digging through his pockets, fumbling, searching for his car keys. After retrieving them, he has nowhere else to look but up. His eyes are glassy. I've hit the nail on the head.

"What happened?"

He sighs. "Nothing really happened, something that's been building." He sits on the bench. He wants to talk, so I wait. "We're going to spend some time apart. She says she needs space."

I've known Magby for two years. He's been married to Donna for four. For the two years I've known him, Magby's been, well, Magby. There's no other way to describe him. Surely this was the same man Donna married two years earlier. Then again, what do I know about the dynamics at play in the Magby household? I recall the last time I saw Magby and his wife together: two weeks ago, the four of us gathered at Amichi's, sharing antipasto and wine. Donna complained about her husband's language. I suppose this was a telling sign.

I sit beside him on the bench. "Sorry. What are you going to do?"

"I told her I'd move out for a while. What else could I say? I couldn't ask her to leave. She needs to take care of Justin, and she's got to do that at home." He pauses, keeping his voice low enough so the others don't hear. "Shit. I wasn't even going to play today, but I needed to sweat out my frustrations. These guys are going to think I'm an asshole now."

"Nah, they already knew that."

He turns from me to hide a sliver of a smile.

"So what's your plan?" I ask.

"Guess I'm going to call my brother in Naperville. Told Donna I'd leave tonight."

"Naperville? You're going to commute an hour to work every day?"

He shrugs his shoulders and I say what I have to say. "You're not staying in Naperville, Magby. You're staying with me."

"I appreciate it, Brian, but you don't have to say that." He shakes his head. "You got a one bedroom and a girlfriend. I don't fit."

"C'mon. I don't see Rachel much during the week."

He sighs, considering my offer.

I nudge him. "Got a couch with your name on it. Go home, get your stuff, and come over. You remember where I live right?"

He looks up and meets my eyes. His mouth curls into a reluctant smile. "How could I forget? Rogers Park, the bowels of the north side. You sure about this?"

"Hell, yeah. But understand, you will get a lesson in Hitchcock."

He grimaces. "Yeah, figured that."

I stand up. "Besides, now I get a ride to work. You just cut my commute from forty minutes to thirty."

He extends his hand. "Thanks, man." Clutching my hand, he glances toward the other men at their lockers, then back at me.

I nod.

"Yeah," he says, "I know. Got to dance the dance."

Magby approaches the others. I can't hear the words, but the gestures speak volumes: first, open palms and shrugged shoulders from Barry Dolan: *What was that all about? Then*, submissive posture and head shaking from Magby: *Sorry guys. Had a really bad day.* Next, a pat on the shoulder from Dolan: *No sweat. See you tomorrow.* Finally, a smile from Magby as Dolan makes his final comment before turning back to his locker: *And for Christ's sake, take a shower, Magby. You smell like shit.*

After showering and dressing, Magby and I step into the yellow afternoon through the back of the school. I start my stroll toward Redding. I haven't made it ten feet before I hear him laugh. He calls from behind. "Whoa, holy shit, Brian."

I turn to face him.

"What is up with those pants?"

Confused, I glance down at my slacks, at first unsure of the source of his amusement. Then I remember: I'm wearing the pants with the Frankenstein stitches on the ass.

"You been wearing those things all day?" he asks.

"No. Just put them on after my shower."

"Why?"

"Because it's Tuesday."

Magby looks at me like I've dropped from outer space. He shakes his head, smiles, and turns toward the faculty lot. I cross the student lot and start down Redding for my usual two-block walk to the el station.

Whoever said, "March comes in like a lion and goes out like a lamb" may have been onto something. A month which, in its infancy, featured a pill-popping teacher waking up on a dark pier has come to an end. Now a woman cares about me, a student trusts me, and a friend needs me. I've overcome a dependency, and I'm ready to take on the world. Yes, Matthew Dials may still be *my asshole*, but I haven't heard from him since he sat on the steps of my building the Friday before last. I realize that during spring break, his teachers, even if they do "have sticks up their asses," may have lightened up on the homework, and I'm aware Matthew couldn't have found me anyway unless he was in cahoots with a horse in a Skokie motel room painting. Still, eleven days have passed, and time has a way of softening harsh realities. Perhaps Matthew Dials will simply disappear.

I'm strolling. I know I need to hurry if I'm going to catch the next train, but I don't care. My cheeks tingle rather than sting. The air is cool, the kind of blue cool causing southern tourists to shake their heads in disbelief at jacketless Chicagoans. Before long the trees on this suburban street will be dotted with golden buds. The birds will sing and the first blades of green will appear in the grass. I close my eyes. I'm in a Robert Frost poem, walking in a green field. I'm putting my life back together, rebuilding a wall by replacing stones felled by the winter swell. Redding Street runs parallel to the Booker Bobcats football field, but for me, the gridiron to my left, the homes to my right, and the school behind no longer exist. This is the best I've felt in months.

"Teach. Over here." The voice comes from the left. One of the stones in my daydream tumbles from the wall and falls on my foot. I don't want to look, but I do. Under the bleachers, Matthew Dials stands beckoning me. A cigarette dangles from his lips, a single sheet of paper from his hand.

Sometimes time seems to stand still. Other times you can't slow it down enough. During my trudge across the end zone, my mind, as it had many weeks ago on a dark pier, becomes overwhelmed with scenarios. What if Matthew does have proof of our dealings? What if someone hid in the woods behind the bleachers filming one of our transactions? Even if he doesn't have proof, his accusations, if he goes ahead with them, will be a pain in the ass. I'll become the subject of rumors among both faculty and students, rumors that will escalate. *Did you hear about Mr. Casey? I heard he was shooting up in the faculty restroom.*

By the time I reach Matthew, who now holds the paper in front of his chest below his smug grin, I've justified my decision to complete this essay for him, to respond to whatever prompt awaits on the single sheet of paper. In a pathetic attempt to mollify my conscience, I've reasoned that the essay will become one more sample to show my classes, one of many I have written to use as teaching tools. More than this though - let's be honest - I'm not prepared to call his bluff, at least not yet. Just this one essay, I tell myself. That's it. Just this one.

I fix my cold stare on Matthew, my hands plunged into pockets. He thrusts the sheet of paper at me. I make him wait.

"C'mon now, Teach," he says. "Take it. I know you love writing this shit."

The sad fact is he's right. I take the paper and read the single argumentation prompt.

"Make it good." He leans close as though plagiarism police have bugged the steel benches. "Make it worth an eight or nine, but keep it real. I'm a good writer, you know that. Make it sound like me. You know what I can do."

Yeah, I know what you can do, you little shit. You can kiss my ass.

"I need it for Thursday so I'll be here tomorrow at 3:30," he says. "Don't email it. Don't text or call, nothing electronic. Just be here tomorrow at 3:30 with a hard copy." He pauses and smiles. "Hey, how about that? Wednesday, 3:30, under the bleachers. Just like old times right, Teach?"

I don't dignify him with a response.

After Matthew turns the corner of the bleachers and disappears down a side street, I go back into the school, to my classroom. I rummage through stacks of papers and find two essays he'd written for me earlier in the year.

When I step back outside, it feels late. My day has become a sandwich. The available time in the middle is squeezed by what has preceded and what is yet to be done. There's an essay to complete, an essay I'd like to have finished before Magby arrives. But even before addressing these two items, I have a rendezvous with a hot cup of cinnamon coffee. I glance at the time on my phone and start for the el station. There'll be no strolling in green pastures this time. I turn from Redding onto Smith. The train is approaching from the north. I run as quickly as my sore knee will allow, slide my CTA pass into the slot. I push through the turnstile, and rush up the steps. Too late.

I stand on the platform, a pawn at the mercy of The Chicago Transit Authority. A gust of wind reminds me that spring, on a whim, can become winter. I take refuge behind an advertising placard but take no solace in the assurance that Nationwide is on my side.

I reach into my briefcase. Glancing through Matthew's old essays, I recall his knack for insight and powerful imagery, his habit of beginning sentences with participial phrases. The vocabulary is advanced, well beyond his years, but just as many gifted thinkers often transcend common sense, I notice he makes some simple mistakes. A few words he commonly misspells, a few modifiers he leaves dangling. All of this will characterize my written response as unauthorized ghostwriter for Matthew Dials. I again summon the comforting quality of denial. I'm doing this for me, a teaching tool. Besides, Matthew's right: I love writing this shit. Damn, I'm such a nerd.

I feel better for ten seconds until denial is exposed as fraud, kicked to the curb by pride. I exhale a long white breath. I need an angle, a way to make this work for me. A connection clicks in my brain. I reach back into my briefcase and retrieve the single sheet Matthew handed me twenty minutes ago. I read the prompt again:

"Use your reading, observations and experience to compose an argument in which you support, qualify, or refute the following claim:"

"After all, life hasn't much to offer except youth, and I suppose for older people, the love of youth in others." - F. Scott Fitzgerald

This little nugget of wisdom comes to us from a man whose life peaked in his 20's. Fitzgerald's life as an adult was clouded by alcohol and his manic love for Zelda, a schizophrenic woman. He died at the age of forty-four.

Given this, one could hardly call the author who became an icon of The *Jazz* Age an authority on *old* age. A seventeen-year-old, however, may agree with Fitzgerald's pessimistic outlook. After all, according to a teenager, what's left after youth except a life full of work, responsibility, and Depends Undergarments?

This is the mindset I try to establish while sitting on the train bound for Rogers Park. I'm seventeen again, invincible, and anyone over the age of thirty is a dinosaur, an invalid, or both. I begin drafting the argumentation essay on my laptop. I'll support Fitzgerald's point of view using teenage logic and basic but proven techniques. I'll attempt to craft an argument worthy of a score of at least eight on The College Board's one through nine scale. Capturing Matthew's voice shouldn't be difficult. Mimicking an author's style is an exercise I have once or twice had my students try. I never thought I would find myself mimicking the style of a student. Irony is a bitch.

I step from the train at Morse. Spring has returned. The sun is shining and shadows on the street below extend into the late afternoon. I know I should get my ass moving, but I don't. Instead, I stand on the platform overlooking Rogers Park. Morse Avenue bustles with new life, colors I haven't noticed before.

What is it about spring?

It occurs to me that even though Matthew's plagiarized essay will support F. Scott Fitzgerald's claim that "life hasn't much to offer except youth," good old Scottie could not have been more wrong. Regardless of age, life offers us spring, nature's renaissance, reminding us that the world is an amazing place. Where and when else in the universe can one indulge in the wonders of daylight extending, grass greening, and female clothes shrinking?

As I descend the steps of the station, I allow this indulgent attitude to guide me. It tells me that even though I should be concerned about timing this afternoon, I will stop and see Clara. I was unable to visit her last week while in "Houston," but it's a testament to her coffee that I could smell it from my motel room in Skokie. Yes, even during day four of detox, my senses, imagined or otherwise, took on superpowers. I imagine Rachel's sarcastic reaction when I tell her: "You could smell my grandma's coffee all the way from Houston? You really are a superhero, Brian Casey."

The smell last Tuesday was of course a cruel brain impulse, a reminder of what I was missing. Today, however, I'm dizzy with the aroma of anticipation. I hurry from the Morse station, my Tuesday bags slung over my shoulder, a Frankenstein scar on my ass. I've reached Clara's building on Lakewood when my cell phone alerts me of a text from Magby:

"Won't be there til 7."

I glance at the time: 5:06. Have I mentioned the second cup of cinnamon coffee tastes every bit as good as the first?

• • •

As always, Clara serves the coffee in china cups with a pink floral pattern. They rest on matching china saucers, arriving on a tray holding two tiny teaspoons, a china cream dispenser, and a small china bowl holding six sugar lumps. I told Clara five weeks ago that I take my coffee black.

Fifteen minutes into my visit, the topic of family has been exhausted. I'm routed by silence to the default. "Still cool outside," I say. "But I can feel spring in the air. Don't you wish the warm weather would hurry up and get here, Clara?"

"Well, I suppose so, but I don't go out much anyway." She gets up, places my empty coffee cup and saucer on the tray and carries it rattling to the kitchen. I follow, ready-handed, prepared to catch a falling cup, an entire tray, or Clara herself if need be. She rests the tray on the kitchen counter. Relieved their harrowing journey is over, the cups and saucers cease their trembling and clicking.

"Don't worry, Brian. It will be warm soon and the birds will fly back from the south." Having bestowed upon me the wisdom of the ages, she turns to face me, looking at me over the round glasses. "I just hope they're friendly, not like the birds in that old Hitchcock movie."

Our discussion of the weather was so mundane, so routine. The words were floating over my head like soap bubbles. Now one of those bubbles has popped, snapping me to attention.

"What?" I say. "You know that movie? *The Birds?*"

"*The Birds?* No, I don't know any movie called that."

"Yeah, the movie you're talking about, it's called *The Birds.*"

Clara's grey eyes wander in confusion before snapping with recognition. "Oh, is that what it was called? *The Birds?* Yes, that's right." She places a palm on her wan cheek. "Oh my. I was so scared after seeing that movie. I didn't go outside for months without looking at the sky."

"Do you know any other Hitchcock movies?"

"Well, let's see, I remember one where a man kills the wife of somebody, a tennis player I think, because he thinks the tennis player wants him to do her in. Then he expects the tennis player to kill someone for him."

"*Strangers on a Train,*" I say.

"What? No, I don't think I know that one."

"Yes, *Strangers on a Train,* that's the movie you described."

She nods absently.

I go on to explain my passion for Hitchcock. We stand in the kitchen discussing various movies. She's no expert, but the fact that she remembers some of Hitchcock's earlier work makes her unlike anyone else I know. I've found another kindred spirit old enough to be my grandparent. Perhaps Rachel was right. Perhaps I was born at the wrong time.

Clara is placing the dirty cups and saucers in the dishwasher. I'm not allowed to help. I rattle off a few more Hitchcock titles. The multitasking is too much for her. She removes one of the stained cups, examines it for clues about *Dial M for Murder*, and returns it to the dishwasher. Sweet lady. She's trying to please me by indulging my passion but it looks like it hurts. I stay quiet until the last teaspoon is loaded.

"Let's go sit down, Clara."

Apparently I've asked for directions. She points to the living room. I let her show me the way.

"Sorry I couldn't visit you last week," I say.

"That's okay, dear." She plops into her chair. "Rachel told me you were out of town."

I choose not to elaborate on my trip. The lies I told Rachel still stir in my stomach. If I tell them again, I may become physically ill. Fortunately, I remember something else I've been meaning to ask.

"Oh, Clara, I wanted to ask you. This his might be a shot in the dark, but do you—" I pause because of her worried expression. "What's the matter?"

"A shot in the dark? I'm sorry, Brian. I don't think I know that one either."

"What? No. I'm not talking about Hitchcock movies anymore." Her shoulders relax. I give her a moment to catch her breath.

"What I was going to say was that I met an old man in the alley about five weeks ago, maybe homeless. Met him two days after I met you, in about the same spot. He was pushing a shopping cart, collecting cans. Do you know an elderly gentleman with only one arm and a long scar on his face? Have you ever seen anyone like that in the alley?" I spare her the minor detail of his corpse decomposing on the floor of Lake Michigan.

Clara is still processing the overabundance of Hitchcock information. She's only caught the last part of what I've said. "Someone in the alley? Yes, your friend, what a good looking young man."

By now I should expect the unexpected from my elderly companion, but once again her words have thrown me for a loop.

"What? Wait a minute. You met a friend of mine in the alley?"

"Well, yes." She pauses, staring at the rabbi hanging on the wall as though he'll provide details of this memory. "I thought this person was you at first because he wasn't very close to me. He was walking away. I even called to him, called your name. He turned around and came closer and I could see he was younger." She hesitates. "Yes, I remember now. He seemed surprised. He said, 'you know Brian?' I told him I did, and he asked if the Brian I knew had the last name Casey, and I said, 'yes I think that's his name.' That is your last name, right?"

I nod. "What did this guy look like?"

"Well, from behind, a little like you, but without the bare tush." She chuckles at her joke.

I reward her with a smile but keep her focused. "What day was this?"

"Last week, I think. Oh I don't know. All the days run together. The only reason I know today is Tuesday is because you came to see me."

Her eyes drift to the photographs on the wall, to Rachel in the cap and gown. A new spark of recognition flashes in her eyes. "Oh, yes, and he mentioned Rachel. That's right. He asked if I knew Rachel. I told him she was my granddaughter. He was so sweet. Said he could see where Rachel got her good looks. I remember now because that made me blush."

My mind is racing with possibilities. Perhaps Matthew attempted to pay me another visit during spring break, waiting for me again on the steps of my building. Then, when I didn't show up, maybe he used the alley as a shortcut back to the el station. Too bad he didn't wander under a falling trash bag.

At first, I find it strange that Matthew would show up again without letting me know he was coming. Then I remember his caution about communication: "nothing electronic." What choice did he have other than to show up and wait? I take a moment to relish the image of Matthew waiting on my front steps for hours, wasting a whole day of his spring break, cursing me for my absence. But it's strange he didn't say anything about this as we stood under the bleachers just over one hour ago. Perhaps he didn't want to give me the pleasure of knowing I'd been the cause of his wasted time.

Clara looks tired, and I'm the reason. I'm a bully. I've beaten her down with movie titles and questions. The floral armchair consumes her. She's smaller than when I arrived.

"Thanks again for the coffee, Clara. I've been thinking about it all day."

She straightens her shoulders and her puckered mouth curls at the corners. I glance at the clock on the mantle: 5:40. Time to go, but not without a word of caution.

I stand up. "Okay, I need to head home. But listen, Clara. I don't think it's safe for you to talk to strangers in the alley. And even though I'm glad I met you and grateful you sewed my pants, you definitely should not invite any more strangers into your apartment. Will you promise me you won't do that again?"

"Okay, dear. I promise."

I'm not sure she's heard a word I said.

In the interest of time, I exit into the alley instead of onto Lakewood. I make my way through the basement and into the stairwell where five weeks ago I'd first encountered Clara and, two days later, Walter. I climb the steps and, as has become habit, take a precautionary peek at the fire escapes above. All safe.

The dumpster sits across the alley, both sides closed. Had both sides been closed five weeks ago, the trash bag wouldn't have been dropped and I wouldn't have met Rachel. Had I not met Rachel, I wouldn't have been here two days later to meet Walter. Had I not recognized Walter in Sheridan Sam's, I wouldn't have followed him into a dark park only to witness his murder. I stare at the destiny-determining dumpster. The Naturalists were right. My life is a series of events beyond my control. I may think I'm making choices, but I'm not. Every choice I make is a manifestation of something that came before: a father deserting a family, a dumpster with one side open.

Today the alley is empty. Slave to sentimentality that I am, I allow my imagination to conjure an image of an old man scraping his boot on the pavement, attempting to dislodge a wet page of *The Chicago Sun Times*. The image doesn't last as I'm distracted by something out of place. A crumpled Burger King bag clings to the base of the dumpster.

Again I repeat Walter's words. "Nobody knows, and nobody cares."

I cross and pick up the trash. I lift one of the dumpster lids and drop it in. Then, to the ghost who may be watching, I give a simultaneous nod and wave.

Glancing to the south, I notice a lone figure in the distance strolling across the daylight glowing at the Pratt end of the alley. He's in no hurry, kicking loose gravel as he paces. I think little of his presence until he does an about-face and strolls across the opening again, then again. He wears a baseball cap. His head is bent to the pebbles he brushes from side to side. I close the dumpster, a task impossible to complete silently. The clang alerts him of my presence. He looks in my direction, stops, pivots, and scampers behind the building on the east side of the opening.

Matthew Dials? No, too tall, but whoever he is, he's here for me. Perhaps it wasn't Matthew to whom Clara spoke last week. My mind jumps to the threatening note I discovered in my mail slot: "Say anything and you're next." I'm frozen with indecision. I consider turning the other direction, exiting the alley on Farwell. Making my way around the block would add ten minutes to my walk home, but at least I'd make it alive, maybe. But I choose not to take this detour because it's spring, and with spring we become young, brave, and stupid.

I sing these three words to myself as I shuffle toward the Pratt opening, but I can't help but feel that young has impulsively skipped ahead and brave has decided to hide behind stupid. This word, stupid, and this word alone, accompanies me. Each footstep crunching the gravel speaks it. A dripping gutter whispers the word as I pass. I step quietly, approaching the opening. I could avoid Pratt all together by entering my building through the back door, but somewhere on my journey stupid has hooked up with his buddy, curious. Together they drag me toward the opening. I slink to the western edge of the alley to put as much distance as possible between myself and my assailant. It doesn't feel like enough. The alley is narrow today, narrower than I recall. I reach the end and peek to the east, straining my eyes toward Sheridan Road. The pacing stranger is gone.

I turn and backtrack, looking over my shoulder as I approach the backdoor of my building. When I reach it, I attempt to laugh away the paranoia.

Get over yourself, Brian. Been watching too much Hitchcock.

Once in my apartment, I splash cold water on my face. Determined to refocus on the task at hand, I take out my laptop and place Matthew's old essays next to me on the kitchen table. I read through what I drafted on the train and glance one more time at the Fitzgerald quote. It occurs to me that while my walk home from Clara's was harrowing, it was also amazing, a heart-thumping adrenaline rush unmatched by any Hitchcock-fueled daydream. For this, I guess I owe thanks to Mother Nature. If it wasn't spring, young, brave, stupid, and curious may have been hibernating while mature, cautious, and boring guided me around the block, stopping to remind me, "zip up your jacket; you're going to catch your death."

Yes, I was correct in my assessment that spring offers us extended daylight, greening grass, and the shrinkage of female garments, but all of these are manifestations of this yearly rebirth, or youth. In the fall, when nature begins its annual golden period, these things are taken from us. Perhaps Fitzgerald was right. Perhaps life "hasn't much to offer except youth." If so, at least life has been considerate enough to give me fodder for the next part of the essay. I begin typing my - or rather Matthew's - next section:

While Fitzgerald's theory qualifies merely as human perspective, it would certainly garner the support of Mother Nature. . .

Thanks to an afternoon of springtime-fueled epiphanies and caffeinated cinnamon coffee, the rest of this section practically writes itself. So does section three, the subject of which slapped me across the face as I stood on the platform of the Smith Street el station.

At 6:40 I finish the essay and read my work aloud. The argument is solid, well developed, easily worth a score of eight. I'm impressed by how I've captured Matthew's voice, touched on the nuances of his writing. With that task out of the way and with bravery, youth, stupidity, and curiosity frolicking outside, I focus on my three new roommates: paranoia, selfishness, and Clinton Magby. The first two have sat beside me for the past hour, reminding me of the perfect timing of Magby's marital problems. If ever I needed the security that comes with a roommate, it's now.

Despite the fact I'm a marked man, I have the intestinal fortitude to order a pizza to correspond with Magby's arrival. The pizza arrives first. The delivery boy gives me a sideways glance. An indentation circles his hair as though he'd recently worn a baseball cap. After tipping him an extra dollar to convince him to spare my life, I close the door and open the box. The pepperoni smells like strychnine, at least what I imagine strychnine smells like. I kick myself for considering the possibility the garlic bread is ticking.

At 7:10 Magby's car finally pulls to the curb.

I buzz him up. He strolls in, duffle bag in hand. "Hey Brian, how are you, buddy?"

Young, brave, stupid, curious, selfish, and paranoid.

"Fine," I say.

Five minutes later, we settle our troubled asses onto my couch. For the time being, I'll spare Magby his lesson in Hitchcock. Instead we stare at the TV, awaiting the beginning of a basketball game between the Chicago Bulls and Boston Celtics. I twist open a beer and hand it to Magby. "Talk to Donna this afternoon?"

The perfect counterfeit of cool, he leans back, takes a swig, wipes the back of his hand across his mouth. "She'll come around. Just needs a couple days to realize she can't live without me." His eyes drop to the Budweiser label, his thumbnail scraping the corner,

"Stay as long as you need to," I say.

Magby looks up at me, mouth agape. I'm speaking in strange tongues. Stay as long as you need too? My own words have taken me by surprise. I value my privacy. Magby knows this. He also knows that his friend Brian, unlike this extra-terrestrial sitting before him in Brian's skin, would make the invitation conditional.

He raises his beer to me. "Thanks, man."

The basketball game begins but the room remains heavy with real life. I can't help but feel the TV play-by-play is a twig lost in a forest of broken marriages and deadly stalkers. Magby slumps on the couch, reattaching the now-severed label to the wet bottle. He clears his throat. "April Fool's Day tomorrow."

I roll my eyes, making sure he sees.

April Fool's Day, I've learned, is an occasion treated by Magby with the reverence of a religious holiday. One year ago on April 1st, I arrived at Booker in the predawn darkness, yawned into my classroom, and flipped on the light. I jumped back with a "holy shit" when I saw the corpse. A life-like plastic cadaver, borrowed from the Booker High School Medical Academy, slumped forward on my desk. A knife was plunged into his back, the white hospital gown bloodied with ketchup. I lifted the head of the dummy and found a post-it stuck to his forehead: "Solve this one, Hitchcock."

I didn't need to solve anything. I'd known Magby for almost a year and knew no one else who would go to this kind of trouble to pull a prank, let alone confuse Alfred Hitchcock with Sherlock Holmes. The murder victim, who for some reason became known as Sam, remained in my classroom all day. AP test preparation took a back seat that day as my classes engaged in their own versions of amateur detective work, attempting to solve what came to be known as The Casey Classroom Killing.

I narrow my eyes with suspicion, tipping my beer at Magby. "Tomorrow huh? What do you have in mind?"

He leans back and laughs. "No worries for you, Brian. You're doing me a solid here. You, my friend, are safe."

I don't believe him.

"The reason I'm bringing it up," he continues, "is because I'm going to share the history of April Fool's Day with my classes tomorrow."

This, I do believe. Magby makes it a daily habit to open each of his Senior AP classes with a fact about the date in history, a tidbit of routine putting his students in a familiar frame of mind as they start class. I understand now, that for the duration of Magby's stay in my apartment, I'll be a guinea pig as tomorrow's historical fact is tested on me today. He leans forward, making sure my eyes are locked on his. I'm about to receive a history lesson.

"Check this out," he says. "A group of jesters once told the Roman emperor Constantine he was doing a shitty job of running the empire. So Constantine decided to let one of them be king for a day. While he was king, this jester - Kugel, I think his name was - passed a ruling calling for absurdity on that day. The tradition stuck."

"Absurdity huh?"

"Yep."

"Ever studied your own genealogy? Maybe this guy Kugel—"

Van Morrison interrupts our conversation by singing the chorus of "Brown Eyed Girl" in my pocket. Magby raises his eyebrows.

Should have changed that ringtone. I'm never going to hear the end of this.

For a moment I stupidly ignore the sha-na-nas coming from my pants.

"Um, Brian, you do know your pocket's singing, right?"

I sigh. "Yeah, it's Rachel," and without taking a breath add, "shut up, Magby."

He's biting his lip, dying to make a wisecrack, but considering the consequences of giving shit to a host who's offered him indefinite refuge. This is going to be torture for him.

I take the call.

"You like baseball?" Rachel asks.

"Sure, why?"

"Chelsea met this guy. He has four bleacher tickets to the Cub's home opener Friday night. He asked if she wanted to give the other two tickets to anyone, so she asked me, and now I'm asking you."

Baseball, another of the rites of spring. My mind drifts to the essay I completed for Matthew Dials one hour ago. The ivy on Wrigley Field's outfield walls will be nothing but bare tangled vines for at least a few more weeks. Then, as Mother Nature works her magic, it will be reborn, becoming thick enough to swallow up ground-rule doubles. It occurs to me that the timing of Rachel's invitation, like the timing of Magby's marital problems, is perfect. There's nothing like rooting for perennial losers to put things in perspective, to help you understand you must plug along no matter how many curveballs life throws at you. Of course, most north siders would gladly sacrifice a little perspective in order to see the Cubs hit a few of those curveballs. Me? I'll take the life lesson.

"Um, hello. Earth to Brian. Still there?"

"Sorry Rachel. Who's this guy Chelsea's seeing?"

"She's not actually seeing him. Just met him a few days ago. His name's Lucas, I think. Anyway, wanna go?"

"To the home opener at Wrigley? Yeah, of course."

"What're you doing tonight?" she asks.

"Watching basketball. Magby's here, going to be staying here for a little while." I slow the last four words for emphasis, aiming them at Magby. He nods, understanding.

Surprised, Rachel says, "Oh," and is silent. Her assumption is that my apartment has become Magby's doghouse. She's right. After a moment she asks, "Is he there with you right now?"

"Yep."

"Damn, you'll have to give me the details later. Guess I'll let you get on with your little bromance. Ciao baby." Again she clicks off before I have a chance to say goodbye.

Magby reaches across the table for another slice of pizza. "What's up?"

"Looks like I'm going to the Cub's home opener Friday night. Double date with Rachel's roommate."

He sits forward, shaking his head. "Christ. Lights in Wrigley Field. Even after all these years I consider that a travesty." He angrily flips his pizza slice into the box. "And now, here's my best friend, selling out, going to watch our beloved Cubbies play their home opener under artificial lights." Devastated by society's indifference to tradition, he jumps up. He throws his hands skyward in exaggerated frustration and storms from the room. Once in the kitchen, he pokes his head around the corner, waves a reprimanding finger in my direction. "I sure hope those lights are bright enough for you gaze into the soul of your brown eyed girl."

I should have known.

SEVENTEEN

ZACH

It's 2:35 on Wednesday. As is its weekday custom, the mouth of West Rogers Park High School regurgitates fifteen-hundred students. They spill down the concrete tongue, hit the sidewalk with a splat, and ricochet in different directions. Zach stands at the top of the steps, paused. He hasn't descended because his finely tuned people-to-avoid radar has detected one stationary object among the moving parts, one body facing the building rather than joining the mass of humanity fleeing from it.

Shit. Is that who I think it is?

Winston Longstreet stands at the foot of the concrete steps cupping his hand to light a cigarette. The Green Bay Packers baseball cap moves to the left and right as he scans the faces moving past. His cigarette and patchy beard say, "look at me. I've transcended high school." He's watching and waiting. But for who? Abe? Anderson?

Zach, having become a student of paranoia, decides it's in his best interest to assume Winston is waiting for him.

Still, I'll be damned if I'm going out of my way to avoid this asshole.

Zach pulls up the hood of his hoodie. He lowers his head and skips down the steps. His earlier designation as a lost puppy had motivated him to master the art of blending in. Now he knows the secret is to move with a sense of purpose, look only in one direction. He reaches the sidewalk and sandwiches himself among a group of bodies. He passes within five feet of Winston, resisting the urge to look his way.

Zach exhales. He's managed to slip by unnoticed.

His first name is called from behind. He slows but doesn't stop. Maybe there's more than one Zach in this crowd of students.

"Hey, Zachary Mondini."

Zach turns. Eyes buried in the shadow of the cap's bill, Winston faces him. The wave of bodies parts as they encounter this fork in the road, creating twenty feet of empty space between them.

"What do you want?"

"C'mon now, Zach. What kind of greeting is that? I thought we were friends."

"I'm not your friend. What do you want?"

Winston closes the distance.

The conversation that follows strikes Zach as absurd. There's no mention of a drowned old man, but Winston has lost a digital camera. Poor guy. How could life be so unfair? Apparently Winston's camera slipped from his pocket at some point during "that night." He says it maybe happened while he was running on the pier or through the park. He was jarred awake early the next morning by one of those feelings that something had been overlooked. He was pretty wasted the night before but remembered using the camera on the beach and felt it bouncing in his pocket as he ran on the pier. He fought through his hangover on Sunday morning, searched the pockets of his coat and jeans.

"It wasn't there," Winston says to the sky. "My fucking camera was gone. I went back to the pier at six a.m. to look for it. Looked everywhere. It was gone. But I'm pretty sure I know who has it." His eyes narrow. They lock on Zach's. "Brian Casey, the motherfucker who had no business being there. That's who's got my camera."

Winston drops the cigarette and grinds it into the pavement before looking up. He steps closer. "You know him, right?"

"Who?"

"Brian Casey, the schoolteacher. You know who I'm talking about."

"Who's Brian Casey? And what makes you think I know him?"

Winston searches Zach's eyes. "Been watching you. Him too."

Zach shrugs.

"My only question," continues Winston, "is how'd you find out who he is? The rest of you pussies were already running when I took his wallet." He cocks his head, again narrows the eyes. "How'd you find out who he is, Zach?"

The word "wallet" has sparked an image in Zach's memory: In the yellow glow of an apartment building lobby, Brian Casey pulls a note from his mail slot. He reads it, pats the empty pocket of his jeans and realizes his wallet was missing.

Winston shoves Zach's shoulder. "Answer my question, asshole. How'd you find out who he is?"

"I followed you. I waited 'til you left Sheridan and followed you. I saw you get into his lobby and put something in his mail slot." Zach holds his breath. Christ, he better be right.

He feels Winston's eyes burrowing through his, searching. He concentrates. *Don't blink. Hold his stare.*

After a ten second eternity, Winston looks away. He digs a pack of Marlboros from his pocket, taps out a cigarette, and removes it with his lips. He cups his hand to light it. After a long drag he exhales the smoke into the sky.

"Doesn't matter. What does matter is this schoolteacher's got my camera. Got pictures from the beach that night."

Zach shrugs. "Sucks for you."

Winston's glares at him. "You too." He leans into Zach's face. "If you don't get it back for me."

Turning against the grain of traffic, Winston walks away. The bodies part, and the human waves left in his wake drift past Zach, alone on his concrete island.

EIGHTEEN

BRIAN

I have a wife. His name is Clinton Magby. It's Wednesday afternoon at Booker High School. My wife hovers over me as I pretend to tackle a stack of rhetorical analysis timed writes. He's pestering me about what time I'll be home, suspicious about my motivation for refusing a ride. It seems the hypothetical bitch I have not yet married has materialized before my eyes. Only one thing out of place: he looks nothing like Jessica Alba.

Magby slaps me on the shoulder. "C'mon, Brian, grade the essays at home. Don't make me go back to Rogers Park by myself. That place is scary." He shivers with mock fear.

If only he knew.

"Nah, want to get them done before I leave. I'm going to be here a while." I wave him off with the back of my hand. "Head back without me."

"You sure? I thought you said my staying with you was a case of you shamelessly exploiting me for rides."

"Yeah it is. But today I've got to stay. I promise to shamelessly exploit you again tomorrow." I sigh, running my fingers through my hair. "I've got a tutoring appointment at Loyola at 4:30 anyway. I'll take the el straight there, be back around 5:45."

He shrugs his shoulders. "Okay. Guess I'll see you later. How do I get in?"

I hand him two keys: the key to the building and the key to my apartment.

"If you go anywhere, leave the apartment key on the ledge above the door. I'll get one of my neighbors to buzz me into the building."

At 3:28 I step under the bleachers. Waiting for Matthew, I read my handiwork one more time. I browse through the first section of the plagiarized essay and wonder where I fall into F. Scott Fitzgerald's concept of youth. I'm almost thirty, the age at which Fitzgerald was at the apex of his life both socially and professionally. Yet Jay Gatsby, a character of Fitzgerald's own creation, was about the same age and wanted nothing more than to "repeat the past." I continue reading:

While Fitzgerald's theory qualifies as merely human perspective, it would certainly garner the support of Mother Nature. For those of us who live in seasonal locations, she takes Earth's life away after a period of annual youth. In the fall months her daylight shrinks, her leaves, once golden buds, shrivel, fall to the ground, and die.

Mother Nature has made sure that humans follow this same cycle. As we age we lose the crispness that characterizes a new blade of grass, the vision that comes with extended daylight, and the bliss that comes with ignorance. In youth, it is this ignorance that allows us to become Daisy Buchanon's "beautiful little fools," Mother Nature's baby birds, unaware that there is a harsh reality beyond the nest.

When we do leave the nest, we fly unabashed into Mother Nature's storm. Then, as the dark clouds gather, we try to umbrella ourselves against the aging and disease she rains upon us. Eventually our umbrellas collapse. We discover there is no pot of gold at the end of this rainbow, only death. The pot of gold, we understand, had been left in the nest many years ago. In fact, it is not our old age that should be termed "our golden years," but our youth. This is when we are golden, and as Mother Nature, F. Scott Fitzgerald, and Robert Frost have so aptly pointed out, "nothing gold can stay."

I lower the paper and glance at the bare trees. The branches mingle and click against each other as a breeze moves through them. When still, they create a mosaic of grey Chicago sky. I'm somehow younger now than I was when I sat on a park bench a few days ago unable to distinguish slats from gaps, positive from negative space. My life is no longer vanilla. I feel it all: the pain, the good, the evil, the love. A strange warmth rolls through me. If nothing else, the past five weeks have made it possible for the sky to surround the branches.

"Fascinating trees, huh Teach?"

My trance is broken.

I turn to face Matthew. He has a shit-eating grin on his face. He's either amused by having caught me in another retrospective moment or he's enjoying the power trip that comes with blackmailing a teacher. I hand him the manila folder with the two typed sheets.

He opens the folder, gives the essay only a cursory glance. "Alright, looks awesome. Thanks, Teach."

"Don't thank me, you little prick."

His mouth drops. He's surprised, even hurt, by my belligerent attitude. What did he expect me to say? "You're so welcome, Matthew. Anytime little buddy."

I keep my eyes locked on him. "The only reason I did this is to get you off my back. I'm done with you."

Apparently having hoped the exchange of a plagiarized essay would be accompanied by the exchange of pleasantries, Matthew is silent. He hasn't anticipated this. It takes him a moment to recapture a combative frame of mind.

"Don't forget I own you, Teach." His words trail off as he realizes this statement may be too bold. He fears another violent reaction on my part, that I may once again grab him, this time slamming him into bleachers instead of a door. In my new detoxified frame of mind this won't happen, but I'm glad he thinks it might.

I step close, glaring into his eyes. "Really? You own me?" He backs away. "Ownership requires proof, Matthew. Deeds, titles, things like that. If you own me, show me your proof. Without it, I'm done with you."

"I don't have to show you anything. You'll find out the hard way." He avoids my eyes, and for the first time I'm confident he's bluffing. I have him on the ropes. He has nothing else to say, but I do.

"You know today's April Fool's Day, right?"

For a moment he looks confused. Has he missed something? He shrugs his shoulders. "Yeah. So?"

I wink before turning to walk away. That ought to give him something to think about.

I feel Matthew's eyes watch me stroll down Redding. I'm tempted to turn around to confirm this, but to turn now would indicate weakness or doubt. I stride with confidence and bask in the glow of my defiance. I'm beholden to no one and nothing. After turning from Redding onto Smith and moving out of sight of the bleachers, my curiosity gets the best of me. So much for being beholden to nothing. Intending to indulge myself a moment longer, I double back to the corner, expecting to see Matthew still standing, mired in the quicksand of defeat.

A thick oak tree, roots buckling the sidewalk in protest, towers on the corner of Smith and Redding. I duck behind the trunk of this tree, glancing toward the bleachers in the distance. Matthew is still there, but he's not alone. Standing a few inches taller, a second figure has his back to me. He accepts a cigarette and a light and gestures toward the manila folder tucked under Matthew's arm. After a few words, Matthew points in my direction, and the newcomer turns. They both face me, but their glance is fleeting and my tree is fat. It is a glance about me but not at me. Matthew shows the folder to the newcomer who opens it, gives the first sheet a glance, and hands it back. The movements of these two young men, their posture, their gestures, tell me they don't know each other.

I watch them for a few minutes. A handshake, an agreement has been reached. Matthew turns away. The newcomer starts in my direction. My oak tree, while conveniently wide, sits too close to the sidewalk. I scurry into a yard on the corner of Smith and Redding, disregarding the notion that a concerned housewife may be peering from behind her living room curtains, dialing 911 to report the stranger scampering through her flower bed.

Taking refuge behind a hedge, I watch through a maze of branches and tiny leaves as the stranger, wearing a Green Bay Packers cap and mirrored shades, passes within twenty feet. I hold my breath so it won't be heard, but this only increases the volume of my pounding heart. I wait until he's moved fifty yards along Smith, one block from the el station, before I step onto the sidewalk. I'll follow, keeping a safe distance. But assuming he's headed for the station, I'll stay close enough to board the same train.

The stranger strides ahead. I'm scampering, ducking behind trees as I follow. For no particular reason, I remember Josiah Coffee, our 4:30 tutoring appointment. I take a moment to curse my father, wherever the loser is, for teaching me responsibility the hard way. I'll text Josiah from the train, tell him I'm running late - no - tell him I can't make it today. If I have to be a no-show for tutoring this afternoon, so be it. There's a mystery to be solved. Alfred Hitchcock would be disappointed if I neglected it in favor of academia.

I aim for the next tree.

The stranger enters the station. For a moment I lose sight of him. Paranoia, never one to miss an opportunity, is quick to take advantage. Suddenly the young man in the green and yellow cap is everywhere, behind trees, peeking from windows, ducking low in parked cars.

I increase my pace.

Stepping into the station, I make the assumption he's taken the steps leading to the southbound platform. An entire city waits in that direction, little in the other. My heart races. Knees weak, I climb the steps. Upon reaching the top, I peek around the edge. A middle-aged woman gasps. She's mistaken my espionage for some weird kind of el platform perversion. She pulls the collar of her coat closed and hurries away from me.

I see him, shoulders hunched, hands plunged into the pockets of his jacket. His long slender profile, the shuffling of his feet on the platform, take me back to yesterday when he paced the opening of the Farwell-Pratt alley kicking at gravel. He stands at the southern end of the station. I take a deep breath and hold it. I step onto the platform and slide the other direction. As I'd done yesterday when seeking shelter from the wind, I duck behind the advertising placard. Nationwide is still on my side.

The train arrives, screeching to a stop. I watch the stranger board one of the front cars. I board close to the back. I have a Hitchcockian plan: I'll hop off at the next stop, peer down the platform to see if he's among the people exiting the train. If not, I'll jump back on before the doors close and complete the same routine at the following stop.

My heart pounds as the train lurches forward. What am I doing? Where will this journey take me?

My window rattles past the southern edge of the station. I see him. He's standing on the platform, the Green Bay Packers cap pulled tight. His head moves from right to left, the image of the train, of my window, of me, reflecting in the mirrored glasses. He nods to me as the train pulls away.

I don't bother texting Josiah from the train. Instead, I continue to Loyola as though a discussion of argumentation will help me reason away the insanity that has become my life.

It's Josiah who arrives late for tutorials this time. He rushes into the library at 4:38 full of apologies and excuses. He drops his backpack and sits, drumming his fingers on the wood tabletop, making no effort to retrieve his practice materials. It's our fifth session together, but today he's different, troubled, not the Josiah Coffee I was hoping for. I'd spent the last thirty minutes on the el, searching the sinister faces of passengers, certain every single one was plotting my demise. I hoped the tutoring session would provide a return to normalcy, but normal has gone AWOL. I consider the possibility I may be imagining Josiah's restlessness, that my paranoia has skewed my perspective.

He glances over his shoulder.

"Everything okay today, Josiah?"

"Yeah, fine." With effort, he redirects his attention, reaches into his backpack.

"Did you time yourself on those multiple choice passages?" I ask.

He plops the practice book on the table. "Yeah, but I know I bombed them. They're ridiculous, Mr. Casey. How you supposed to answer all those questions in one hour?"

"I told you they're tough. But we're going to talk about some strategies for pacing yourself today.

He looks over his shoulder again.

The session, to say the least, is unproductive. I attempt to explain how to analyze question stems, how to identify the most difficult multiple choice items that should be left until last so the test taker doesn't run out of time before answering the easy questions. I've been through this several times with my classes, but today each time I point out the stems containing "all of the following except" or "which of the following do not," the rest of the question takes on a life of its own:

Brian Casey has spent the day hiding behind all of the following except. . .

Which of the following people do not want Brian Casey dead?

As I struggle to maintain my focus, Josiah's focus remains on the library's entrance over his left shoulder. We're going through the motions. During the second half of the hour we attempt to disguise our mutual paranoia by discussing argumentation, specifically the use of reason and logic rather than examples for developing an argument.

"I don't know, Mr. Casey. I don't really get it." He pauses, tapping his fingers on the table as though providing a metronome to speed up the second hand of the clock to our left. "Do you have, like, a sample essay or something I can look at?"

I understand Josiah's desperation. He wants to fill the rest of the hour with an excuse to avoid my eyes and academic conversation. I feel the same way. It's clear nothing more will be learned today, and having him pretend to read a sample would provide the silence, the distance, we both seek. Remembering my pledge to use my - or Matthew's – "Life hasn't much to offer except youth" essay as a teaching tool, I locate the file on my laptop.

"Take a look at this, Josiah. Check out the reasoning and use of concrete details, how they contribute to the argument." I turn the computer to face him.

I watch him read and feign interest. It's a slow half-hearted process. His eyes reach the bottom of the screen. His reluctant fingers slide on the track pad as he scrolls down to continue. Then, as though called to attention, his shoulders stiffen and he swallows hard. He leans in close, focused. His mouth moves silently, forming the words that appear on the screen. He looks up at me with a new expression. The apathy has become confusion.

"Who wrote this?"

The question takes me by surprise, but being a master of creative avoidance, I manage to sidestep a direct lie.

"There's a name's at the top. Why?"

He doesn't respond, but scrolls to the top of the essay. I watch as his mouth forms the name Matthew Dials. He's searching, trying to place the name.

"Josiah? You okay? Why do you care who wrote it?"

"No I don't care about that." He swallows the words. "I just think it's really good and, um, like I told you, I know some people at Booker." He pauses. "I was wondering. Have you read this whole essay, Mr. Casey?"

"Of course I've read it. Why? What's wrong?"

"Nothing wrong. It's just really good."

Our strange hour together comes to an end. This time Josiah is the one reluctant to leave. My curiosity peeked, I offer to sit and talk as we've done in the past, but he says no. He's got other homework and he might as well sit here and do it before heading home.

"Alright, Josiah." I stand up. "Have a good afternoon. I'll see you on Friday."

He doesn't respond. He lifts a Social studies textbook from his backpack, opens it to a random page. I'm supposed to believe he's found the correct page by dropping a 350 page book on the table and, like a magician completing a card trick, flipping it open to the page he seeks.

"Josiah," I repeat, "see you Friday?" Something, intuition perhaps, prompts me to phrase this as a question.

"Oh yeah. Friday. Later, Mr. C."

I leave the library, but not the campus. Instead of cutting across the quad to where the entrance to Loyola opens onto Sheridan Road, I wait, absorbing the stares of curious coeds as I peek around the red brick corner of the student center, forty yards from the library. I'm unsure what I'm waiting for because I'm no longer sure what to expect. I consider the possibility that the past three and a half weeks of my life have been a dream that started on a Saturday night with an innocent visit to a bar called Sheridan Sam's. The dream has taken some unusual turns and now includes spying on a young man who, until today, had provided me with something lacking in my life, a comforting sense of predictability.

Apparently, Josiah's other homework wasn't much. He emerges from the library five minutes after my own exit. He pulls up the hood of his sweatshirt, hunching his shoulders so it can extend forward, hiding his face. He ducks his head and strides across the quad toward Sheridan Road. I follow. Once he reaches Sheridan, I hear a barely-decipherable name called. Matt? Jack? To my surprise, Josiah reacts only as one bearing that name would react, instinctively stopping and turning. The caller steps into view and my heart skips a beat. He wears mirrored sunglasses, a brown leather jacket, and a Green bay Packers baseball cap.

I'm standing behind the cement pillars marking the entrance to the university. The mystery man jabs his finger at Josiah's chest, reprimanding him. He turns to walk away, pivots on his heels, and points at Josiah. "One more chance, asshole. I'm watching you."

Josiah stands, watching the stranger walk away.

I step from the shadows. "Who was that, Josiah?"

He jumps back. I'm a ghost, appeared from nowhere. "Mr. Casey. What are you still doing here?"

"Who was that?" I ask again.

"Just a friend." He avoids my eyes.

"A friend? Didn't look like he was being very friendly to me. What's going on, Josiah? You okay?"

"I gotta go, Mr. Casey." With this, he dashes into the rush hour traffic on Sheridan Road. We are mid-block, at least forty yards from an intersection or crosswalk. The driver of a Toyota Camry slams on his brakes, honks as Josiah darts in front of him.

"Josiah. Wait."

Watching him dodge six lanes of impatient traffic is torture. I'm helpless, anchored to the sidewalk. I cringe as he stops, starts, and stops again as though performing a poorly choreographed dance to the cacophony of honking horns and screeching brakes. A driver berates him from an open window, "What the fuck, dude," as he rushes by Josiah, paused in the middle of the street, waiting for an opportunity to make his next dash. Unaware that I had been holding my breath, I'm startled by the gasp of air escaping me once he reaches the safety of the opposite sidewalk.

He turns and looks at me. The world is moving between us but we're frozen in time. I raise my palms in question as his image flickers in and out of my line of sight with each truck, van or SUV that rushes past. He says something to me. His words are lost in the traffic, but I don't need to hear them. I know what he's said.

"I'm sorry, Mr. Casey."

Now Josiah is running. He heads south on Sheridan. I move parallel to him on the other side of the street, determined not to lose sight of him. When he turns right on Devon, the street running perpendicular to Sheridan, I know he's gone. I can't cross the street without waiting for the light to change. Even if I could, I'd never catch him.

I look to the south. The stranger, the green and yellow cap, is barely visible a hundred yards away. He's approaching the left hand turn where Sheridan wraps around Loyola. Now it's my turn to run. I weave through the throng of Rogers Park rush hour pedestrians. I reach the intersection and look to my left. Too late.

• • •

Josiah Coffee is a sixty-two-year-old African-American male living in Portland, Oregon. Originally from New Orleans, his interests include carpentry and zydeco music. He graduated from Booker T. Washington High School in 1968 and is a proud new grandparent.

Funny, I wouldn't have guessed Josiah was into zydeco. Of course, my Josiah Coffee may have foregone the entire Facebook route, but it's strange that Google would produce the same results, or lack thereof. I'm not completely surprised he's not who he claimed to be. If nothing else, the past five weeks has taught me to expect the unexpected.

By Thursday morning I'm convinced that not only does my Josiah Coffee not attend Howard High School, but he fails to exist. I will, however, try one more thing.

At first, the name of the student he claimed gave him the recommendation eludes me. I dig deep into the recesses of my memory, pulling out a snippet of conversation from the first time we met.

"Who's your friend at Booker?" I asked.

"Malory Carstons."

I'm confident this is the name he mentioned, and as I check the student database at Booker this is confirmed. Malory is a freshman and according to her grades, an average student at best. She's not enrolled in any pre-AP classes, hardly the profile of someone from whom a junior would solicit a recommendation for AP tutorials.

During my conference period I go to Malory's Algebra class and knock gently on the door. I apologize to her teacher for the interruption, ask if he'd mind letting me talk to her for a minute. He begrudgingly calls to her.

Malory is an overweight girl. She looks at me like deer in headlights, unsure what kind of trouble she could be in with a faculty member not one of her own teachers.

"Hi, Mallory. I'm Mr. Casey."

"Okay."

"I want to ask you about a student - not from here - from Howard High School. Says you recommended me for tutoring."

"I don't know nobody at Howard,"

"You don't know Josiah Coffee?"

"Who?"

"Josiah Coffee."

"What kind of a goofy name is that? He said I recommended you? Why would I do that? You're not even my teacher, and I got no idea who you're talking about."

"Maybe that's not his name. Did you talk to anyone about AP tutoring?"

"What's AP?"

"Never mind, Mallory. I guess I got the wrong person."

NINETEEN

ZACH

It's over. Zach hoped he could keep up the charade until May, when Josiah Coffee, the average student from Howard High School, would overcome incredible odds and pass the Advanced Placement English Language and Composition exam. Zach knew passing this exam wouldn't be a problem. He passed it last year in Atlanta, and now, with Brian Casey's additional tutelage, he was more prepared than ever.

While completing his assignments as Josiah Coffee, Zach had been amazed how difficult it was to dumb himself down. The all-important step of revision had never before included a transition from active to passive voice or the removal of overly-insightful observations.

Interestingly though, becoming Josiah Coffee during his interactions with Brian came quite naturally. While in his tutor's presence he simply met Brian's expectations, became the person Brian expected him to be. Zach recognized this as the Sociological theory of *the looking glass self*, a theory applying to impressionable people who unknowingly become what they think others perceive them to be. In Zach's case, however, he allowed - even encouraged - Brian's preconceived notions of Josiah Coffee to feed his ability to stay in character.

In a perfect world, Josiah would stroll into the AP testing room in early May and pass with flying colors. Zach hadn't yet worked out the logistics of this. He'd have to register as Zachary Mondini, but this shouldn't present a problem. No official documentation of results would be sent to a private tutor. Josiah would simply tell Brian he passed. That was it.

In fact, Zach considered not taking the test at all but realized Brian would become informed of the exam's essay prompts and Josiah Coffee would need to be prepared for this. Besides, he reasoned, perhaps I can improve on last year's score. Zach decided to make this his personal challenge. After all, Brian had given him new insight into the test and the subject matter. It would be a shame if it went to waste.

The credit for Josiah Coffee's remarkable accomplishment would go not only to Josiah himself, but also to his amazing tutor, the man who showed the ability to turn a subpar student into a scholar, lifting a heavy load to incredible heights.

As a result, Brian Casey's life would once again have purpose. The renaissance wouldn't be much, probably not enough to make him forget his failed attempt to save a drowning old man, but it could be enough to let him know there are people out there who he can help, people who need him. Then, having restored Brian Casey's sense of relevance, Zach's penance would be complete. Brian would be a new man, a man worthy of Rachel's love. He and Rachel would be happy, both of them owing a debt of gratitude to Zach, their secret guardian angel.

All of this was to occur before the end of summer when Zach would pack his suitcase with clothing, toiletries, and peace of mind and head to The University of Pittsburgh.

Josiah Coffee would simply disappear. Perhaps his family would move from Rogers Park and Brian Casey would receive a letter without a return address, a letter thanking him for changing a young man's life

TWENTY

BRIAN

Opening night at Wrigley Field. Two uneventful days have passed. No sign of a Green Bay Packers cap, no sign of the student formerly known as Josiah Coffee, and no sign of my asshole, Matthew Dials. Thanks to Magby and his "this day in history" obsession, I now know that the first motion picture theatre opened in Los Angeles on April 2nd, 1902. And thank God I'm finally blessed with the knowledge that on April 3rd, 1953, *TV Guide* was published for the first time. Still, these invaluable tidbits of information have failed to fill the void left by the absence of blackmailers and stalkers.

Spring, for Chicagoans, is a tease, a date who dashes your horny hopes with a goodnight kiss on the cheek. And baseball, a naïve victim of this tease, has been seduced into believing it can play outdoors - at night - in early April - in Chicago. The day's balmy high temperature of fifty-two degrees has plummeted along with the sun that one hour ago forsook us all by becoming bored with baseball and disappearing behind Wrigley Field's third base stands.

The centerfield bleachers rise from the Earth like the exposed ruins of a Roman Coliseum. The four of us squint into the bitter wind as the flags snap above our heads. No blanket of cloud cover protects us from the cold night sky. The temperature, however, does come with the silver lining of women seeking shared body warmth. Rachel snuggles close to me.

"How old is this guy Lucas?" I whisper, glancing past her to where Chelsea and her date jostle playfully. She elbows him in the ribs, laughing.

"Why?" asks Rachel.

"Looks kinda young. Is Chelsea robbing the cradle?"

"I don't know how old he is. I think Chelsea said he's twenty-three. But she's only twenty-six. I'd hardly say that makes her a cougar. Besides, you're four years older than me. Does that make you a dirty old man?"

Honesty tempts me, but I answer, "of course not."

I look again at Lucas. Twenty-three? He doesn't even look that old. He catches my glance and, to my surprise, holds it with a wry grin and a raised finger. I'm intrigued. He wants something, wants me to watch him. He unzips his Cubs windbreaker, reaches inside with great ceremony and withdraws a green and yellow cap.

What the—?

I can't look away, but I can't tame my eyes. I feel them darting between his eyes and the cap, now unfolded in his hand, the Packers logo turned to face me. He lifts the cap. With a slow-motion slide over the back of his head, he puts it on and pulls it tight. He turns back to the game.

My cell phone rings, causing my already racing heart to floor the gas. I juggle the phone as I pull it from my pocket, anchoring my hand against my thigh to stop the trembling. I look at the screen: Magby. He'll have to wait.

Rachel throws a curious glance my way as I return the phone to my pocket. "You okay? Why didn't you answer?"

I lean forward, looking past her toward Lucas. Chelsea blocks my view. She leans into him, laughing again.

"I've got to tell you something," I whisper. "But not here."

My phone rings again. God damn it, Magby.

Rachel keeps her eyes fixed on mine. I've whet her appetite and now she's starving. What can't I tell her? Why can't I tell her here? I raise a finger to put her unasked questions on hold and to let her know I'm about to put Magby's annoyance to rest. Knowing Magby, it could be anything: Monday's historical fact, a dirty joke. Doesn't matter. Whatever it is, the calling won't stop until I answer. I press the phone to my ear, cupping a hand over the other. "What is it, Magby?"

His tone catches me off guard. It hints of responsibility, significance. But because the Cubs have chosen this moment to stage a rare rally, his words are lost among the cheers of bleacher bums.

"What? Can't hear you. Hold on. I'm gonna call you back."

I stand and turn to Rachel. "I'll be right back." She clutches my sleeve, looks up at me. She wants answers. I gently remove her hand. "I'll be right back."

Our bleacher seats are right of center. The shorter distance to the aisle is past Rachel, Chelsea, Lucas, and four others to my right. I head to the left.

When I reach the concourse, I move without purpose. I'm striding to nowhere, drumming my hands on my thighs. I find myself surrounded by coconspirators, all wanting me dead. A ten-year-old kid wears a giant foam finger to disguise the fact he's packing heat. A popcorn machine fires off machine gun rounds as I pass. The questions in my head jostle for position, fighting for answers: Why is he here? What does he want from me? Should I be worried for Rachel? For Chelsea? For a minute I forget why I'm here, pacing this concourse. I look my hand, the phone in my palm.

I make the call. "This better be important, Magby. This is not a good time."

"Okay, well, I thought you might want to know—" His voice is lost again as another roar comes from the bleachers.

I slow to a walk. "Speak up. Still can't hear you."

He raises his voice: "I'm trying to tell you that you had a visitor to your apartment tonight."

"A visitor? Who?"

"Your father."

I stop walking. The voices of the concourse have become ghostly echoes. I must have misunderstood his words.

"Sorry, what did you say?"

"I said your father came by." Then, because of my silence, thinking he's lost me: "Brian? You still there?"

"I'm here."

I'm leaning in a corner of the concourse, my forehead resting against the wall, my face buried in the dirty corner. The world has stopped. The outside noise has disappeared. I hear only Magby's voice.

"It was weird," he says. "I opened the door and your dad just stood there staring at me, looking confused. I think for a minute he thought I was you. But why would he think that? When was the last time you saw him?"

"Twenty years ago."

Now silence hangs on the other end of the line as Magby processes the magnitude of what I've told him.

"Wait. Did you say twenty years?"

"What did he want?" I ask.

"He said to just tell you he was here." A pause. "Christ, Brian, I had no idea. I told him you were at Wrigley, wouldn't be home for hours. I asked him if he wanted to come in, offered him a cup of coffee. He said he'd come back another time and then he left."

Another pause.

"You okay?"

"Yeah. I just. . . I gotta go. I'll talk to you later."

I step from the concourse. I'm standing at the base of our section, section 102. At least I think that's where I stand. Guess I could be anywhere. It's all a dream anyway, right? I scan the hundreds of heads in front of me. All these people, none of them know trouble.

Our row in the crowded bleachers has become lost. I search for a landmark and spot the green and yellow cap. I'm reminded of Lucas, his dramatic gesture eight minutes ago, so significant then. I enter our row, this time on his side. He doesn't matter anymore. Nothing matters anymore, not the green and yellow cap, not the fact that the Cubs have scored their first run of the season, not even Rachel.

I sidle past the people in our row. Lucas watches me approach. He still wears the cap, the same expression below the bill, narrowed eyes, wry grin. Idiot. He has no idea he's an ant knocking on a giant's door, a distant second place finisher in the evening's shock Brian Casey contest. When I reach him, I stand a moment facing him. His expression changes to one of confusion. I take the cap from his head and drop it in his lap. Chelsea and Rachel look at us, baffled. Chelsea scoffs and waves a hand to dismiss our nonsense. She doesn't get the whole sports rivalry thing. Guys are just too competitive. Lucas's eyes drop from mine. I've made him uncomfortable. It was supposed to be the other way around. He returns the cap to his head and feigns interest in the game.

I sit down. I'm eight years old. It's 1991 and my father, John Casey, sits beside me. He points to the second baseman kicking the infield dirt. This is Ryne Sandberg, my favorite Cubbie. Then it's the seventh inning stretch. My father and I stand and sing along with that old man, Harry Carry, as he leads the Wrigley Field faithful in his own drunken version of "Take Me Out to the Ballgame."

Rachel, recognizing I'm far away, snaps me from my trance. "Brian? You okay?"

I turn to her. For a moment she's a stranger.

"What's wrong?" she asks. "Do you want to leave?"

I want to answer "yes" or "maybe" or "I don't know." Does it matter what I answer? Is anywhere safe? Perhaps I should crawl back into a pill bottle. It felt safe in there. Beyond Rachel, the green and yellow cap sneaks into my line of sight. I force myself to focus on the now, the imminent threat of Lucas. We can't leave Chelsea alone with him.

"No," I say. "We need to stay."

We do stay, but only for one more inning. The score is irrelevant. I guess the Cubs have fallen far enough behind to justify an early exit. The four of us step onto the street. I turn for a moment and look back at Wrigley Field, the baseball stadium formerly known as The Friendly Confines.

. . .

The train from Addison is packed with fair-weather Cub fans, historians, aware that a seventh inning multi-run deficit is a game lost. We stand clutching the rail above our heads. I'm shoulder-to-shoulder with Lucas, but my head is turned to Rachel. The train lurches forward. She's looking up at me, her eyes pleading, agonizing with anticipation. She's waiting for news too delicate to share with Lucas, Chelsea, or the Dick Butkis look-alike breathing on the back of her neck.

The train booms ahead, the interior lights flickering on and off. It occurs to me that earlier in the evening Rachel and Chelsea had boarded at Berwyn because Rachel kept an appointment in that neighborhood, a job consultation, at five. Chelsea tagged along. They left Rachel's car parked in the area and waited on the Berwyn platform until I texted Rachel to let her know I was on the next train heading south toward Wrigley. Lucas met the three of us as we disembarked at Addison. But now, as we rumble north into the night, here he is, on the same train. I have no idea which stop is his. If Chelsea and Rachel exit at Berwyn, Lucas and I will be left on the train. Or will Rachel suggest Chelsea and Lucas take her car home while she stays on the train with me? I can't let that happen. It's my fault he's here. I don't trust him with Chelsea.

Lucas's shoulder rubs against mine as the train rumbles ahead. I can't share my dilemma with Rachel. He's too close, and the playfulness he shared with Chelsea has gone to bed. They're quiet. It's been a long day. Chelsea's cheek rests against his chest, her eyes heavy with the motion of the train.

We screech to a stop at Lawrence, two stops short of Berwyn.

"I'm getting off here," Lucas says to no one in particular. "Got to stop and see a friend about something." He looks down at Chelsea. "I'll give you a call." He kisses her. His abrupt announcement and the kiss both take Chelsea by surprise. Her cheeks flush and her mouth drops. Lucas turns to us. "See you, Rachel." His eyes linger on me for a moment before he adds, "Brian."

Just like that, he's gone. I wait for the bomb he's slipped into a stranger's backpack to detonate, for his evil twin brother to appear in a Milwaukee Brewers cap. Surely I should be waiting for something. Security is not one of the cards I've been dealt today.

Somehow, we reach Berwyn in one piece.

"You're going to walk us to my car, right?" Rachel says, with an insistent gaze as the train grinds to a stop.

"Of course."

. . .

"It's just one more block and around the corner," says Rachel as we stroll toward the Dominick's parking lot where she left her car. We're hand-in-hand. She slows our pace, trying to create enough distance from Chelsea to accommodate a discreet question or two.

Chelsea, after realizing she's surged five steps ahead, whirls around, walking backwards. "C'mon guys. It's freezing." She dances in place, waiting for us to catch up.

Rachel rolls her eyes at me. She'll have to wait a little longer.

Chelsea is on top of the world. "What do you think of Lucas? Cute, huh?"

The question, I assume, is for both of us. I don't have the answer she wants. I leave it for Rachel.

"Yeah, cute," she says.

"How long you been seeing him, Chelsea?" I ask.

"We met last week. He came into the store. Didn't even look at any of the clothes. Just started flirting with me. I kind of blew him off at first, but he came back two more times. Said he was going to keep coming back until I agreed to have dinner with him." She shrugs. "Hey, what can I say? He was persistent and I caved."

"What's his last name?" I ask.

"Laramy. Lucas Laramy. Pretty cool name, huh? Sounds like a movie star."

Too much like a movie star. I make a mental note and tag it to the physical features I've sketched in my brain. I'll check on the name later. We reach Rachel's car. Chelsea agrees to give us a minute. "Take your time. I'm turning on the heat. Gotta defrost the tip of my nose."

Rachel waits until Chelsea has closed the door. We lean against the trunk. "Okay, spill it, Mister. What's going on?"

I've known since we left Wrigley Field that this question was coming. I was torn about which of the evening's bombshells to drop on Rachel, reasoning that exploding both of them together may minimize the impact that each deserves. The decision was made for me as both Lucas and the imminent threat he represented made early exits from the train. The ghost of my father, on the other hand, has accompanied me every step of the way.

"I don't understand," I say to Rachel after telling her about Magby's phone call. "Why would he show up now? Out of the blue?"

"Maybe he wants you to forgive him. How old is he now? In his sixties?"

I take a moment to do the math. "Seventy-two."

"Okay, so he's getting up there in age. Maybe he wants to leave his life in order."

"Why? You think he's sick?"

"I don't know, Brian. But I think you need to give him a chance - to talk to you I mean - to explain anything he needs to explain." She pauses. "I told you my own father died when I was eighteen, right? He never had the chance to know me as an adult. Maybe you need to give your father that chance."

She puts her hand on my arm and invites me to her apartment.

"Nah, don't think so," I say. "I'm going to go home and think."

"Okay. Well, it's pretty cold out here. Get in. I'll drive you back to the station."

I open the passenger side door. Chelsea, in the front seat, crosses her arms defiantly. "No way, Brian. I just got warm. I'm not getting out."

She leans forward and I squeeze into the back seat of the two-door Honda Civic. Chelsea continues chatting away about the cold or Lucas or some other aspect of her happy-go-lucky life. I catch Rachel's concerned glance in the rear-view mirror and we drive into the night.

• • •

Back in Rogers Park, the dark walk home from the Morse el station is eternal. I reach the Farwell-Pratt alley and pause – no, can't do it – too many surprises already for one day. I continue past the opening and turn on Lakewood.

As I pass the front of Clara's building, I'm reminded once again of Fitzgerald's quote: "Life hasn't much to offer except youth and, I suppose for older people, the love of youth in others." I stop and stare at the building. It houses an old woman whose greatest pleasure comes from serving cinnamon coffee to a young Tuesday visitor. In the alley behind, an old man smiled as a member of a younger generation helped him restore a little Rogers Park pride by picking up trash around a dumpster. And now, around the corner, an elderly father has knocked on a strange door, hoping to win back a long-lost son. The love of youth in others? Maybe Fitzgerald was right after all.

I reach my building and stand under the yellow light, digging in the pocket of my jeans for my key. A trembling voice, distantly familiar, comes from the darkness behind.

"Brian."

My heart leaps into my throat.

I don't turn or answer. I can't. Ten thousand epithets I've saved for him are gone, my hard drive wiped clean. Behind me, his footsteps shuffle closer, reluctant weary scrapes on gravel. I shouldn't be able to hear them. Farwell is too quiet. Where are the tires grinding on the puckered street? The wind singing through the trees? I face the door motionless, frozen. The warm yellow glow of the lobby has never been more inviting yet more inaccessible. It should be easy to reach. Just dig deeper into the pocket. Find the key. Slide it into the lock. Step inside.

The footsteps behind shuffle closer. His shadow, elongated by the streetlight, peeks in my periphery. Where the fuck is that key? I fumble in my pocket. Got it. I aim for the lock but the key is a coward. It takes a suicidal plunge from my unsteady hand, bouncing on the cement step with a clang that is far too loud on a night far too quiet.

The creak of bending knees and a small grunt from behind, right behind.

A hand reaches around me, extending the key from a thumb and forefinger. I take it without turning. Our fingers brush. The footsteps shuffle again, backing away, giving me space. I take a deep breath and insert the trembling key and step into the lobby, leaving my father alone in the cold night.

•   •   •

It's Saturday morning. I spent the night tossing in my bed, becoming entangled in sheets that would five times be thrown aside as I made my way to the living room, tiptoeing past a sleeping Magby to peek through the blinds, scanning the street below. I finally drifted into a restless sleep, must have been some time around four.

Now, at nine a.m., I'm trying to make sense of it all. Up for hours, Magby sits on my living room couch, his bedding uncharacteristically folded on one end, a stack of ungraded essays on the table in front of him.

"Coffee in the kitchen," he says. "Probably cold now. Want me to zap a cup for you?"

"Nah. I'll get it."

Last night I entered my apartment and found Magby dozing on the couch, a *Law and Order* rerun keeping him company in his half sleep. Playing the part of the concerned and dutiful friend, he sat up abruptly as the door clicked closed behind me.

He dug a fist into his eye. "Hey, what time is it? You okay?"

"Yeah. Hell of a night."

I didn't tell him about encountering my father outside moments earlier. Instead I dismissed his "sorry you missed your dad, Brian" with a tired wave of my hand and went to bed.

Now, this morning, he's trying too hard. He doesn't understand I've had it with strange encounters. I want to tell Magby to just be Magby, but I'm not sure I could deal with that either. No, let him think his strange attempts at compassion are helpful. Maybe tomorrow I'll get breakfast in bed.

I carry my zapped coffee to the couch and sit down. Magby turns his body to face me, waiting for information I didn't give him last night. I take a deep breath and begin.

"My father walked out on my mother and me when I was nine. . ."

He sagely nods. My friend, who became my wife, has now become my shrink.

. . .

After treating Magby to my life story, I'm anxious to call Rachel, not only to tell her about encountering my father, but also to drop bombshell number two, exploding the legend of Lucas Laramy. The call will need to wait though. Last night Rachel mentioned a job consultation she'd scheduled for this morning. To let her foolishly believe her life isn't all about me, I wait until noon to make the call.

"Something I didn't tell you about last night," I say, closing my bedroom door and stretching out on the bed, prepared to wrap her in the blanket of my troubled life.

"Something you didn't tell me? What a surprise." I'm not sure what she means by this but her tone reeks of sarcasm.

Undeterred, I prop myself on my elbow. "Lucas Laramy doesn't exist."

Rachel had started to speak but cuts her words short. I've taken her in an unexpected direction.

"What?"

I go on to explain that my internet search for Lucas this morning drew no results of anyone resembling the young man who graced our presence at Wrigley last night. It's not until Rachel asks why I'm checking up on him that I tell her about his connection to me and about the green and yellow cap.

"Does all of this scare you, Brian?" There's the attitude again.

"What? Does it scare me? Well, it is pretty unsettling."

"Maybe you should go hide in your closet, or are you scared of the skeletons in there too?"

Uh oh.

A wave of panic washes over me. I sit upright on my bed, at full attention, prepared to defend myself against accusations not yet made. I look at the closed door, the painted-shut window. No escape routes. I say the only thing that comes to mind.

"What's that supposed to mean?"

She lets silence amplify the absurdity of the question before responding. "That kid we met in the restaurant a couple weeks ago? What's his name? Matthew Dials? He was your student, right?"

I catch my reflection in the mirror. The terrified stranger staring back at me is urging me to plead ignorance until there's no turning back. "Matthew Dials? What's this got to do with Matthew Dials?"

"My meeting this morning – that's who I met."

I'm standing now, pacing the room. I gaze upon the grey alley. I've forgotten why I called.

"Yeah," she says, "I thought that might surprise you. Anyway, he wants me to do a painting of some classic rock musicians for his bedroom. His parents said he could commission someone and he called me. Called me back on Thursday to ask if we could meet to talk about this painting."

She pauses, I suppose to give me a chance to come clean. My mouth is open but unable to deliver the words my brain is trying to form.

"Anyway," she continues, "I was surprised when I got to Matthew's house this morning to find out he was just a kid. But he looked familiar. I asked him if we met before. He reminded me we met at that restaurant, Amichi's. His dad owns a pharmacy." She pauses. "But you already know that, don't you, Brian?"

The question is rhetorical. I don't answer.

"Chatty kid, that Matthew Dials," she says. "We struck up a conversation. I asked how he liked his new school. Said he missed Booker. Said you were an awesome teacher, but then he said something curious."

She waits. I have no choice but to ask. "What'd he say?'

"He said you never gave extra credit."

"Extra credit? So what?"

"For anything." Belligerence has crept into her tone. She's losing patience. "He said you never gave extra credit for anything, Brian. He made a point of emphasizing the word anything, and he gave me a look and it was clear he wasn't talking about schoolwork. I asked him what he meant. He didn't answer. Just randomly started talking about the pharmacy. Made it easy for me, like he wanted me to know without actually telling me. Then I remembered seeing an unlabeled pill bottle with 'Dials Pharmacy' stamped on the lid in your medicine cabinet. I remember thinking that was kind of strange."

The line is silent for a seven second eternity. My forehead rests against the window pane.

A heavy sigh on the other end. "Why didn't you tell me you have a problem?"

"Because I don't."

"That's what I thought you'd say. Goodbye, Brian." Finally the goodbye she'd never given me. I guess she was saving it for when she meant it.

"Rachel wait. I did have a problem, but not anymore." I'm pacing the room, delivering the words on foot. "Don't hang up. Let me explain. I didn't go to Houston." The words pour out, reaching, trying to pull her back. "I spent the week at a motel in Skokie - detoxing - for you. I wanted to be a better person for you."

Silence.

"Rachel?"

I'm not sure how much she heard because I'm not sure when she clicked off.

·   ·   ·

It's Sunday morning. My world turned upside down, I find myself pacing a sidewalk in Lincolnwood. The daylight reflecting on the grimy windows fronting the red-brick building makes it impossible to see inside. I know Rachel's apartment is on the third floor but which window is hers?

I need more eyes, can't watch all of them at once. If her face does appear, I can't miss the opportunity to make eye contact. Unless she's stopped reading my texts, she knows I'm out here, knows I've come eighteen city blocks to grovel. Surely that's worth a sympathetic glance of acknowledgement from a dirty window.

The front door opens and my heart jumps. Chelsea steps out. Never before have I been so disappointed to see a gorgeous blonde.

"She doesn't want to talk to you," Chelsea says. "And neither do I. Rachel told me what you said about Lucas, and you're wrong, Brian. How big is your ego anyway? Does the whole world revolve around you?"

Apparently yes.

"His name's not Lucas," I say. "He's not who you think he is, Chelsea. Please promise you'll be careful with him."

She looks at the sky, holding back tears. She fears I'm right but is fighting the notion.

She sets her jaw and glares at me. "I've got an appointment. Go to Hell." She turns and storms away.

I glance again at the windows above. The sun has emerged,

176

brightening the day but rendering them less transparent. I gaze up and down the lazy Sunday morning street: a few cars, none in a hurry, fewer pedestrians. A kid sitting at a corner bus stop on the next block glances my way before turning his attention to a family man emerging from the deli across the street. The man opens a brown bag and smells what I imagine are hot fresh bagels within.

I reach into my back pocket. I unfold and read the letter. What's the point? It says nothing new, nothing I haven't already said in twenty-two hours' worth of unanswered texts and emails. But I'm old-school and I'm desperate. A hand-written letter personally delivered eighteen city blocks demonstrates a greater level of commitment to groveling than any impersonal electronic communication.

Again I gaze at the windows above. I'll wait five minutes, no more. Five minutes later I make the same promise. Finally, I crumple the letter, toss it in a trash can, and walk away

TWENTY ONE

ZACH

Playing detective and guardian angel at the same time was no easy task. The two hours Zach spent parked across the street waiting for Brian Casey to emerge from his apartment building were interminable. He felt conspicuous to say the least. This particular Sunday morning was far too overcast to be wearing the shades, and his Atlanta Braves baseball cap pegged him as an outsider to the Cub fans strolling by.

Finally, Zach abandoned his father's car when he saw Brian step outside, fold a piece of white paper, and slide it into the back pocket of his jeans. Zach watched as his former tutor turned the corner onto Lakewood, heading toward Morse. It was time to follow on foot, or by bus or train if need be. He wasn't sure where this morning's exercise in espionage would take him, but he had to follow. He needed answers and, in some capacity, Brian Casey needed him.

The bus ride was not only an unforeseen expense but also an exercise in discretion. Brian, nervous and unhappy, looked over his shoulder again and again. A couple of times his glance seemed to fall on Zach but without recognition of his former tutorial student, Josiah Coffee.

By 9:10 the neighborhood signs alerted Zach of their destination:

Lincolnwood. Of course, Rachel's neighborhood. Brian was going to see Rachel, maybe to pick her up, perhaps a date for brunch. Zach decided to follow just long enough to see where Rachel lives. Then he better make himself scarce, disappear before they see him. The two of them together would double his chance of being recognized. And how awkward would it be if Rachel introduced him to Brian as her cousin, Zach Mondini?

No, don't let them see you.

By 9:30, Zach's espionage had led him to a corner bus stop in Lincolnwood. He watched Brian step from the bus and turn to the west. Zach exited and pretended to move the opposite direction. After a dozen steps, he peeked over his shoulder. Brian was a safe distance away. Zach sat on the bus stop bench.

Brian reached the next block and paused. He approached the door of a red brick apartment building, pressed one of the buzzers several times and stood in the doorway. When no one answered, he backed onto the sidewalk, looking up at the windows. There must be some misunderstanding. That had to be Rachel's building, but why hadn't she come down when Brain buzzed? Maybe they got their signals crossed. It wasn't until Brian began pacing the sidewalk, that Zach suspected trouble in paradise.

Before long, a blonde – smokin' hot from even a block and a half away - emerged from the building. She spoke to Brian for a moment, but stormed away after an obviously unhappy encounter. Brian remained, pacing and gazing at the windows. He glanced in Zach's direction. Zach turned quickly away. Across the street from the bus stop, a customer came out of Kamar's Deli and paused. The man dipped his nose into the open bag, then lifted his head, eyes closed. A smile of sheer satisfaction encompassed him. Zach envied the man. Hot bagels on a Sunday morning, one of life's simple pleasures. Zach wished he still had room in his own life for simple pleasures. He returned his attention to Brian, still pacing. Zach wished the same for Brian.

Brian stopped. He removed the white paper from his pocket, unfolded it and read. After pacing for ten more minutes, he crumpled the paper and tossed it into a nearby trash can. Head hanging, he turned the corner and disappeared.

Now, at 9:45, Zach is alone. A CTA bus pulls to the stop. He shakes his head at the driver. The bus pulls away. Zach sits forward. He's here, in Lincolnwood, Rachel only a block and a half away. Why not just stroll up and buzz her apartment? Tell her to forgive Brian for whatever he's done to piss her off. She'll ask Zach how he knows Brian. But really, this would be a relief. He could get it all off his chest, tell her everything: the pier, Winston, the tutoring. Surely she'll understand when he tells her to keep it all to herself. She'll probably be touched by his compassion.

Zach leans back against the bench and looks at the sky. Who's he kidding? Rachel would be on the phone with his parents in a matter of minutes, concerned that her sweet young cousin is mixed up in some dangerous business.

Zach rises and digs his phone from a pocket. The GPS will guide him back to Rogers Park, to the car he told his father would be gone just long enough to complete a homework assignment with a friend. He's been gone way too long, but he puts the task of creating an excuse on hold. Plenty of time for that on the trip back. For now, his focus must remain on the best way to stroll down a sidewalk, a lone pedestrian, and inconspicuously remove a crumpled paper from a trashcan. He pulls the Atlanta Braves cap a little tighter and steps from the bus stop.

TWENTY TWO

BRIAN

"I'm going home," Magby announces when I return from my wasted trip to Lincolnwood. His duffle bag, packed and zipped, rests by the front door, this morning's coffee cups, stained on the rims, sit on the table where we left them.

"Donna wants me back. Told ya she can't live without me." The real Clinton Magby has returned just in time to say goodbye.

I pick up the coffee cups and start for the kitchen. "I'm happy for you. Hope things work out."

Magby springs from the couch, jubilant. He's respectfully waited for me to return. Now he can't wait to leave, to get back to his wife, his son, his quiet suburban street. He follows me into the kitchen, extending his hand. I take it and he pulls me to him, giving me a quick man hug, two pats on the back.

"Thanks for the hospitality." He releases me and starts for the door. His words trail away from me. "To tell the truth, not sure how long I could stay here anyway. Rogers Park is way too much drama for me. Long-lost fathers showing up. Dead bodies in the lake. Strange noises in the alley."

At first, I dismiss Magby's words as his usual meaningless banter about my "seedy" neighborhood. It's not until he's slung the duffle bag over his shoulder that it hits me. I hurry from the kitchen. "Hang on, Magby. What did you just say?"

He stops and turns. "Too much drama?"

"No. A dead body?"

"Yeah, you didn't hear? One of your neighbors told me it was on the news last night. An old man floating in the lake." He opens the door. "Great neighborhood you got here. Thanks again, man." The door clicks shut behind him.

. . .

It's 4:12 Sunday afternoon. I'm late for my appointment but don't care. The afternoon shadows of this Northbrook suburb stretch before me with a Sabbath lull. A train, as though apologizing for the interruption, softly rumbles into the Smith Street el station behind me.

I pause at the oak tree on the corner of Smith and Redding. Booker High School sits one hundred yards to my left, a slumbering Sunday giant. Two cars, belonging to teachers with no lives, hobnob in the faculty lot. Across the brown football field, the hard metallic stripes of the bleachers pinstripe the soft woods behind.

I see movement under the bleachers. He's there, pacing, his head cut from my vision by one of the steel benches. He ducks and sees me. I slow my pace. He knows I'm in no hurry.

My call two hours ago had taken Matthew Dials by surprise. "I'll be at the bleachers at four today." I said. "You need to be there too."

"Why?"

"Trust me. You don't want to miss this."

I stroll across the end zone, approaching Matthew. His fists, visible between the benches, are clenched. He suspects I've come to confront him about driving a wedge between me and Rachel. He's battle ready, prepared for a confrontation. I turn the corner and step under the bleachers, my eyes fixed on him.

"You watch the news Matthew?"

The question takes him by surprise. He cocks his head. "The news? Not really. Why?"

"Should really watch the news. Interesting story this weekend."

He shrugs.

I reach into my jacket and extend the folded piece of paper, a printed news report. He's hesitant, but takes the paper and reads. I move beside him and read over his shoulder.

The body of an elderly man was recovered from the water at a Rogers Park Beach Saturday afternoon, the Rogers Park Fire Department said.

At about 5 p.m., firefighters received a call from residents in the area of Farwell Avenue and Sheridan Road, reporting a body floating close to the pier, said Captain Patrick Bannon.

When officials arrived, there was no need to attempt resuscitation of the man whom Bannon estimated to be in his 70s. He was transported to Evanston General Hospital, where he was pronounced dead.

Bannon said that while Rogers Park police continue to investigate the incident, the man "appears to have ingested a lot of water and suffered trauma in the form of a contusion to his forehead which may have been caused by a fall from the pier. Foul play has not been ruled out."

Bannon added, "The indication was the person may have been in the lake for a substantial amount of time, but due to the cold water temperature, the body is remarkably well-preserved."

"The identity of the man remains unknown as police continue to investigate," Bannon said. "A forensics team is doing all they can to identify him. He has been described as missing his left arm below the elbow and he has a deep scar extending across the right side of his face. He was wearing a long wool coat and black rubber boots. I would appeal to anyone with information to contact the RPPD."

Matthew finishes reading and raises his head. "So what?"

I take the paper from him. "Really? Still nothing?"

Again he shrugs.

I fold the news report and return it to my pocket. "Last week, on April Fool's Day, I gave you an essay to turn in to your new English teacher, 'Life hasn't much to offer except youth.'"

"Yeah. So?"

He's confused, has no idea where this is headed. I pull another folded sheet from my pocket. "In fact, I happen to have a copy of your essay right here." I hand him the sheet. "You don't need to read the whole thing. After all, you wrote it, right?" I wink, tap the sheet in his hand. "Start here."

Again, I read over his shoulder.

In our old age, we become dispensable, rusty jalopies broken down on a youthful Formula One race track. We wander down life's cold pier. The decades have been unforgiving. The years have left us with a jagged scar on our cheek, a missing limb.

The further we walk down the pier, the deeper the water surrounding us. This water is black with mortality. We might try to turn back, but when we turn, we see a group of young men laughing, following us. Unburdened by mortality, their steps are light and their water shallow.

We love the young men because we have been them, but because they haven't been us, they don't love us back. They know that once they dump us from the end of life's pier, they'll be free of us. Our rubber boots, designed to protect us from Mother Nature, are no match for human nature. They fill with water, ultimately anchoring us in our wet grave.

When Matthew looks up at me, I'm reminded of the expression on Josiah Coffee's face when he read this same paragraph. I allow Matthew a moment of painful realization before I speak.

"Terrific essay by the way. I'm guessing you turned this in online, right? To turnitin.com?"

The wheels are spinning in Matthew's head. He understands that his essay, describing a murder victim who wasn't discovered until Saturday, has been floating in cyberspace since Thursday. The foul play that Fire Captain Patrick Bannon has not "ruled out" is clearly laid out in an essay bearing the name Matthew Dials.

His eyes lift to mine but his gaze is blank. He's processing, looking at me but failing to see. Gone is the smug grin, the defiant posture.

"What do you want, Mr. Casey?"

The name sounds foreign. Apparently I'm no longer "Teach." I consider the shortcomings of an education system in which teachers have to frame their students for murder in order to gain respect.

I expect Matthew to ask how I knew about the dead man before the body was dragged from the lake, but he's consumed by his own survival. His carefree life has ended because he asked a teacher to plagiarize an essay. His eyes plead for mercy, beg forgiveness. I can't help but feel sorry for him. I'd planned to do more with the whole April Fools angle, but as I watch his lip quiver, I decide enough is enough.

Matthew's eyes scan the horizon for answers before drifting to the dirt beneath his feet. I make an effort to conceal my compassion, keeping my voice steady.

"Matthew, look at me."

He raises his head.

"Your teacher's unlikely to make a connection between this essay and the dead body. You have nothing to worry about as long as you do what I say."

He nods, his eyes vacant.

I continue. "I'm guessing you're going to be contacted by someone, seventeen or eighteen-years-old, good-looking kid. Might say his name's Josiah, maybe something else."

I point to the paper in his hand.

"He's going to want to know how you know about this, about the old man." I turn my reprimanding finger to him, slow my words for emphasis. "When you hear from him - from anyone you even think might be him - you're going to tell me."

A spark of realization flashes in Matthew's glassy eyes. "Zach Mondini."

"What?"

"His name's Zach Mondini. I'm meeting him tomorrow."

TWENTY THREE

ZACH

It would be easy getting Brian off the hook. All Zach needs to do is tell Winston about the essay he read on Brian Casey's computer. Winston would realize there was another witness, someone else at the pier that night. He'd consider. Maybe it wasn't Brian who picked up the camera after all. Maybe it was a kid named Matthew Dials.

This may be enough for Winston, but it's not enough for Zach. Still too many unanswered questions. Why did Matthew give the essay to Brian in the first place? The kid doesn't even go to Booker. Was he blackmailing Brian? Was the essay his way of letting Brian know Matthew saw what happened? Maybe he had some kind of proof, perhaps a video or another witness. Zach wouldn't put any of this past Matthew Dials. Hasn't even met the kid and already knows he's an asshole.

Three days earlier, on Friday evening, Zach had taken a chance by sending Matthew a friend request on Facebook. Well, maybe not so much of a chance. Anyone with over fourteen-hundred Facebook friends was probably in the habit of accepting all requests and, sure enough, Matthew accepted Zach's. No alias was necessary this time. He was Zachary Mondini, a friend of a friend of a friend who claimed to have met

Matthew at a Christmas party which Matthew publicly admitted was "lost to his memory thanks to the wonders of spiked eggnog."

From reading Matthew's posts and likes and dislikes, Zach knew he'd encounter a kid with some smarts, but a kid with an attitude. Matthew's latest status read "mired under the oppression of lesser minds." And before that, "they say that those who can't do, teach. But where does that leave those who can't teach? The answer: Northshore Preparatory Academy."

The online communication, initiated by Zach, went like this:

"Matthew – don't know if you remember me from Skyler's party back in December - found your name on a post-it stuffed in my wallet. Talked about classic rock."

"Don't remember you but WTF. What's up?"

"Doobie Brothers reunion – got two tickets – can't use them. Interested?"

"F yeah."

And that's all it took, the possibility of seeing some washed up 70's rockers trying to keep their guitar straps on their sloped shoulders. The boys made arrangements to meet at Matthew's school where they would exchange cash for tickets.

Now it's Monday afternoon. Zach sits in his father's car, parked at the curb beside the manicured lawns of Northshore Prep. He wears the Atlanta Braves cap he told Matthew would identify him. He has no concert tickets. The most awkward part of the encounter will be when he tells this to Matthew, who will be confused, pissed off, want an explanation. It won't take long for the chump to realize their rendezvous has nothing to do with The Doobie Brothers, not once Zach mentions the name Brian Casey.

After that, Zach will ask Matthew about the essay, tell him about a deranged maniac named Winston Longstreet. Finally, he'll warn Matthew to leave Brian alone unless he wants this maniac coming after him.

The front doors of Northshore Prep burst open. As happens at West Rogers, students pour down the concrete steps. Zach gazes toward the building's entrance. At the top of the steps stands Matthew Dials. Easy to pick out, the shock of blonde highlighted bangs, the skinny jeans. Looks exactly like the images on his Facebook page.

Zach watches Matthew skip down the steps and pause at the bottom. Matthew looks left and right scanning the surroundings for a stranger in an Atlanta Braves baseball cap. Zach waits until most of the students have cleared. He steps from his father's car. Matthew spots him and nods. The two strangers approach each other. When separated by fifty feet of pavement, Matthew peels off to his left, striding away, looking at Zach over his shoulder.

What? Where's he going?

"Hey," Zach calls. "You're Matthew, right? It's me, Zach Mondini. Where you— "

Zach is jerked backwards. The hood of his sweatshirt is being pulled, choking him, propelling him backwards. A hand is placed on the top of his head. The back of his legs hit something, a car. He falls into the seat. The door is slammed and clicked locked. His heart races. Chest heaves. He turns to identify his assailant but the figure is circling the rear of the car, head lost from view. *Winston? Shit. Find the unlock button – get out and run.* Too late. The driver's side door is thrown open. Brian Casey ducks in.

What the—

After the initial shock, Zach exhales a sigh of relief. Thank God it's not Winston. The relief doesn't last long as Zach notices the expression on Brian's face, an expression he hadn't seen on the laid-back teacher who tutored him as Josiah Coffee.

Brian's eyes burn into him. "First things first," he snaps. "Zachary Mondini. That's your real name, right?"

Zach looks away, images from Brian's letter to Rachel swimming in his head. It's time to come clean. He turns back to Brian, lowers his head. "Yes." A wave of relief washes over him, an incredible burden lifted.

After this, Zach makes it easy. He doesn't wait for questions, but lets the answers pour forth. He purges, cleanses himself. A couple of times he's tempted to mention Brian's letter to Rachel, now neatly folded in Zach's back pocket, but checks himself. The questions generated by the letter will have to wait. It's Brian's turn for answers.

The answers come in droves. Within five minutes Brian knows the details of the night at the pier. He knows the name Winston Longstreet. He knows about a lost camera. He knows Winston believes the camera is in Brian's possession. After this unsolicited shower of information, Brian sits silently, considering. His fingers tap the steering wheel. He turns to Zach. "Where's this camera now?" His tone is less angry, more understanding.

Zach reaches into the pocket of his jacket. He withdraws the silver camera.

"I keep it with me. Never know when I might see him." He pauses. "But I have seen him, a few times. I just can't bring myself to give it back to him, Mr. Casey. It's all I've got against him, you know?"

Brian extends his hand. "Give it to me."

Zach remains motionless.

Brian moves his palm closer. "He thinks I have it right?" A pause. "So give it to me. You're off the hook."

Zach hands him the camera. "The memory card's in there, Mr. Casey. I downloaded the photos to my computer. But I don't think he cares about the pictures from the beach that night. He's got to know they've already been copied."

Without comment, Brian flips open the camera's viewfinder. He scrolls through the images.

Zach watches him. "There's other stuff on there too. Personal stuff. This guy, Winston, his little brother died about a month ago. I think he took it real hard, kind of lost it. There's a bunch of pictures of the two of them."

Brian continues to scroll silently. Zach gazes through the passenger-side window. Beneath one of the oak trees stands Matthew Dials, watching the car. He isn't smiling. He's taking no satisfaction in having been a successful accomplice in Brian Casey's act of abduction. Zach can't help but feel Matthew, like him, is a victim.

He turns back to his former tutor, intending to ask him about Matthew's essay, but hesitates. Brian is unshaven. His eyes heavy with lack of sleep. While sitting in the Loyola library as Josiah Coffee, Zach had been impressed by his tutor's youthful appearance. Brian obviously stayed in shape, took care of himself. But now, rubbing his temples, blinking tired eyes as he scans the images, he looks much older.

"I'm sorry about everything, Mr. Casey."

Brian looks up from the camera and their eyes share a moment of understanding. Brian's face wears a new, kinder expression. He's fighting the expression but losing the fight. He's once again Mr. C. and the young man before him needs his help. Realizing he's been exposed as a softy, he turns away for a moment, then back, a half smile on his face. "Tutoring?" He raises his eyebrows. "What was all that about?"

Zach shrugs. "I don't know. I wanted to get to know you. Wanted to help somehow." He considers mentioning Rachel, but hesitates. Too many secrets already revealed. Let Brian believe Zach's involvement in his life ended with a rush-hour dash across Sheridan Road.

Brian slides the camera into his jacket pocket. "Josiah Coffee, huh?"

"Yeah, stupid name, I know." Zach lowers his head. "First thing that came to me."

Brian nods, again tapping his fingers on the steering wheel. "What about the AP test? You really plan on taking it?"

"Nah. I'm a senior. Passed it last year."

Brian shakes his head. Duped by a kid, but at least one with good intentions. They sit a moment in silence, staring from opposite windows. Zach gazes toward the oak trees. Matthew Dials is gone

TWENTY FOUR

BRIAN

Jay Gatsby dies during third period at Booker High School. He's shot by a grief-stricken widower, an undeniable consequence at the end of a string of events resulting from his attempt to "repeat the past." His elderly father, Henry Gatz, has come to New York to bury his son, unaware that Jay's millions were acquired through the sale of liquor during prohibition, the 1920s' gift to gangsters.

My classroom, in all its cinderblock glory, is my sanctuary. I gaze upon the sea of young faces before me, every seat occupied by a welcome distraction from my own life. Matthew's empty desk, placed in the hallway last week, has been carried off by a custodian unaware of his contribution to my sanity. The desks in that row are spaced evenly to fill the void, to mollify my conscience.

This is where I belong, strolling the aisles of my kingdom, lording over the nation's youth. Here I can find my life by losing myself in literature, a paradoxical practice allowing me to bury my troubles beneath those of predictable old friends.

"Who's responsible for Gatsby's death?" I ask the class. I stop strolling and punctuate the question with two open palms. "Sure, Wilson pulled the trigger, but when you look at the big picture, who's really responsible?"

"It's Tom's fault," a voice calls to my right. "He led Wilson to Gatsby and let him believe Gatsby was sleeping with his wife."

"Nah, it was Nick," someone else chimes. "He knew everything, could have prevented Gatsby's death if he shared all the stuff he knew. He's guilty by omission."

The words strike me and I'm whisked away. *Guilty by omission.* I see myself walking from a dark pier with someone else's murder tucked in my back pocket. I shake myself, snap my momentary trance. My students wait, confused by my silence. Ryan Peters has given the response I hoped for. It's my turn. I could - should - elaborate on Nick Carraway's role in Gatsby's death, but something, fate perhaps, prompts me to steer the conversation in a different direction.

"Okay," I say. "Answer this for me. Should Nick have shared the truth about Gatsby's shady business dealings with Gatsby's father?"

"What good would that do?" says David Hanratty. "Let the old guy believe his son was some brilliant businessman. He's a lonely old man. Pride in his son is all he's got." Wisdom sometimes comes from unexpected sources. The accidental prophet, David Hanratty, has spoken. Again, the words wrap around my conscience and carry me away.

A lonely old man. I hear an unsteady voice call my name from a dark sidewalk after a twenty year absence.

Pride in his son is all he's got. The door clicks closed as I leave my long-lost father standing outside, alone in the dark.

I'm wandering, lost in my own classroom. The class is silent until a solitary voice slices through the fog. "Mr. Casey? You okay?"

I locate my body at my podium, but my mind remains far away. I lift my head.

"Life hasn't much to offer except youth, and I suppose for older people, the love of youth in others."

I'm not sure, but I think I've said this aloud. The curious stares of my students would indicate such. They look from me to each other, trying to determine the significance of this seemingly pointless remark I've addressed to the ceiling.

The bell rings, dismissing third period. I sit at my desk and rest my forehead in my palms. Pride is a monster. It chews up forgiveness and spits out spite. I will find my father. I will forgive him.

TWENTY FIVE

WINSTON

Facing the street, Winston Longstreet stands in the doorway of an apartment building on Lakewood. Golden buds dot the tree limbs. April is bringing Chicago back to life, but Micah is gone forever.

Winston shivers at the thought of the approaching spring thaw. He's already haunted by Micha's death. How bad will it be when he's surrounded by new life in the spring and summer?

God has no sympathy for those left behind.

He closes his eyes. *You're not alone Micah. I won't forget about you.*

He turns and lifts his gaze to the brown brick building rising in front of him. He's familiar with the alley behind but has never seen the front. Ugly-ass building really. Old, even older than most of the residents he's watched coming and going during the hour he's spent pacing the sidewalk.

Like most of those residents, at least the building's an easy target. Should be no problem getting in. No intercom system. Just a column of buzzers like tiny round welcome mats next to a column of names. No way for the fossils inside to even know who's ringing their doorbell.

Press a few buttons, he'll get in.

He puts his index finger at the top of the column of buzzers and runs it down. He reaches for the door handle and waits for the buzz. Within twenty seconds, he's in the building.

The lobby is typical. A wall of mailboxes. Subtle wallpaper, some ancient floral design. A large mirror in an ornate frame hangs opposite the mailboxes. Winston pauses at the mirror. At first he doesn't recognize himself. He's noticed this type of thing before. Weird, how when seeing your reflection in unfamiliar surroundings, the surroundings are familiar, and the reflection is a stranger. He moves closer to the mirror, searching for the familiar. He finds it in Micah's features. Never noticed them before, the traces of his little brother in his own face. Something about the curve of his jaw, the curl of his lips.

"Thank you for taking care of me, Winston," Micah says from the reflection.

A door clicks closed on the hallway to his left. Footsteps approach the lobby. Winston shakes himself, turns from the mirror, his back to the approaching footsteps. He steps to the wall of mailboxes, fumbles in the pockets of his jeans as though searching for a key. The footsteps pass behind him. The door opens and the unseen person steps outside.

He turns back to the mirror. Micah's gone, again.

Winston balls his fists but checks himself. *Save the rage. You'll need every ounce of it in a few minutes.* He raises his palm to the mirror, touches the empty features in the reflection. How many times will his little brother be taken from him?

Again, a stranger stares back.

"Micah is still here," The stranger says. "Remember, this is all for him."

A flash of movement in his periphery, someone outside turning from the sidewalk, approaching the building. The figure is blurred by the beveled glass door. Winston turns away, but he's turned toward voices. A couple pushing a stroller approaches from the hallway to the right. A wave of panic washes over him. Too many people converging on him. He glances at the mirror.

"Quick. Do it now." says the stranger.

Winston sets his jaw. He turns and strides onto the hallway toward the approaching couple. He pulls the black hood over his head, far enough forward to conceal his face, but not far enough to raise any red flags. His heart races. The couple is within twenty feet. He's prepared to give them a nondescript nod, but no need. They move past him, their attention focused on the annoying little bundle-of-joy squirming in the stroller. Winston watches them over his shoulder, waits until they've turned into the lobby.

Nothing can stop him now. He's done his research, knows the apartment number and the name. It's time to let the power take over, let the voices guide him.

He continues around the corner and down the dim hallway

TWENTY SIX

BRIAN

It's Tuesday afternoon. I left Booker at three. Faculty basketball has taken a back seat to real life. When composing the email to my colleagues explaining my absence from this afternoon's game, I was tempted to type, "Can't play today because I framed my drug-supplying former student for murder because he caused my girlfriend to leave me at the same time that my long-lost father returned which distracted me from the homicidal lunatic who's been stalking me." I decided this was a little wordy and settled on "got the shits."

Yes, I will make amends with my father. But because I have no choice but to wait for him to step from the shadows on some quiet night, my list of fences needing mending will start with Rachel. Operation Make Brian Irresistible, OMBI, has been relaunched, and once again it begins with cinnamon coffee. My absence from basketball will facilitate an early visit to Clara. Perhaps Rachel will be there if she assumes I won't. If not, I'll once again count on Clara to sing my praises to her granddaughter.

· · ·

It's 3:35. Spring has brought its healing powers to Rogers Park. The sidewalk in front of Clara's building is cracked by winter but bathed in April. I stand a moment basking in the season. Then, emboldened by the crisp air, I skip up the concrete steps and aim my finger at Clara's buzzer, but no need. My newfound optimism as well as my intentions of waging an irresistible surprise attack on Rachel is validated when a couple with a stroller pushes open the door, allowing me to step inside.

I pause at the mirror in the lobby. It's a new me. Sure, the sandy hair is still starting to thin, but in a dignified, mature way. The face under the hair has accepted, even embraced, this new maturity. The jaw is strong. Blue eyes brim with confidence and compassion.

I turn onto Clara's hallway. As always, the corridor is dimly lit. I follow it around the corner. I'm about to knock on the apartment door when I hear a gasp, a faint cry from inside.

"No, please no." Clara's voice.

I try the knob, pound on the door. "Clara?"

A crash from inside. Something falling. Another cry from Clara.

I drop my briefcase, pound harder. "Clara?" I'm yelling now. "Clara?"

More scuffling and cries from within. I slam my shoulder into the door. Not enough. I step back, anchor my hand against the opposite wall and kick. The door crashes open. Momentum throws me off balance. A dark figure from within the apartment lunges at me, slams me backwards. My head cracks against the wall. I crumble to the floor. Through the pain I see him running: tall, black jacket or sweatshirt, black hood. All black.

· · ·

My concussion does not go unattended this time. My hearing returns before my vision. The black has become a thick white fog from which voices fall.

"Put something under his head."

"Careful, lift his head gently."

The first voice, familiar but whimpering: "Is he okay? God, please. Is he okay?" Through the throbbing in my temple, my brain registers the voice as Clara's. My vision fights through the white haze. Her face materializes above me. "Oh, Brian." Her whimpering turns to sobs. "Thank God you're okay."

She's on her knees, tears streaming down her face. My first instinct is to help her up. She's in her eighties, on her knees. I try to shake the cobwebs from my head, but common sense objects by plunging a dagger into my brain. I wince and lie still. The details return: Clara's cries, kicking the door, my head against the wall.

My peripheral vision fights through the fog and a second figure comes into focus. I roll my head toward the face. I start to speak.

"Shh, stay still, Brian. But don't close your eyes. Stay awake."

Good advice. I won't close my eyes. If I do, she'll disappear again.

"Rachel, I—"

"Shh, don't talk."

•   •   •

The paramedics and cops arrive at the same time. Rachel is sitting on Clara's couch, her arm around her grandmother's shoulder. A portly cop, who has introduced himself as Officer Sam Rosetti, has pulled up and straddled a chair, putting himself at Clara's level.

"Can you tell me what happened, Ms. Wiseman?"

"He attacked me, pushed me down."

"How'd he get in, Ma'am?"

"Well, I let him in."

"Why?"

Clara's mouth opens, but no words escape. Her vacant eyes drift to the crooked rabbi on the wall, to the rug at her feet, and finally to the sagging gladiolas in a floral vase on the coffee table. "Brian," she says.

"What?" asks Officer Rosetti. "Who's Brian?"

Clara and Rachel turn to face me. Rosetti turns.

I lift the ice pack from my head and sit forward. "I'm Brian."

Clara's eyes widen. "I remember now. There was a knock on the door. I asked who it was. He said, 'Brian.' I opened the door but it wasn't Brian. It was—" Fear flashes in the old woman's eyes. She shivers.

Rachel tightens her grip on her grandmother's shoulder.

"It was someone else." Clara whimpers. "Tall, with a hood. I couldn't see his face. He pushed me inside and slammed the door." She swallows hard. "I think he was going to kill me." The words morph into sobs. Rachel draws her close.

Rosetti pauses, purses his lips. He turns his attention to Rachel. "Anything you can tell me, Ms. Gold?"

"I got here - guess it was a few minutes after - and found them in the hallway. Brian was lying in the hallway and my grandmother was knocking on doors, crying, trying to find help. She already called 911." Rachel bends her face to Clara, speaking softly. "You did the right thing, Grandma. You did everything you could."

Rosetti turns to the EMT and tips his head toward me. "He okay?"

The paramedic nods toward the open door. "In better shape than that wall out there."

"You up to answering some questions?" Rosetti asks me.

I nod.

"What happened?"

I return the ice pack to my head. "I heard Clara – Ms. Wiseman - crying for help from inside. Then a crash. I kicked the door open and he came at me, so fast, I didn't know what hit me."

"Get a look at the guy?"

"No. It was too quick."

"Any idea who it was?"

I shake my head.

"Sounds like this guy knew you'd be showing up. Used your name to get in. Who else knew you were coming?"

I catch Rachel's knowing glance and look away. Rubbing the back of my head, I shrug and grimace. Too many questions for a guy in obvious pain.

Rosetti mumbles something unintelligible, glances at the broken door, then turns to Clara. "You got somewhere to stay tonight, Ms. Wiseman?"

"She'll stay with me," Rachel responds. "In Lincolnwood."

Rosetti glances at his watch. "I can give you a ride."

Rachel hesitates. "I'll call a cab."

Rosetti looks again at Clara who seems about to shrink into the couch's cushion gaps. He hoists himself from the chair and turns to Rachel. "Help your grandmother get her stuff together, Miss Gold. I'm going to drive you."

Rachel looks at me. "Brian? Will you come too?"

The words wrap themselves around me like a warm blanket. I smile and nod.

.   .   .

Compliments of the RPPD, we arrive at Rachel's apartment around five p.m. I guess it's been a while since Clara's been here. She looks around with fascinated eyes. She wanders to the easel and the table with the plastic cloth, lifting one of the paintbrushes from the cup of cloudy water. She's absorbed, fascinated. It's beautiful to watch. Discovery has trumped fear. An old woman is being introduced to a granddaughter she's known for twenty-five years, experiencing what F. Scott Fitzgerald referred to as "the love of youth in others."

Clara drifts toward the painted canvases stacked against the living room wall. Rachel seizes the opportunity to engage - distract - her grandmother with an impromptu art show. We sit for hours, talking about the paintings, looking at family photos. For a while I manage to forget about blackmailers and stalkers and killers. For the first time in years, I feel part of a family, a family enjoying an evening of artwork, hot tea, and denial.

By 9:30, Clara is tucked into Rachel's bed.

"Where will you sleep, dear?" Clara asks Rachel, clutching the blanket to her chin. "Will you be close?"

"I'll be on the couch, Grandma, in the living room." She sits on the edge of the bed. "But I'll stay in here 'til you fall asleep."

Clara looks up at me, lips quivering. "Thank you for being there, Brian." She reaches for my hand. "You saved my life."

I take her hand and gratitude like a thief in the night. I glance at Rachel. She's reading my mind. If not for me, her grandmother would have been in no danger. Then again, if not for me, her grandmother may be dead. I'm the disease and the cure.

I lay my other hand on top of Clara's. "You don't have to thank me, Clara." I smile. "How could I not be there? Can't resist your cinnamon coffee."

Rachel and I sit with Clara as she falls asleep. Even after she drifts off, the toll of the day's events rest in the lines on her face, catch in her unsteady breath. We tip-toe from the room. I'm overwhelmed by the moment, the vision of what could be. Rachel and I have just put our baby to bed.

Carrying her blanket and pillow, Rachel stops in the dark hallway and turns to me. She tucks her hair behind her ear. The horizontal light from the living room brushes her cheeks and touches her lips. She leans close. I relax my mouth, ready for the kiss.

She hits me with the pillow. "You've gotta be the lamest superhero ever."

She turns and saunters down the hallway.

We sit in the living room and talk for an hour. I purge, cleanse myself. The written confessions I left crumpled in the trash can outside a few days ago pour from me. My cell phone rings three times. I ignore it, determined to show I'm fully vested in what matters most: the beautiful woman beside me, the old lady in the beautiful woman's bed. I search Rachel's eyes for signs of forgiveness. I'm not off the hook yet.

At 10:45 Chelsea comes in.

"Hey Rach—" Her mouth drops when she sees me on the couch, Rachel's pillow and blanket by my side. She shoots Rachel a disapproving look. How could her best friend allow this lying scoundrel back into her life?

Chelsea puts a hand on her hip. "What's going on?"

"Shh." Rachel beckons her closer. "My grandmother's asleep in my room."

Chelsea turns to the hallway and back. "Why?"

Rachel slides over, making room on the couch.

Eyes blue and wide, Chelsea listens to Rachel's account of the day's events. Like a true artist, Rachel attempts to paint me a hero, even tries to deflect blame from me by avoiding the names Lucas Laramy and Winston Longstreet. Doesn't matter. It's clear by the expression on Chelsea's face that she's connected the dots.

"It was him, wasn't it?"

Rachel and I both nod.

Chelsea picks up her keys and without another word goes to bed.

Rachel doesn't invite me to stay, and I don't ask. Baby steps, I tell myself, reaching for my jacket.

TWENTY SEVEN

ZACH

It's Tuesday night, 11:30. Zach sits on the living room couch, a paperback Hamlet on the table in front of him. He's supposed to read Act III by tomorrow.

Whatever.

He lifts his foot, kicks the book aside, and crosses his feet on the coffee table. Funny, how schoolwork used to matter. He's not alone in feeling this way. Most of his classmates also suffer from the academic apathy known as senioritis. But not like Zach. For him, it's about priorities, and centuries-old literature might as well be, well, centuries old. Besides, he's got other problems: for one, the guilt that's consumed him for the past sixty-one hours.

Sixty-one hours? Is that all?

He turns his head from the white paper resting beside him on the couch, but finds himself face-to-face with Jesus Christ, who instead of minding his own business, is busy dying for Zach's sins. The crucifix taunts him:

And you deny your Catholicism? What a joke. You're a perfect Catholic, Zach: Yield to temptation, torture yourself with guilt, then do it all over again. Your parents must be so proud.

Zach looks away. It's true. For sixty-one hours he has hated himself as only a perfect Catholic can. For sixty-one hours, he's been a slave to temptation, whipped by guilt.

Unlike his young Catholic counterparts, Zach's temptation is not the ever-accessible porn on his laptop, nor is it the bottle of Johnny Walker Red staring at him from his father's unlocked liquor cabinet. Instead, Zach's temptation is a white sheet of paper lifted from a Lincolnwood trash can sixty-one hours ago. The paper rests beside him on the couch. The crumples have been carefully smoothed, an attempt to nurse the wounds found in the words. Zach hoped this action would ease the guilt too, help justify the fact that he's already read the letter a dozen times. Or has it been fifteen? To be honest, he's lost count.

He places the paper on the coffee table in front of him, flattens it again, and runs his palm over the cracks like a skilled masseuse.

Fuck the guilt. He's doing the right thing. If Brian's letter to Rachel had taught him anything, it taught him that the well-intentioned schoolteacher needs a guardian angel, and if not Josiah Coffee, why not Zachary Mondini?

He turns to the crucifix. *Put that in your grail and drink it.*

He picks up the paper and reads, the thirteenth or sixteenth time:

Dear Rachel,

I'm a fool. I'm not going to make excuses. You were right about Matthew Dials. I started getting Vicodin from him before he became my student, and I didn't stop until I had no choice. I'd like to tell you I made the decision to detox on my own, but it was made for me when he stopped supplying me. I didn't go to Houston on Spring Break. I spent the week weaning myself at a dive motel in Skokie. I should have told you, but I wasn't sure how you'd react.

Zach lowers the paper to his lap. When he first read these lines on Sunday, Brian's addiction had come as a shock, but perhaps it shouldn't have. After what the poor guy went through at the pier, who could blame

206

him for wanting to dull the pain? Even more shocking was that Brian used Matthew Dials, a student, to feed his addiction. How did that start? How did Rachel find out? And what about that essay? How did Matthew know about the incident at the pier? Why had he so clearly referenced it in an essay written for his English teacher? Was this connected to their business dealings?

So many questions – so few answers.

A door clicks open behind Zach. His heart jumps. His father's slippered footsteps brush the wood floor in the hallway. Zach quickly folds the paper, tucks it under his leg. He reaches for *Hamlet*, flips it open to a random page, leans back and listens: the rattle of ice cubes and a rush of water in the kitchen. The footsteps retreat and the door clicks closed. Zach exhales. He tosses the book onto the couch and retrieves the folded paper. He continues reading:

The night at the pier changed me. This may sound melodramatic, but I can't forget the sight of Walter's body disappearing over the edge. I don't think I'll ever shake that image.

These words came as a shock to Zach. He'd spent the past month under the assumption that Brian was at the pier by chance and had witnessed the murder of a stranger. But no, the old man was someone Brian knew. What a horrible night that must have been. But who was this man, Walter? A relative? A friend? Why had Walter wandered onto the pier alone with Brian in the distance behind? Perhaps Brian was looking out for an old friend, following him to make sure he was okay. And then Winston Longstreet showed up. . .

Zach takes a deep breath and exhales.

Back to the letter:

When I returned from Wrigley Field on Friday night, my father was waiting outside my apartment. I panicked. I didn't take your advice, Rachel, didn't even speak to him. Instead I left him standing outside in the cold. Twenty years without seeing him. He gave me a chance and I blew it. I don't

know how to find him. I don't know if I'll ever see him again
.

Zach looks up. A twenty year absence. He's already done the easy yet disturbing math. During one of their early tutoring sessions, Brian told Zach – alias Josiah Coffee - that he was about to turn thirty. Twenty years. Brian was nine years old when he last saw his father.

Zach cranes his neck. He stares down the hallway toward his parents' bedroom. His dad can be a real asshole, but at least he's here.

He continues reading:

Do you remember convincing me to tutor that kid, Josiah Coffee? Well, that's not his real name. He's involved in this too. He was either there that night or he knows what happened. What I don't understand is why he'd go to all the trouble of sitting through tutorials. Was he setting me up for something? Trying to get me out of my apartment?

On Sunday, Zach was hurt when he first read these words. His intentions as Josiah were so honorable. How could Brian feel otherwise? He had to put himself in Brian's shoes, become the sum of Brian's parts, to forgive his former tutor for this lack of appreciation. Now, having explained everything – well, almost everything - to Brian as they sat together outside Northshore Prep, Zach feels much better.

He skips to the final paragraph.

Josiah Coffee? Lucas Laramy? Is anyone really who they claim to be?
My life has become consumed by uncertainty. The only thing I'm certain of is that I'm in love with a woman named Rachel Gold - assuming that's her real name.
Love,
Brian

Nice touch, ending a troubled letter with an expression of love. But who the hell is Lucas Laramy?

Zach sits back and smiles. He'll find a way to get this letter to Rachel, anonymously. She'll be moved by it, understand that she's loved, the kind of love that's hard to find. She'll forgive Brian and Zach will be cool with it, even happy about it.

He glances again at the crucifix, the tortured Christ figure in the thorny crown. He lays the paper on the table and massages the creases. He understands now. His pursuit of Rachel was the pursuit of a grail, and now with his blessing, someone else will drink from that cup. Rachel will love and be loved as she deserves. Everything will be alright.

TWENTY EIGHT

WINSTON

The blue lights on the dash read 11:30 p.m. Winston shifts in the seat of the Mustang parallel parked on Pratt Avenue. Ahead on the left, the lights in Brian Casey's third floor apartment remain off. Winston turns the key and the car is quiet. He'll fire up the ignition and run the heat again in twenty minutes when he starts to feel the cold. Eight hours of waiting – he's learned the routine.

The Mustang faces Sheridan Road. He was lucky to find this space, perfect for spotting the schoolteacher if and when he approaches from that direction. The side-view mirror is positioned so he'll notice if for some reason the loser turns the corner from Lakewood to the rear.

Winston's hand again wanders to the hard object in his jacket pocket. Why does he keep doing this? The gun's not going to disappear. Where's it going to go?

Ten feet ahead, a streetlight rising from the dead grass drops light through the windshield. Winston shifts again, catching his reflection in the rearview mirror: the Packers cap, the face below submerged in darkness. But what's that? Behind his own image, movement, a shadow in the back seat, a whisper.

He spins around. "Micah?"

He stares at the empty seat. The visions are coming more often. He lowers the driver's side window and shivers. The cold air seems to ground him, keep the visions at bay. The chill from the open window sends a signal to his groin. He steps from the Mustang, into the opening of a narrow walk slicing between two buildings. He unzips and aims at the base of a trash can. Fourth piss in the last eight hours. Zipping up, he backs from the opening onto the Pratt Avenue sidewalk. There's movement to his right. A distant figure, on foot, has turned from Sheridan. .

He ducks into the Mustang, slides low in the seat. The figure moves half a block closer but turns from the sidewalk and disappears into a building.

Winston sits up. His fingers drum the steering wheel. What an inconvenience Brian Casey has become. Showing up at the pier, taking the camera, all those images of Micah. Might as well be holding Micah hostage in that shit-hole apartment.

Then there was the night at Wrigley Field. What a waste. The point was intimidation, to convince the schoolteacher that nobody was safe until Micah was set free. But Brian Casey seemed distracted more than anything else. The four opening-day tickets had cost Winston a full-day's pay at the shop. Ten hours in the oil change pit for nothing.

Killing the old woman would have been perfect for letting the schoolteacher know what Winston's capable of. The old hag's going to kick it soon anyway. And with Brian Casey going there every Tuesday around five, his prints must be all over the place. But this time he showed up early, didn't give Winston time to finish the job. In fact, the schoolteacher probably emerged a hero.

Winston fixes his stare on the sidewalk ahead. Eight hours. Is he wasting his time? After what happened this afternoon, who knows if the guy's even coming home tonight? Might be in the hospital. The fucker hit that wall pretty hard. But it had to happen tonight. Another night prowling Chicago's north side for elderly victims wouldn't cut it. The power that's surged through Winston all afternoon and evening is too good to waste on another fossil. He's ready to explode and the schoolteacher is the only one worthy.

Again, in the rearview mirror, a ghostly shift of shadow in the back seat. He doesn't turn.

Focus. Got a job to do tonight.

Back to business, Winston replays the scenario, a rehearsal of sorts: When he spots the schoolteacher, he'll approach him, show him the gun. He'll force him into the apartment. The schoolteacher will give him the camera, laptop, anything else with the pictures. Micah will be set free.

Then he'll finish the job.

His heart races with the thought of killing the schoolteacher. He touches the gun again, but knows he won't use it. No bullets anyway – just a prop. Besides, the rush will be greater, the high higher, if the power comes from within instead of from the barrel of a pistol. He raises both hands in front of him. *All I need. My own weapons of mass destruction.*

In the side mirror, movement. Someone has turned the corner from Lakewood, approaching through the alternating moonlight and shadows. But again, not the schoolteacher. The dark figure is slow footed and stooped, each step painfully thrust forward from the hip. Another of Rogers Park's useless old farts. Place is just teeming with them. Winston takes a deep breath and exhales. Any other night this would be perfect - easy prey - but not tonight.

Be strong. Let the geezer go by. Remember why you're here.

The old man shuffles next to the Mustang, his feet dragging the sidewalk. He's within ten feet, so tempting, such an easy target. Winston's left hand twitches the door handle. He's holding himself back, resisting the irresistible.

Micah's voice whispers from the back seat. "Help me, Winston."

Winston's right hand grips the steering wheel. He's losing control. He avoids looking at the old man, concentrates on the grip, the streetlight touching the white curve of his knuckles.

Hold on tight. Let him go by.

He closes his eyes, counts to twenty - slowly - should be enough.

He opens his eyes. The old man has moved thirty feet past the Mustang but stopped in front of the schoolteacher's building. He makes a slow right turn and shuffles toward the entrance. Winston loosens his grip on the steering wheel, sits forward. The old man lumbers toward the building. He's within fifteen feet of the concrete steps, approaching the warm yellow glow of the iron and glass door. Winston's right hand slides from the steering wheel. Blood races to his heart. Impulses click in his brain. One of Brian Casey's neighbors. This is too good to pass up. The schoolteacher loves these fossils.

Obeying the voices within, he throws open the door of the Mustang and swings his legs out. The old man has reached the base of the steps. He's clutching the handrail, hoisting himself toward the yellow glow.

Winston's body has taken control. He's floating toward the old man. His long legs are those of a thoroughbred, the inner voices wind at his back.

The old man stands at the door.

Behind Winston, Micha's voice urges him forward. "Stop him, before he gets inside."

Winston turns toward the building. The old man has reached the top step. "Excuse me, Sir." Winston's words boom through the quiet night.

Startled, the old man turns. He takes a step back, confused, even frightened by the tall figure approaching him.

Winston stops. "Sorry for scaring you. Just need some directions."

The old man relaxes his posture. Winston removes the Packers cap and looks up at the stars. He feeds his victim a disarming smile. "Cold night huh?" He glances left and right. Pratt Avenue is quiet and lonely and dark.

Micah's voice whispers in his ear. "Take him now, big brother."

TWENTY NINE

BRIAN

I'm on the el from Lincolnwood. Clara is tucked into Rachel's bed, Rachel asleep on the couch. I'm alone on the train, fingering the torn vinyl of the bench, trying to decide if the milky glob on the floor across the aisle is a wad of saliva or a used condom.

I need a car.

I'm on my way back to Rogers Park. I don't want to go home tonight, but I will. I'll exit the train at Morse, duck my head into the cold, and stride the three block minefield to my apartment. I'll double bolt the door, crawl into bed, and get my five hours. In the morning I'll pour myself a cup of strong coffee and pretend today never happened. I'll drag myself to work and stand in front of my classroom trying to convince my students that being able to analyze rhetoric will make them rock stars.

I glance at the time on my phone. Almost midnight. Was it only seven hours ago that Officer Sam Rosetti straddled the chair in Clara's living room? Feels like another lifetime. It was bizarre watching the grizzled cop get choked up. He clearly had a soft spot for Clara, had to bite his lip when she started crying. A cop with a heart. Go figure.

My cellphone rings in my hand. My heart jumps. I take a deep breath and look at the number. Blocked. Maybe the same caller I ignored at Rachel's. This time I answer.

"Hello?"

"Showed up just in time to save that old bitch," the voice says. "Think you can do it again?"

I sit forward. "Who is this?" Stupid question. I know the answer.

"It's your worst nightmare." The cliché is on cue, rehearsed. I've set him up. "I'm the empty pill bottle in your medicine cabinet. All your Hitchcock villains rolled into one."

He's quiet on the other end, waiting for me to respond. I'm supposed to ask how he knows these things about me, but I won't. Two can play at this game. I take a deep breath, steadying my voice.

"Winston Longstreet."

He starts to speak, but stops. I've deviated from his script. How do I know his name?

"Listen, motherfucker." The smugness has deferred to anger. "Be at the pier in twenty minutes and bring the camera. Be on time, or your neighbor's gonna end up in the lake with the other fossil. And when they find him, they'll find your wallet."

"Twenty minutes? I don't—" A beep. I look at the screen: Call ended.

At night, there's nowhere to hide on an empty train. The cold white light has turned the windows into mirrors. I can't see out, but the world sees in. A million eyes watch me, all peering from under the bill of a green and yellow cap. The interior lights flick off, plunging me into seconds of terrifying darkness. When they come back on I expect to find Winston Longstreet sitting beside me. But no, it's only me, and my refection rattling in the mirrored window. At least I think the window's rattling. Or am I trembling? I'm not sure. I beg the reflection for answers. The personal stuff - Hitchcock, the pills – how does he know these things? From Rachel? Not a chance. But who else knows about the pills?

Of course. Matthew Dials.

I remember watching the two of them under the bleachers at Booker on April Fool's Day, shaking hands and pointing my direction. I should have asked Matthew about the encounter when I had him on the ropes on Sunday.

But what did Winston mean by my neighbor? And my wallet? Christ, I forgot he had my wallet. I look at the time on my phone: 12:02. I stand and pace the empty car. He said be at the pier in twenty minutes. I'll never make it, but I have to try. I can't let this can't happen again.

12:04: The train crawls to a stop at Thorndale, two stops short of Morse. The door slides open for nobody. I'm emboldened by the rush of cold air, taunted by the seven seconds of open space in front of me, tempted to plunge into the dark night, sparing my destiny from the cold hands of The Chicago Transit Authority. The door closes.

Think. Calm down and think.

I look at the transit map above my head. Could reach Morse in ten minutes. A sprint to the lake will take about seven. But the camera is in my apartment. Even using the alley as a shortcut, that's at least a four minute detour. I'll never make it.

For the next several minutes, I'm a slave to the CTA. I can only move as fast as the train will take me. Another stop. Nobody gets on. Nobody to get off. I sit and drum my hands on my thighs. I remove the spongy black case from my phone, returning the phone to its silver origins. I put it in my pocket because checking it every thirty seconds has failed to slow down time.

The train rumbles to a stop at Morse. My phone is back in my hand. 12:14: eight minutes left. I bound down the steps and spill onto the street. To the east. Sheridan road is a distant three blocks away, Farwell one block south. The park, a block beyond that. Then the beach, the pier.

I start to run.

12:16: I feel I'm dreaming. I'm running in the middle of the empty street. I know I've made this choice because of the cracks in the sidewalk, the low tree limbs, but I don't remember processing the information.

12:17: I've never felt Rogers Park so still, so quiet. Nothing but my breath sucked in through my nose and expelled from my mouth, my feet slapping the concrete. I'm against the wind. It blows cold in my face. I lower my head and focus on my legs flashing in front of me. I'm still wearing my loafers and khakis.

I approach Lakewood. Decision time. I consider turning right toward my apartment, the camera. But it's 12:18. Only four minutes left. I cross Lakewood without breaking stride. No time for detours. Ignoring the stitch in my side, I increase my pace. Sheridan Road glows yellow one block ahead. A few soundless cars move across the intersection. I won't wait for the light to change. They'll have to wait for me.

12:20: I reach Sheridan and cross. I run past the Old Style beer sign glowing in the window of Sheridan Sam's, past the White Hen Pantry, the Farwell brownstones. Every landmark is left in my wake.

12:22: I leap over the cul-de-sac curb and plunge into the darkness of the park. My chest heaves, my heart races. I have no camera, no plan. The lake and pier take shape before me. I stop running when I reach the graffiti wall. I bend over, hands on knees, and vomit. Wiping my sleeve across my mouth, I squint toward the wet horizon. Something in the distance, a shapeless shadow at the end of the pier.

I'm not too late.

I step from the sidewalk onto the open beach. I'm exposed. The shadow at the end of the pier is too far to tell, but Winston must be watching. He knows I'm here. It's time to stall - slow down time - walk.

Two minutes later I'm on the pier. The shadow at the end becomes two. I wipe the cold sweat from my eyes and squint toward the shadows. I shuffle my feet on the loose gravel. The air is still, the night dark and quiet. I move closer, within a hundred feet. The two figures take shape, one on either side of the steel rope. The one on the inside is Winston. I recognize his height, his posture, the cap pulled tight. The other is much older. He struggles, clutching the rope and pawing at Winston's arm to avoid falling into the cold water.

A voice calls from the shadow. "You're late, asshole. Hurry up."

No more stalling.

I walk toward them, a slideshow of images from the digital camera playing in my head: Winston and his little brother mugging in a bowling alley, eating hotdogs at some amusement park. The boy, gaunt and bald, propped in a hospital bed.

I'm within fifty feet.

"Stop," he calls. "Show me the camera."

Try talking to him. Worth a shot.

"I'm sorry about your brother, Winston. But none of this is going to bring him back." I'm a trembling voice of reason. "Why don't you let the old guy go? I'll give you the camera. Just let—"

"Fuck you, schoolteacher." The words slice through the darkness like a knife. He's losing patience. "You don't know shit about me. Show me the camera." He grabs the old man's collar, thrusts him over the water and shakes. The old man gasps.

Out of options, I reach into the pocket of my jacket. I locate my phone, hard and cold without the spongy black case. I clutch it, mostly concealed in my hand, but with a silver edge revealed. I raise it high into the night. "Want your camera? Go get it." With this, I heave the phone into the black water of Lake Michigan.

Winston's guttural scream reaches me before the tiny splash. He shakes the old man's grip from his arm. The old man flails his arms but catches hold of the steel rope. With a violent thrust, Winston swings an elbow. It connects with the old man's chest. A grunt and a terrifying cry. The old man disappears over the edge. I charge toward Winston. He roars, braced for impact, legs apart, shoulders lowered. Umph. We collide. I drive him back, slamming him against the unlit tower. The impact bounces me backwards and for a weird moment we stand regarding each other.

He comes at me. Another collision. We wrestle each other to the concrete. My cheek and mouth scrape gravel. I spit out the cold dust. He swings. I cover my face but his fist connects with the back of my head, the same spot I hit the wall. Pain shoots through my skull. Another blow, this time to my mouth, knocking something loose. We're wrestling again. I taste blood with the gravel dust. I spit to avoid gagging. He swings and I raise my arm to deflect his blows. *Go for his eyes. Wait for the right time, and go for his eyes.* The blows keep coming to my shoulders, my ribs, but with less velocity. He's winded, slowing down. I press my thumb and fingers together, a makeshift spear, and aim for his face. He screams, throws his hands over his eyes, and falls from me.

I lie on my back, chest heaving. Dark clouds sweep across the night sky. For a weird moment I'm at peace.

A cry from the water.

Spitting blood, I struggle to my feet. My head is throbbing, my world spinning. I stagger to the rope. The old man's head bobs in and out of the cold water. His fingers, desperate for a hold, scrape the edge of the drenched concrete. I climb over the twisted steel rope and perch on the three-inch ledge. I lower myself to a knee, bend to him. I clutch the rope with my left hand, stretch with my right. "C'mon. Take my hand."

He reaches, two inches short, before sinking into the water.

I work my way lower. I hang over the edge, gripping the rope with my hand, the iron post with the crook of my knee. He resurfaces, gasps for breath, reaches.

I stretch and yell. "C'mon."

Our hands connect but the grip is wet and weak. The fingers slide apart and he goes under. I'm about to go in after him when his head again bobs to the surface. I can't get any lower. My face is pressed against the wet concrete. I lunge. I've got him by the wrist.

"Hold on," I yell. "Don't let go."

I close my eyes and roar. Every decibel feeds the grip, empowers the muscles in my right arm and shoulder as I pull. I open my eyes. His torso is out of the water. He lifts his knees, trying to gain traction with his feet. They slide from the wet concrete. Almost there. One more pull. One more roar into the night.

He's up, clutching the bottom steel rope with his right hand. I release his left and grab him under his arm. He gasps for breath, his face inches from mine. Our eyes meet. Time stops.

It can't be. . .

We struggle over the railing and collapse in a wet heap.

219

I prop him against the light tower. He shivers, violently inhaling and exhaling sobs of cold air. His thin hair is plastered wet to his head, water running down his face. He looks at me, lips trembling, and ties to speak. "Your mouth. . . bleeding. Brian, I. . ." The words give way to shivers.

"Shh. It's okay." I take off my jacket and wrap it around him. We sit in silence, his head on my heaving chest, my arm around his trembling shoulder. I wipe the cold sweat from my eyes and gaze to the west. In the distance, Winston Longstreet, in a drunken weave, stumbles from the pier. He clutches his face with one hand, blindly gropes for support or balance with the other. He crosses the beach and like a ghost, disappears into the shadows of the park.

I hold my father close. He tries to speak several times, but I stop him. There'll be plenty of time for words, apologies, forgiveness.

Twenty feet away, an object rests on the pier. I secure my father against the light tower and struggle to my feet. Legs like rubber, I stagger and pick up the green and yellow cap. I hold it a moment, gazing toward the empty park. Then, turning to the lake, I fling the cap like a Frisbee. It floats through the air and lands softly on the water. Without a care in the world, it lounges atop Lake Michigan, rolling gently with the waves, inching toward the shore.

I help my father to his feet. We start toward the beach. At the pier's halfway point, we stop. I pause and look up. I'm not sure why. If I'm looking for stars, there are none. If I'm looking for God, he's hiding behind the thick blanket of charcoal sweeping across the sky. I turn to the south, toward downtown Chicago, the twinkling lights of Navy Pier. I close my eyes and feel the breeze on my face. Two weeks ago I stood in this very spot, brushing the windswept hair from Rachel's cheek, kissing her under a billion stars.

Forgive me, Rachel. I want to stand here with you again.

I turn to my father. He's watching me, still shivering, but with a warmth, a peace in his eyes. He doesn't speak. His mouth curls into a crooked smile.

I understand now. F. Scott Fitzgerald was wrong. My father's smile is so much more than "the love of youth in others." It's life wrapping him in a warm blanket of forgiveness, filling the empty spaces between slats of a bench. It's life, whispering in the ear of Walter's ghost: Somebody does know. Somebody does care.

My father and I turn and face the remaining stretch of concrete pier. Beyond the beach and the oak trees, Rogers Park awaits. We lean on each other and begin our new journey together.

THE END

Purchase other Black Rose Writing titles at www.blackrosewriting.com/books and use promo code PRINT to receive a 20% discount.

Made in the USA
Middletown, DE
11 June 2015